STRONGER THAN HOPE

KATHERINE MCINTYRE

HOT TREE PUBLISHING

ALSO BY KATHERINE MCINTYRE

STRONGER THAN HOPE

KATHERINE MCINTYRE

HOT TREE PUBLISHING

For information, contact the publisher, Hot Tree Publishing.

www.hottreepublishing.com

Editing: Hot Tree Editing

Cover Designer: BookSmith Design

E-book ISBN: 978-1-922679-06-2

Paperback ISBN: 978-1-922679-07-9

To Rob and Riley, my Linc and Beckett.

CHAPTER 1

NATE CRANKED THE RADIO AS HE DROVE DOWN THE highway, unrestrained boxes bouncing around in the back of his Hyundai Sonata. The Cure had popped on, and he needed the dose of comfort as the trees crowded on either side, the road signs all unfamiliar.

He'd been on the road for seven? eight hours now? They'd all started to blend together, and his ass was going number by the second, but with the GPS counting down, he couldn't bring himself to stop by the side of the road or take a break. Not when he was so close to his new city, his new home, his new life. Nate rolled down the window, letting the sweet breezes float through the car. They juiced his veins with the hope of something different than the monotonous slog he'd been crushed under.

He tapped his fingers along the steering wheel to

the beat of "Friday I'm in Love," his heart pounding a million miles an hour as he raced along the open highway, following the signs toward Chesapeake City, a tiny town nestled in Maryland. It was a far stretch south from Massachusetts, further down than he'd traveled before. The sensible part of him should be terrified, but his heart hadn't gotten the memo.

After Sam dumped him six months ago, he'd been desperate for a change, for something different to grab hold of and follow skyward like some aimless kite.

In a way he was. Gone was the job, gone was the suburban town he grew up in, gone was his group of friends, and gone was every safety net he'd ever bounced back on as he cut his own strings.

In the distance, he caught sight of an arched bridge guiding the way into town. It stretched over water that glittered under the sunlight, a small town lying at the opposite end. The breath snagged in his throat. This wasn't the chaos of Boston on a Saturday night—the pure opposite. Verdant trees surrounded the town on either side, and the river sprawled out, lazy boats chugging along the canal. The spring breezes brought the sweetness of fresh water, a mesmerizing scent he couldn't stop inhaling. Half of him was tempted to stick his head out the window like a golden retriever to get more of the view of the new place he planned on calling home.

Once upon a time, he'd loved the fast pace of the city, hitting bar after bar and then heading to work at Awake Industries to power through one marketing meeting at a time. However, three years away from thirty had him questioning everything he'd ever believed.

The radio slipped in another Cure song, and Nate counted himself lucky for the twofer as he jammed out on the road, coming in closer and closer to all the bright, shiny, new. Promises whistled on the breeze, and he wanted to reach out and clasp them in his hand. He soared across the bridge, slow-moving freight boats making their way through the canal. As he emerged on the other end, the sight of the small town before him caused his breath to hitch. He'd seen pictures of his new apartment, of the town, the quaint, historical buildings, but getting the view up close got his pulse pounding in a way the club scene failed to summon of late.

His heart twisted a little bit. He wouldn't mind doing this whole adventure with someone beyond himself. Maybe he needed a dog, or five. Sam had pretty much hammered in his head that he wasn't long-term material—no ambition, no drive, no roots.

Part of him needed to prove the asshole wrong.

He slowed as he began to wind down the small streets, people walking to and fro along the sidewalk during this gorgeous day. Folks took their big, lumbering St. Bernards on walks or carried kiddos on their shoulders as they headed around town, ducking in and out of the small businesses lining the way.

Soon, he'd be running one of those tiny establishments.

Hopefully not into the ground.

Nate made the left and then the right onto a side street, minutes away from his new place. He slowed to a crawl as he scanned the buildings, trying to find the gray one with the cranberry door that would be his latest home. The sun struck his windshield, causing him to squint as he crept forward.

A loud curse snapped his attention front and center. Nate slammed on the brakes. The blinding light cleared in time to reveal the guy he'd been two seconds from flattening.

"What the fuck, man?" the guy called, slapping a hand on the hood of his car.

Nate let out a groan. Here for two minutes, and already he was mowing down pedestrians. If what he'd heard about small towns was true, he'd have a reputation as the asshole city slicker by tomorrow morning.

He poked his head out the window. "I'm so

sorry," he yelled. "I didn't know which house was mine." Nate gripped the steering wheel a little tighter, resisting the urge to slam his head into it. Now he sounded like an idiot.

The guy wove around to the driver side, and Nate caught his first real glimpse of him. The man looked to be early thirties, and the tank top and jeans he wore displayed a muscular body that made Nate bite back a whimper. Goddamn. He possessed a deep tan and dark tousled hair, his Italian heritage clear by his thick brows, his strong nose, and full lips meant for smirking.

Not only had he almost run over someone, it was one of the hottest guys he'd ever seen.

"Are you drunk?" the guy asked, his voice deep and gritty. "Why can't you find your house?"

Nate feebly jerked a thumb to the towering boxes in his back seat. "Hey, I'm Nate, and I'm new in town. I swear I'm not normally this bad of a driver— just trying to figure out which place is mine."

The guy arched a brow, an effortless motion that looked hot as hell on him. He leaned against the side of the car. "Don't suppose it's the house two down with the For Rent sign still up? I heard old man Fletcher found a tenant."

Nate glanced to the picket sign on the small front lawn and caught sight of the cranberry door and the number on the outside he'd been looking for. This close, he caught the guy's scent, all sunshine, earth, and musk. A flush lit his cheeks.

"Ah, yeah, apparently that's my place. I should pull off the road now and drown myself in mortification privately," Nate babbled, his cheeks bright red.

"The name's Linc. I'll see you around," the guy said, clapping a hand on the side of his car. His lips quirked in a half grin.

Nate's brows drew together. "Oh yeah?" he responded, hoping he didn't come across too eager. Not like seeing more of the man would be a hardship.

"Yeah, I'm three houses down," he said, tossing a hand in the air before he strode off in the direction of the place Nate braked in front of. Before he committed any more almost-vehicular manslaughters, he pressed on the gas and pulled into the open street parking in front of his new place. His heart still pounded like he'd run five miles without pause, and he took a moment to glance up the street.

His hot neighbor stepped into his house, closing the door behind him. Nate took another few minutes to come down from his embarrassment. He had a car full of boxes to unpack, but he needed a moment. Nate rested his forehead on the top of his steering wheel and let out a groan.

Only a few minutes into arriving at his new place, and he'd already made an ass of himself in front of the sexy new neighbor.

He only hoped this wasn't a sign of what was to come.

CHAPTER 2

THE EARLY SUNLIGHT STREAMED THROUGH THE windows, pale beams lighting the oak flooring. Lincoln had already pocketed his wallet and keys, and he waited by the door in his usual morning ritual.

"Beck," he called. "I'm going to close my eyes and count to five. We need to get you to school on time." The steady pulse of impatience thumped inside him, one he squashed down every time.

Linc didn't bother closing his eyes as he heard the rustling from the other room. "One," he counted out, making sure his voice projected through the house. "Two, three."

The rustling grew louder, and he shut his eyes for when Beckett burst out of his room. The patter of those socked feet pounded against the hardwood as the little guy raced toward him, a bundle of explosive energy. Beckett rarely missed the "count to five."

"Four," Linc said, a note of warning in his voice. Beck smacked into him, those small arms wrapping around his leg with a death grip. Little ones were a force of nature all on their own. Linc reached down to muss the kid's dark brown hair as he blinked his eyes open. "Okay, shoes, kiddo."

"Samwise wanted to play," Beck said, plopping on the ground. The fluffy Maine coon in question slunk out of the room, tail tick-tocking back and forth as his golden eyes scanned the room.

Linc crouched to help him speed up the shoes situation. "You know he'll play at any hour of the day, even two in the morning."

He arched a brow as he looked at his kid, those big brown eyes pure Marissa. The sight caused a twist in his chest, the way the grief sucker punched him at random, even six years later. Still, Beckett had gotten the rest of his looks from Linc, the Italian genes dominating, all dark curls and olive skin. Beck even had the misfortune of his prominent nose, which would take him some years to grow into.

Linc straightened, passed Beckett his Crayola-red backpack, and jangled the keys. "Time to go." He cast a glance through the open layout of the main floor, unable to help how his gaze lingered on the kitchen table where Marissa used to sit back with her black coffee, and the shabby couch they'd bought together when they first moved in here. Now the couch was covered in crumbs most days because Beck kept sneaking crackers there.

He and Marissa had formed a thousand memories in this place, and even a small human together—one she'd never gotten to meet.

The word preeclampsia still sliced like a knife every time he thought of how fast what should've been the happiest time of their lives turned into a tangled web of grief.

Linc squeezed Beck's hand a little tighter as they exited the house, stepping out into the bright sunlight. Beck squinted as he skipped alongside Linc. Warmth flooded Linc's chest at the sight of his little guy who'd become his entire world. Beckett grinned wide, his face full of sweetness and an innocence Linc couldn't help but protect.

They headed over to his black Toyota Tacoma, and he buckled Beckett into the back before climbing into the driver seat. Today he had an agenda a mile long, but the morning and afternoon drive with his son was sacred, a time he refused to let work take away from him. He kept busy enough with his contracting business, and after he dropped Beck off, he'd be meeting with a new client.

"Daddy, why are bricks red?" Beck asked from the back seat.

Linc's lips lifted in amusement. The barrage had begun. "Not all bricks are red, kiddo, but you see a lot of them that color because they're made from a reddish-brown clay found in nature."

"Can we make bricks?" he asked again, a never-ending fountain of curiosity.

"I can find a way for us to play around if you want to try," Linc offered. "Or we can visit one of the places where they make those materials." Beckett always wanted to know about "Daddy's work," which was perfect, because he would happily let the kiddo muck around with the safer stuff. He started the engine and began the quick drive over to Beckett's school, Chesapeake Elementary. Along the way, Kyle McReady gave him a wave from the sidewalk, and Beckett's former nanny, Marjorie Jennings, blew a kiss to the munchkin as she strolled by.

Small town like this, any time he needed help, he knew just who to go to.

Small town like this, and everyone knew his damage. "Widower" might as well be stamped across his forehead.

Small town like this, and sometimes he felt like the past would coil around him and squeeze until he suffocated.

He pulled in front of Chesapeake Elementary, the familiar stone building with the white-and-black sign out front. Beckett let out an excited trill from the back seat. He'd hold on to these years as long as he could, because sooner rather than later, the excitement would turn to groans. At least, if Beck was anything like him.

"Got your backpack? Your coat?" he asked as he pulled into place. Kids were already walking up to the door, some skipping and laughing, far more awake than a lot of the adults. He caught Beckett nodding in the rearview mirror, his bright eyes gleaming as he bounced in his seat.

"Love you, kiddo. Have a good day at school." Linc turned to look at him.

"Bye, Daddy," Beck called out as he cracked the door open. "I love you!"

With that, he scampered out to join the rest of the kids heading inside, his backpack slapping his back as he went. Linc couldn't help the grin quirking his lips. He watched until Beck entered the building, filled with the sort of kinetic energy he wished he could bottle and tap into on the longer days. He squeezed the steering wheel for a moment and let the warmth saturate him before he popped out of park and hit the road again.

Time to get his head in gear for the jobs lined up

today. First stop was for coffee though, because despite being a morning person, he'd need the extra energy, unlike his son. Since Chesapeake Brew had closed for remodeling, Eliza's café, Cozy Corner, was where all the locals flocked to at the moment. The little café boasted scalloped white trim on the exterior and a charming wooden sign hanging from the front with delicate script.

Linc pulled into a spot along the side of the road and exited the car. He clapped a hand to his back pocket to check for his wallet, jangled his keys in reminder, and headed toward the front door of Cozy Corner. Not the best place for a quick in and out, but until the main coffee shop reopened, the café was the sole option available.

Folks from the town filled most of the two- and four-seater tables, and Eliza patrolled back and forth behind the counter he made a beeline toward. This time of day, a single stool was all he hoped to claim.

Jeremy waved at him from a nearby stool, beckoning him over. The Port of Call bartender was the sort of hot that demanded a chance, all tawny, ripped muscle, sparkling green eyes, and perfectly styled ear-length hair. When he'd asked Linc out a few years back, they'd gone on a couple of dates. Unfortunately, the fling ended up like all of his attempts—going nowhere. Linc settled into the seat next to him and met Eliza's eyes before offering a nod. She took the cue and began filling a cup for him.

Depending on who you asked around town, he was still mourning his wife, he'd married his job instead, or he'd taken himself off the market for good. A thread of truth existed in all the rumors, but the whole truth was that he didn't muddle around in shallow water. No one he'd met ever came close to clicking with him like Marissa had.

"I don't understand why you come here for a single cup of coffee." Jeremy gave him the side-eye, hunched over his plate of eggs, toast, and bacon, with a cup of orange juice and a mug of coffee to complete the meal.

"Not much of a breakfast person, but if I'm going to get any work done today, I need the kick start," Linc said, switching his attention to Eliza as she hustled on over and slid the steaming mug of coffee his way. "Thanks, Liza," he said, wrapping his palms around the warm porcelain.

The woman had owned this place her entire life, and he couldn't imagine anyone else behind this counter. Eliza was one of those people who emanated sunshine, and the smile lines around her eyes, her soft brown-and-gray hair pulled into a bun, and her dimples brightened everyone's days.

"When are you and your boy stopping by again?" Eliza asked. "Miss seeing his sweet face in here."

"I'll make sure to bring him out for breakfast on the weekend," Linc promised. He loved and hated the way everyone knew each other here. Folks like Eliza made things easy for him, but when Mrs. Cutter suggested for the thousandth time that he consider dating her niece because his son needed a mother in his life, he wanted to take a sledgehammer through drywall.

Linc brought the steaming liquid to his lips, desensitized to temperatures a long time ago. He'd cut his teeth working construction, and after that, cold and heat rarely affected him. The rich liquid coursed down his throat, the ritual waking him up as much as the caffeine.

"I'm glad." Eliza patted the counter before heading over to another customer needing attention.

"What's on your agenda today?" Jeremy asked, chewing on his scrambled eggs as he talked. It was a damn shame things hadn't worked out between them, because the man loved to fill in sentences as much as Linc loved leaving silences, and he seemed to get hotter every year. Yet while there had been some chemistry, the comfort was missing.

"I'm meeting with a new client, and then I'm going to continue the project over at Parkridge in the afternoon," Linc said, taking another sip of coffee. "Are you working tonight?"

"Always, always," Jeremy replied. He cast him a pointed glance. "Did you hear the new owner of the coffee shop arrived in town? What do you think he'll be like?"

Linc shrugged as he drank the remainder of his coffee. "I'll let you know. That's the new client I'm meeting with next." He slipped a few bills onto the table and rose. "I'll see you around, Jer."

"Eliza?" A voice sounded from behind him right as he turned around. "I brought you the—"

Linc didn't make it a pace before something solid smacked straight into him. A second later, the scorch of liquid on his chest followed, seeping into the fabric of his shirt.

"Oh, shit."

Linc looked in front of him to see the guy who'd almost run him over the day before holding a paper cup of coffee, half empty. Because the rest of the liquid had spilled onto Linc's shirt.

Nate's mouth dropped open in horror. "I'm so, so sorry." He placed the cup of coffee onto the counter and then groped around in the air.

Linc lifted the fabric off his chest to ease some of the burning. Thankfully the liquid hadn't been piping hot.

Jeremy reached over and passed a wad of napkins into Nate's grasping hands.

A blush stained Nate's cheeks as he approached with the napkins. Before Linc could tell him he was fine, just a mess for his next meeting, Nate dove in and started blotting at his shirt. This close, he got a better glimpse of the guy than the brief view from the other day.

Goddamn, Nate was pretty enough to give Jeremy a run for his money.

His dark brown hair was long enough to tug, and his big heartbreaker eyes were a bright blue that drew immediate attention. He had a wide jaw and thick brows, but he emanated this boyish sweetness. Linc couldn't help but linger for a moment on his features, a flicker of attraction lighting his chest. Well, that was inconvenient.

Nate furiously dabbed at his chest. "You must think I'm the worst person on the planet," he mumbled.

"You'll have to try a little harder to earn that title," Linc said, placing a hand on the guy's broad shoulder to try and stop the onslaught of dabbing. The gesture worked. Nate stopped, his gaze whipping up to greet his. Linc continued, "Unless you're saying that because you cut my brake lines."

Nate's eyes widened as he shook his head. "I

STRONGER THAN HOPE   19

swear, I'm not out to get you. I just have the worst timing in existence." He looked a little bit miserable, and Linc couldn't help the urge to reassure him.

Linc met his gaze and glanced to his chest. "I'm pretty sure my shirt's dry enough. You're okay. I'm not burnt."

Nate rifled his hand through his thick hair, those blue eyes pleading as he glanced up at him. "Right." He retracted the wad of napkins from his chest that was far from dry. Nate glanced to his shoulder, and Linc realized with a start his palm still rested there. He licked his lips on reflex, forcing his gaze away from the distraught guy who looked too damn pretty for his own good. Linc pulled his hand away.

He needed to get out of here before this scene got any more awkward.

"I've got to get to my job, so unfortunately your window to trip me or shut a door on my hand is closing," Linc offered the dry joke. At first, Nate stared at him like a kicked puppy, and Linc regretted making the crack, but a second later Nate's expression relaxed.

"I think I can manage the rest of the day without trying to injure or maim you," Nate said, taking a step back as he brought the wad of napkins to the nearest trash can. He grinned, the earnest sort that lit up his eyes, and Linc shook his head, unable to help his own smile.

"See you around, neighbor," Linc said, tipping two fingers at him in a lazy wave. He offered Jeremy and Eliza a nod, both of them still staring between him and Nate. Guaranteed, half of Chesapeake City would be talking about the incident by dinner time, because this town and its gossip were legendary. Linc headed for the door, restraining his hefty sigh. The last thing he needed to be was a part of the never-ending rumor mill.

Time to get to work.

CHAPTER 3

NATE'S SHOULDERS HEAVED AS HE STEPPED IN FRONT OF Chesapeake Brew. He'd inherited this coffee shop from his late uncle Howard, not because they'd been close, but because no one else in the family wanted anything to do with it. The place would need an overhaul if they expected to stay relevant in modern times. He carried a hefty bag of Eliza's cookies he'd be sampling as a part of their planned exchange. While he'd sell some of her wares at his shop, she'd be using his coffee at her café. Too bad most of his coffee sample ended up on his ridiculously hot neighbor.

Both times Nate had run into Linc, he'd managed to make a mess of himself, and he was pretty sure Linc either hated him by now or at the very least thought he was a complete idiot. It didn't help that

Linc was so hot, Nate was constantly flustered around him. Seriously, Linc was all Italian good looks, dark curls, and oozing machismo that caused his cheeks to flush after a second glance.

Nate skimmed a hand through his hair as he approached the front door. The lights were on, which meant his uncle's old store manager Daria must be inside. That was all he could guess, because no one else had keys to the place. What she was doing here so early mystified him, but he needed to get his head in the game. He had another meeting on the agenda, this one more than important.

Nate pushed the door open and stepped inside, the scent of roasted coffee beans greeting him front and center. He hadn't walked two steps in when he smacked straight into a big metal something.

"Whoa," a deep voice sounded from above.

Nate's hands shot out on reflex, his grip curling around the structure in front of him before he realized he'd walked straight into a ladder. He spread his stance out and steadied the ladder. Jesus, he needed to pay more attention. With his head in a thousand different places, he'd been making more sloppy mistakes than ever.

He glanced up to see who'd been climbing the ladder in the first place, and embarrassment splashed over him like the coffee he'd spilled earlier.

Linc stood near the top of the ladder, his hands braced on the unstable light fixture he'd been working on.

How? How the hell did he keep fumbling around this guy?

Nate winced. "I'd apologize, but I'm pretty sure we're past that by now, right? I can skip straight to groveling for forgiveness, if that works."

Linc's brows drew together as he glanced down. "Don't tell me you're the guy who's taking over the coffee shop?"

Nate nodded, taking a second to survey the room around him. Daria stood behind the register, watching, arms crossed, though he still wasn't sure why she'd showed up today. Linc stood above him on the now-stable ladder, dressed in the same clothes as fifteen minutes ago when they'd literally run into each other at Cozy Corner. Except now he had a tool belt strapped around his waist and some sort of screwdriver in hand. As if the guy could possibly look hotter.

The lightbulb blinked on in Nate's head.

"And you're the contractor I hired…" Nate trailed off with the realization. "Great first impression I made." The words slipped out before he could help himself. Mortification didn't cover it. The floorboards could swallow him whole right now, and he'd be just freaking dandy.

Linc's mouth twisted into a wry smile. "It could've been worse...."

Nate blinked. "Jesus, Mary, and Joseph. I don't know how. Accidentally setting the town ablaze?"

Linc shook his head and climbed down from the ladder with a creak. "Yeah, please don't do that."

Nate gripped the ladder even tighter as Linc descended, as if he could make up for running head-first into it upon entry.

"Sorry," Daria called from behind the counter. "I was having him try to fix the light that hasn't been working for ages. Figured since he showed up, we might as well get the thing repaired."

Nate sucked in a shaky breath. Well, at least one of them was composed here, though it should've been him. He was taking over as the owner of this place and already his manager ran laps around him, responsibility-wise, and he'd almost run over, spilled coffee on, and nearly knocked down his contractor. A flush crawled up his neck, one he tried to ignore even though the prickles intensified. *Don't cry. Definitely don't cry.*

"I just came to work on the espresso machine. The steam wand needed some retooling before our temporary shutdown, and I thought since people would already be here, it'd be nice to have the company," Daria continued.

Nate nodded. If only that didn't make him feel out of his depth. He was so grateful for all of Daria's knowledge about this place, even if he came to more of a realization of how little he knew about running Chesapeake Brew. Nate sucked in a deep breath, trying to steady himself. This was his shop now, so how they used to do things didn't matter. He'd worked in enough coffee shops through college to understand how they operated.

He glanced up right as Linc reached the ground, still tall enough to loom over him. Nate's heart leapt in his throat with the guy mere inches from him. This close, he caught the guy's earthy scent, all musk and sandalwood with a splash of coffee. A sinful ripple of attraction rolled down his spine. Because of course he had to utterly embarrass himself in front of the first hot guy he met in town. He couldn't help but linger on the way Linc's triceps flexed as he brought his arms down, the corded forearms straight out of a fantasy. Even those large, callused palms made him salivate.

Down, boy.

When Linc's gaze landed on his, the man's lips quirked into a half grin. "So, as long as you don't have any more accidental surprises in hand, why don't we go over your thoughts on the remodel?"

"Right," Nate muttered, running his fingers through his hair for the thousandth time.

Daria kept peering over toward them, which made him feel the slightest bit uncomfortable. Daria seemed so damn competent and in control here, and the idea of just stomping in and mixing up the territory she'd worked in for so long made his stomach churn. Yet he needed to do just that if he wanted to update this business into the modern era. His uncle had run an okay business, but there had been zero online presence, and he'd failed to give the store a cohesive coffee shop front—too many dusty knick-knacks crowded shelf space that could be utilized to forge connections with the other shop owners, like he planned on doing with Cozy Corner.

"Let's go talk in the office," Nate said, tilting his head in that direction before his feet followed. The steady thump of Linc's steel-toed boots sounded behind him, a reminder that he was bringing this gorgeous man into an even smaller space when he could already barely stop ogling the guy. He didn't even know if Linc was gay or not, yet his libido hadn't got the memo. Christ, he needed to get his head in gear.

He ducked into the office still crammed full of his

uncle's mess. Stock filled the wire racks—everything from cups and lids to the five-pound bags of fresh roast they got wholesale from a local vendor. That spot had been well taken care of, unlike the area around his uncle's desk covered with paperwork piled up on top of the surfaces, spilling out of the drawers, and completely disorganized. From what he'd gone through, he could see his uncle's business had been on the decline.

That didn't intimidate him in the slightest—he'd done his research on the area, and with some necessary updates to the business, he believed he'd be able to turn this place around.

"Looks like you've got a lot to go through," Linc murmured as they settled in front of the trash heap of a desk.

Nate scrunched his brows as he skimmed over the back room. "This paperwork shouldn't be too bad. It's the remodel that's going to take more time."

"Depends on what you're looking to do," Linc said. "I'm a one-man shop, though I can subcontract out if need be."

Nate's gaze traveled over the back room. This wasn't what he needed to fix—it was the outdated flooring, the walls sorely in need of a paint job, and the fixtures that looked like they'd been installed in the seventies and never changed. "What do you think about bringing the front of house to modern times? I'm picturing a rustic look, not the industrial style you'd find in the city."

Linc's lips quirked in the half smile Nate all too fast found charming. "Surprising. I thought a city guy like you would want the stainless steel and black look all up and down this joint."

Nate placed his hand over his heart and took a stagger step back. "City guy? Is that the reputation I've got around here after a few days?"

"You're lucky that's the only reputation you've got with the way gossip flies around here," Linc responded, cracking his knuckles as his gaze swept to the rafters along the ceiling. For a moment, the half smile vanished, and a pensive expression replaced it. Nate couldn't help the curiosity percolating inside him.

"I'm sure they'll have plenty of fodder against me after a week," Nate replied, breaking up the quiet.

Linc's brow lifted in a wicked curve. "If you're single, you're screwed. The old ladies are harpies who will try to pair you up with anyone possible, especially their daughters or nieces."

"I might be single, but that's not my speed, even if the daughters and nieces were total sweethearts." The words slipped out of Nate before he could process what Linc's reaction might be. In any new town, he needed to gauge how approachable they were. Back in Boston, he had plenty of rainbow-friendly spots to visit, but he always had to roll the dice in smaller towns.

Linc's smile returned, those dark brown eyes growing a little more intense. "Even though I like more variety than the women of this town, I'm damned sick of getting set up."

Nate's lips went dry with the realization. The way Linc stared at him wasn't innocent, and he needed to suck in a shaky breath to try and regain his senses. So, his hot neighbor was bi—message received. As if this didn't make it harder to maintain professionalism.

"Chances are, they'll shove their one gay nephew my way," Nate joked. Not like he hadn't been there with his own family whenever his mom's coworker had a gay son or his aunt's best friend knew a younger man who happened to be of "the same persuasion." It got old fast.

"Oh, so you know these ladies," Linc responded with a heartbreaker of a grin. "And here I thought you'd need the warning."

The casual flow of the conversation between them made Nate's heartbeat step up to double speed. He hadn't expected to meet anyone who put him at ease so quickly, even after he'd made an idiot of himself a thousand times over in front of this guy.

"You'll have to point out who to avoid," he responded, leaning against the desk as he crossed his arms over his chest. "Can't be seen having any successful setups if I want to continue my reputation as a human disaster when it comes to relationships."

"Lofty claims," Linc responded. "Sounds like you're trying to give my bad rap a run for its money. I'll warn you, I'm competitive." His scorching gaze locked onto Nate's before switching to the shelving he ran his fingers along.

Christ, the proximity to this guy made him dizzy. And Linc was not only going to be working for him over the next month, but he lived a few houses down. As this town had already proved, avoiding him would be an impossibility.

He snuck another glance. Linc's navy T-shirt looked glued to his sculpted chest, the coffee stain from earlier still on the front. Even the fluorescent lights back here didn't affect the man's rich olive skin, so different from his own paler shade. The dark scruff along Linc's jaw and those thick brows made Nate's pulse speed up, and he forced himself to look away before he got caught drooling.

Rustling sounded from the door to the front of house as Daria stepped into the back room. Her gaze darted to them as she made her way to the wire racks. The woman couldn't be more than a few years older than him, but every time they'd interacted so far, he felt like he'd been called into the principal's office and was somehow in trouble. Her brows drew together as she snuck another few glances their way while rooting through the five-pound bags of coffee.

The sight of her offered the splash of cold water Nate needed. He was here to plan out the remodel with Linc, not flirt with his contractor.

"Right, so, rustic," Nate sputtered out, as if they'd been talking about that this whole time. His cheeks flushed, because he was incapable of hiding any damn response. "Have any ideas on that front, boss-man?"

Linc lifted his brow again, and Nate tried to ignore the thrill that rose inside him at how sexy the move was. *Stop looking. Stop drooling.*

"Pretty sure you're the boss here," Linc said, wrapping his hand around the end of the metal rack. "But with this space and that concept, I've got a couple in mind already we can go over."

Nate brightened at Linc's confidence. Clearly, he'd chosen the right guy for the job, and not just because he was smoking hot. "I'll place myself in your competent hands," Nate said. Linc's smirk widened, and those dark eyes devoured him. A flush raced up Nate's spine as he realized the misspeak. "My business, I mean," he spluttered, wanting to melt into the floor for the thousandth time today. "I trust you'll do a great job with the remodel."

Nate glanced to see Daria peeking at them from over by the five-pound bags of coffee. Probably judging and cursing his lack of professionalism. He withheld his groan.

"Glad to hear the vote of confidence," Linc responded, the rich, husky voice doing things to his libido.

"Let's head up front, and you can show me what you're thinking," Nate said, pushing up from the desk and making all but a mad dash to the store section of the building, as if he could race away from his embarrassment.

He managed to outpace Linc and Daria, plunging into the main area of Chesapeake Brew. Nate scrubbed his face for a moment in a last-ditch effort to regain his composure.

The next month was going to be one hell of a challenge.

CHAPTER 4

LINC WALKED TO WHERE HE'D PARKED BY THE WATER, his black Toyota Tacoma shining under the midafternoon sun. He'd finished with a couple of quick jobs a few blocks away, caulking a bathroom for Mrs. Withers and then changing out bulbs in the Newbury house. Both required minimal supplies, so he just carried them in his workman's bag to and from. The crisp spring air drifted his way, bringing with it the scent of fresh water and lilacs.

Next, he'd be heading over to Chesapeake Brew. Today they'd be nailing down the plan and starting to look over materials for the renovation, and he'd be lying if he said he wasn't looking forward to it. Not only did this project allow him to exercise more creativity than usual, but he'd also get to see Nate McAllister again.

Linc cracked the passenger door to his car open and slung the bag in. He might not do serious relationships, but he was still human. Nate was the sort of hot this town didn't see often, and Linc's sex drive kicked into second gear every time the guy entered the room. Between Nate's ear-length dark hair, the slight cleft chin, and those puppy dog earnest blue eyes, he ticked all of Linc's boxes.

Linc shut the door and looped around to the opposite side as his phone began to ring. Unknown number. He picked it up, always hopeful for new work. He might have a monopoly on this town, but that offered limited pickings apart from regular small jobs.

"Lamp Post Contractors," Linc answered. "What can I do for you?"

"Hi, is this Lincoln Lane?" a deep voice came from the other end. "We're looking to discuss a business opportunity."

"This is he," Linc responded as he settled into the driver seat and stuck the keys into the ignition.

"I'm Jensen Millner with Millner and Associates Construction. Your associate Rob Greene recommended you. We're a construction company out in Baltimore, and we could use some extra hands on deck for a large project that's a bit behind. We're trying to subcontract the remaining work so we can reach our deadline—should only be a few days on site."

Rob was someone he'd grown up with who specialized in masonry, and given the chance, the guy had moved the two hours out to the city a few years ago. Normally, Linc wouldn't think of taking even a short job further away, but his house had gotten more oppressive of late, the memories haunting him more than ever. Linc wasn't lonely, per se—Beckett illuminated every day for him—however, he was alone.

Alone in his job.

Alone in running his house.

Alone in raising his son.

Lately, those feelings had gone from a subtle thump to a pounding roar.

"What are the days you'd need me?" Linc asked before he could think on the offer for too long. Mom and Dad would happily take Beckett if he needed to stay overnight for a few days in Baltimore—that, he didn't worry about. What made him hesitant was the way stepping out of his small pond got his gears turning in the direction they had as of late. Maybe Rob Greene had the right idea.

"Three weeks from now, Monday through Wednesday," Jensen replied. "I'll call you back with more details if I'll be putting you on the roster."

"Yeah, throw me on," Linc said, one hand squeezing tight to his steering wheel even as he sat in his parked car. A weight settled in his chest. Something about taking this gig felt like an inevitable step in a direction he still wasn't sure about. The only thing he knew was that he couldn't keep existing in this cycle of the same—of the house he'd shared with Marissa and the responsibilities he shouldered alone, ones that grew more crushing by the day.

"Glad to hear," Jensen replied. "I'll be in contact soon. Talk to you later." With that, the man hung up, the silence echoing in Linc's car.

Linc turned the key in his ignition, and the engine roared to life. He pulled out of the parking spot and turned to glide onto the road, heading toward his next job: Chesapeake Brew. A prickle traveled down his neck, but for the life of him, he couldn't tell if the direction he headed would be a lifeline or would fuck him further.

———

Linc adjusted his seat in one of the uncomfortable orange chairs, all plastic bucket and metal legs that were going to get replaced in this remodel. Thank god too—Nate wasn't wrong about how outdated the business had become. No one had complained, at least not to Harold McAllister, because it was the lone coffee shop in town, but the place still needed updating.

Nate sat across from him, a circular once-white table stacked with plans and ordering books between them. The white undershirt and navy button-down paired with jeans looked beyond mouthwatering on the man, showcasing a lithe, toned body and an ass that deserved attention. Nate chewed on a pen as he skimmed over the stain colors for the hardwood to give it a more uniform look with the replacement wooden counters as well as the table and chair sets they'd picked out.

This was the most fun he'd had on a project in a long while. The amount of free rein Nate gave allowed him to tap into years of expertise in the field, unlike so many other jobs where the parameters were strictly dictated—often to a headache-inducing point. If he had to hear Francine Kimber complain that the shade of paint was a degree off one more damn time, he was tempted to throw the whole bucket at the wall.

"Figure out which stain you want for this place?" Linc asked, reaching out and skimming his fingertips across the samples Nate perused. He shouldn't be flirting with the guy—especially since he was working a job for him—but he couldn't help himself.

Nate had one of those expressive faces that showed everything, and Linc hadn't missed the lingering glances or how he flushed during most of their interactions.

Nate chewed on the pen, glancing up with it still hanging out of his mouth. Those beautiful blue eyes fringed with dark lashes glued on him, a surprising hunger flaring in them. Linc resisted the urge to bite his fist, the look sending a kick to his libido. It had been far too long since he'd gone on a date or hookup, and his body's immediate reaction to Nate left a clear reminder.

"Right, stains," Nate said, shaking his head as if blinking out of a trance. "Do you think walnut would be too dark?"

Linc nodded, despite the way other parts of his body were distracted at the moment. "If you're looking at the dark walnut color, yeah. That would fit more in a city coffee shop. I'd recommend sticking with an oak or something lighter though not too robust—a bit of an ash gradient to meld with the fixtures you have picked out."

"I know Edison bulbs are the cliché, but…," Nate started, pensiveness on his face.

Linc lifted a hand. "But they're classic for a reason, and it'll fit the combination of new rustic well as long as you pick the warm-toned ones. Since we already have some exposed brick along the wall to boost the aesthetic, the wooden additions will complete the look."

Nate's hesitation burst as a bright smile overtook his face. The guy had such a gorgeous grin that Linc needed to force his gaze away for a moment. The way his eyes lit up, how he radiated his emotions had Linc's pulse quickening.

"I'm so relieved I hired you," Nate said, plucking an oak stain from the pile. "I might've had a vision in mind, but I didn't have the technical knowledge to make it happen. No wonder you're the best-rated contractor in town."

Linc's lips twisted into a wry smile as he tried to ignore the warmth Nate's praise brought his way. "I'm also the only contractor in town; at least the only one who's stuck around."

Nate shrugged. "Yeah, but you're clearly talented. You listen to your clients and engage with them. Besides, I've seen the work you've done around Chesapeake City. It's beautiful."

Goddamn, this man was so toothache sweet it threatened to break through Linc's cool exterior. Folks as earnest and open as Nate were rare.

Linc scratched the back of his head, not sure how to respond. "Just doing my job" was what he ended up forcing out after a bit too long had passed. "Let's finalize what chairs we're ordering to replace this crap," he said, in a hurry to distract. Not to mention, his ass had gone numb after sitting in this one awhile. The shop needed the upgrade, bad.

He passed the magazine over to Nate right as his phone began to buzz. Linc glanced down to the number—Beckett's school.

"Do you mind if I take this?" Linc said, lifting his phone. Nate offered a nod as he plucked through the pages and brought his pen out to circle the chairs they'd discussed. Linc rose and strode away, swiping to answer his phone. "Hello?"

"Mr. Lane?" A familiar voice sounded over the line—Jen, the school administrative assistant. "There's been an incident we wanted to inform you about."

Linc's insides turned to ice. No, no, no. Those words were ones he dreaded hearing from the school —incident could encapsulate so damn much, but from his experience, it delivered the worst.

Had Beck gotten hurt? Was he in trouble? Linc sucked in a deep breath, forcing himself to answer.

"What happened?" he asked, the words sounding wooden.

The pause before Jen continued seemed inter- minable. In that moment, all he could hear was the beep-beep-beep of the hospital machines, all he could see was the fatigued look in Marissa's eyes, and all he could feel was how her skin got colder and colder. His surroundings tunneled out, and he waited on the single response.

"A fight broke out with the kids, and Beckett was involved. From the sounds of it, a few of the boys were picking on him."

The breath caught in Linc's throat, a complicated mix of relief and rage flooding through him like the flu, to the point he couldn't process either. "He's okay?" was all that came out.

"Your son's fine," Jen said, "but we don't think this is the first time he's gotten picked on. He got a few cuts and bruises, and we're sending all parties home for the day to cool off. I'm calling to see if you can come and pick him up."

The relief faded fast, and full-blown fury pumped through him like an injection. "He's getting sent home? What's happening to the kids who did this to him?" His grip tightened on his phone, his jaw working overtime as he tried to keep his voice level. The simmer threatened to turn into full boil.

"We're sending him home because he's had a tough day and could use a break from the excitement," Jen said, her voice taking on the calming tone she'd probably used a thousand and one times to soothe angry parents.

Linc tried to suck in a deep breath, but the rage in his chest was a trapped moth, battering around in its cage. His sweet boy had gotten pushed around. Hurt. He swallowed hard.

Jen continued, "As for the other kids, we're investigating the situation, and their parents have been alerted. If it happens again, we'll be taking more severe action."

Linc's mouth glued shut. He wanted to scream, wanted to demand they take action now, wanted to talk to these parents and smack some sense into them to raise better kids.

Right now though, the most important thing was getting to the school as soon as possible to pick up his son.

"I'll be right over," Linc said, sucking in a sharp breath. He finished the conversation with Jen, barely able to focus on the words coming out of his mouth, not while this fury pounded through him louder and louder. He hung up his phone and slipped it into his pocket, his fingers feeling a little numb. He glanced over to where Nate still sat, his shoulders hunched as he pored over the magazine, scrutinizing a little too hard for Linc to believe he hadn't listened in.

Linc settled into the shitty seat across from Nate, who glanced up with some hesitation.

"I'm sure you overheard that," Linc said, heaving

a sigh. "Great acoustics in this place."

Nate ducked his head with an apologetic wince. "Wasn't trying to. The secretary at… your son's school? Well, the secretary speaks really loud."

As much as he didn't want to share the knowledge about his son with the guy he currently lusted over—those two worlds were always kept separate—he didn't have much of a choice now. "There was a situation at school, and I need to go pick him up. If you want, I can swing by after to get your choices on everything so I can place the order for materials."

Nate shook his head, a soft grin on his face. "Go, get your son. We have email for a reason."

Linc rapped his knuckles against the surface of the table. Gratitude flushed through him as he rose. "I'll see you tomorrow then." Not like he'd expected Nate to give him grief, but each client was different, and he never quite knew how folks would react. For him though, Beck always came first, before the business, before dating, before *anything*.

Linc reached down to grab his tool belt and his messenger bag, which he slung over his shoulder, and then he headed out the door, stepping into the bright spring sunlight. He booked it to his car, turned on the ignition, and started the couple minute drive toward Chesapeake Elementary.

The short drive was a blessing and a curse. A

blessing, because he could get to Beckett fast, and a curse, because a few minutes didn't offer enough time to compose himself as he pulled in front of the place where he'd dropped his son off this morning. The place he believed would be safe for his kid, a place where Beckett wouldn't be getting beaten up and bullied.

Linc swallowed bile, the acidic tang leaving a bitter aftertaste. He wanted to scream, wanted to thrash, wanted to punch something.

Fuck, he wanted Marissa here.

Instead, like always, he was in this alone. Linc squeezed the steering wheel as if the motion might stand a chance at levelling him before he hopped out of his truck. He raked fingers through his thick hair as he approached the entrance of the building. Once he stepped inside, he could hear the steady thump, thump, thump of his heart in his ears, as if it bounced off the linoleum floors of the school to echo louder.

The sounds of teachers' voices rang out from the classrooms, along with the small voices of all the kids contained in this place. Something ugly twisted inside at the thought that any of them could hurt Beckett. He strode over to the offices. A few of the kids sat on the benches right outside, hunched over.

He spotted Beckett on one of the benches by himself, leaning against the wall. The moment he saw his son, the anger took a backseat. His throat tightened, and his emotions formed a fist in his chest. He should've protected him somehow. Should've taught him to look out for this, even though Beckett was sweet and idealistic on his roughest days, like his mom. Nothing like his cynical, jaded father. Fuck.

Linc walked up to his son and sat on the bench beside him, taking in the bruises along Beckett's arm and the scrape on his knee, the sight like swallowing razor blades. He knew from experience that the end results could be much worse, but what sucker punched him harder than the physical scrapes was the quietness from his bright, sunshine son, how Beckett's lips remained shut, how he looked at the ground. Linc leaned down and wrapped an arm around Beckett's shoulders.

"Hey, kiddo," he murmured, his throat still tight. "We're gonna go grab some late lunch, okay?" He pulled him in for a hug.

Beckett stared up at him, those dark brown eyes wide and sad. Linc glanced away, not wanting to let the emotion twisting inside escape to the surface. His eyes burned. Then Beckett pulled away from the hug, casting a wary glance to the other kids waiting around. Linc's gaze followed to the few bigger boys with scowls on their faces. He set his jaw. Best he get Beckett out of here now, for multiple reasons.

Linc pushed up and peeked into the office where Jen sat behind the main desk. The middle-aged woman offered him a nod, an apologetic half grin on her face.

"Going to take Beckett?" she asked. "I'll be in contact with you soon about all of this."

Linc nodded, not able to voice anything without betraying the complicated tangle of emotions that roared in his chest. Without a word, he returned to where Beckett slumped and offered his hand. Beckett pushed off the bench without taking it, walking past him. Linc swallowed.

He was supposed to protect his son from the shittier aspects of life. He was supposed to keep him safe. Reality ground away at his bones, truths he never wanted his son to know.

They headed out to the car in silence, one that felt so unnatural. Normally, Beckett filled them all up, jabbering about Dinobots or asking whatever weird questions bubbled up in his mind, whether it was about how many stars were in the sky or why ducklings had fuzz. Marissa had known how to fill the quiet too, something he'd never excelled at. Linc could listen, but he'd never been talkative in the slightest, and that hadn't shifted as he got older.

Beckett sat in the back seat while Linc climbed into the driver seat and settled in place. He turned on the ignition and glanced in the rearview mirror at his son. He'd taken for granted how easily Beckett offered his feelings and thoughts. He would need to make the move on this one. Not for the first time, he missed Marissa something fierce. She would've known how to handle this.

"Hey, kiddo," Linc said. "Do you want to talk about what happened?"

For a moment, the quiet spread until it grew smothering.

"We can go get pizza from Benny's," Linc offered. He wouldn't make his son talk if he wasn't ready, even if the sight smashed his heart to pieces. That prompted a reaction from Beckett, who looked up at last.

"They told me I was too weird," Beckett murmured. "Because I don't like going out and running with everyone at recess. I was drawing a story with a superhero who rides dinosaurs."

Linc nodded even though he didn't think his son could see. "Captain Courage?"

"Yeah." Beckett brightened another notch—Linc grasped onto each shift for dear life. He shrugged a little then. "They started pushing me around, calling me… stuff."

"Kids can be jerks," Linc said. "Even if you're only ever nice to people, sometimes they just respond by being mean." He sucked in a sharp breath, trying to control his anger. Beckett was hurt and didn't need him throwing his own oil spill of emotions into the pond.

Beckett's lower lip wobbled. "Why?"

Linc blew out a long breath. So, now the heavy questions began. Fuck, he still didn't know why some folks inherited the asshole gene. "Sometimes they're upset about themselves, or sometimes their circumstances haven't been kind," he started, feeling like every bullying PSA he'd heard as a kid, the same ones he'd rolled his eyes over. "Sometimes they don't know how to be nice. But you do, Beck. You've been caring from the moment you were born, and that's a gift of yours. They might hurt your feelings, and it's definitely not fair, but don't let them take your gift away."

Beckett bobbed his head, looking at him from the back seat.

Linc turned around. "I know they called you weird and other mean things, but that's because they don't understand you. The right people are going to love your Captain Courage drawings, and they'll sit right beside you with a crayon and paper."

Beckett met his eyes and offered a soft smile. "Thanks, Daddy."

Goddamn, his kid slayed him every time. He

might've had energy before, but after this situation, he just felt zapped. Linc wished he could text someone other than his parents about this, to see if he hadn't fucked up the first big bullying talk, but he and his close friends either didn't have that sort of relationship, or they didn't have kids.

What he missed more than ever was the partnership he'd had.

His phone buzzed, and he slipped it out. Nate had sent an email. He skimmed over the contents, the choices all laid out in bullet point. He scrolled to the very bottom.

Good luck with the school issue. If you're as competent a dad as you are a contractor, I'm sure you'll do great.

Linc's chest tightened at the words he'd been longing to see. Goddamn, Nate McAllister's combination of hot and considerate was dangerous. He slipped his phone into his pocket.

"Who wants pepperoni and pineapple pizza?" he called as he began to pull out onto the road.

"I do," Beckett called back, his voice lighter than before.

He'd take the win and run with it. Still, uncertainty nagged in the back of his mind. If the issues at school continued… well, they'd make the call when they reached that crossroads.

CHAPTER 5

Nate had about twenty papercuts at this point, and he didn't feel like he'd gotten halfway through the stacks of bills and old documents back here. What had his uncle been doing with the business? He knew the guy was up there in his years, so he'd probably only stayed open due to Daria's diligence. Nate sat back in the seat and stretched his arms overhead, listening to his spine make a snap, crackle, and pop. The scent of freshly roasted coffee beans was his sole comfort here in the stale corner that comprised the office.

He glanced at the clock. Crap, the hours had flown by. As if on cue, his stomach grumbled. He'd been back here for hours sorting through the stacks of folders. Daria had popped in and out during the day and currently worked up front, sorting through the shipments he'd brought in. So far, the woman was beyond competent, even if she came off a little crisp at times. She probably just needed time to adjust to the whirlwind of changes.

Nate sipped from his now-cooled cup of coffee and then set down the papers he'd been perusing. The old financial reports would still be here tomorrow, so he should take a breather for tonight and grab some dinner.

The sound of footsteps echoed as Daria popped into view. Her dark brown hair was pulled into a bun, and she wore a zipped-up gray hoodie and a stained pair of khakis that had collected streaks of dust. As she approached, she gripped a piece of paper harder.

"What's this?" she asked, a new thread of tension in her voice.

Nate frowned as he tried to see what was on the paper. He'd left several out front while working on some new logistics for the shop.

Daria smacked the paper onto the desk, the sound snapping him out of his exhaustion. He sat up in his seat and placed his cup of coffee down. The piece of paper was the new price breakdown he'd come up with for when they reopened.

"That's our new pricing," he said, his brows knitting together in confusion. What was she so enraged about?

"This is robbery," Daria said, crossing her arms and glaring at him. "Your uncle kept the same prices for years, and his customers are going to be furious when they see how much you're charging for a cup of coffee or a latte now."

Nate frowned. His stomach turned at the idea of trying to scam customers or doing anything unfair, but his uncle's prices had been so low they weren't even competitive anymore. He no longer questioned why Uncle Harold's business had been sinking under more and more every year. "I'm not trying to hurt anyone," he said, rubbing his nape. "But we do need to operate as a business if we want to stay afloat."

Daria's frown increased in intensity by the second. "Right. So that's the way we're planning on operating? Cold business sharks? You'll run this place into the ground."

Nate blinked. Damn, he was not prepared for her vitriol right now. Part of him knew he should be taking command and being all boss-like. This was his business, and he needed to act like it if they had any hope of being a success. But he got stuck instead in a spin cycle of the anger radiating off her.

Nate sucked in a deep breath. He didn't want to

dismiss Daria outright—she knew this place better than he did—but he would be stuck paying the bills if the business failed. "We're going to have to increase the amounts some, but maybe there are strategies we can try to offset the cost or to help people who might have a hard time affording a cup of coffee. Like a fund people can donate to so we can offer free cups to those in need? Or we can do regular discount days."

Daria's frown didn't budge, her arms folded as if she were some imposing statue. "Those all seem like backpedaling," she said, an edge to her voice that wasn't promising.

"We've got a bit of time until we reopen, so why don't we revisit this when it's not the end of a long day?" Nate asked, not wanting the woman to chew his head off. Probably wasn't the most manly reaction ever—at least not by the shitty standards of the society they lived in—but he'd never succumbed to those anyway. He just wanted people to be happy, for folks to get along.

Daria tapped her shoe on the ground twice, but she bobbed her head in a nod. "I just think making the change is a bad idea" was all she said before striding away.

How was he cowed by his uncle's old manager? He would never get this place off the ground if he couldn't take control. In his gut, he knew upping the prices was the right business move, but convincing her of that would be a whole different hurdle.

Nate chugged the rest of the cold coffee in his mug, cleaned it in the sink, and grabbed his messenger bag. He needed to get out of the office. After Daria had delivered her outburst, she must've left for the night, because she was nowhere to be found in the front of the house. They hadn't even opened yet, and already he was getting into disagreements with the manager.

Times like these, he missed Boston.

The sun had set, and when Nate stepped out, the stretch of town was all lit up. The historical buildings, the waterside view, and the gorgeous bridge all captured his attention, a slice of the pristine. Gentle breezes swept through, cooled by the night and sweetened by the rhododendrons blooming in the yards. This city seemed unreal at times, and for brief moments, Nate could taste hope in the air, threading throughout—that this could be somewhere he called home.

Nate strolled down the sidewalk, firing off a text to Laura.

My uncle's old manager and I are already butting heads. Joy.

He tapped the side of his phone, not bothering to slip it into his pocket. Out of everyone back in

Boston, Laura was one of the people he missed the most. She was a steel-boned-corset sort of woman—a whip-smart lawyer who could navigate murky terrain with the best all while being the most loyal friend he'd known. His best friend had been devastated when he told her about the move, and while she'd understood, she still tried to lure him back any available chance she got. His phone buzzed with the return text.

You do realize you're allowed to hire whoever you want, right? Why not just fire her?

Nate swallowed hard. He hadn't even broached the idea. Of course Laura would though—the woman was the logical balance he'd always needed when he mooned over relationships or ideals the world never seemed to follow.

I'm not a monster, Laur.

His house lay a street away, close enough he could walk to work daily. While he'd walked a lot in Boston, he'd always taken the subway to his job, and already, the convenience seeped into his bones. Even if Daria would be a challenge, there were so many other amazing things about this town he was still discovering. Like a certain neighbor of his that kept popping up everywhere.

His phone buzzed again.

You could let her run you out of town and come home then.

Nate rolled his eyes. Maybe he just needed to make some friends in the area. Not like he could hit up a club in a tiny town like this. His usual spot of coffee shop chats wouldn't happen until he opened Chesapeake Brew, but he needed to try something.

He approached the line of houses and couldn't help but cast a wayward glance toward the one Linc had pointed out. He'd be lying if he said the guy wasn't on his mind more often than not. Even though he worked with Linc on the remodel, he was also his closest thing to a friend in this town right now. Besides, any time the guy's molten gaze raked over him, Nate's fantasies ran wild.

The front light was on at Linc's house, casting an apricot glow, and as Nate walked past, he caught sight of a familiar figure leaning back in a wicker chair on the porch.

Nate lifted his fingers in a hesitant wave as he caught Linc's eye.

"Hey, neighbor," Linc called, his deep bass tone rumbling through Nate. "Coming back from the coffee shop?"

Nate shoved his hands in his pockets as he strode up the walkway to Linc's house, not wanting to shout. Today had already been too loud, especially after Daria had all but chewed him out. "Lost track of time there," he said, stopping in front of the steps.

Linc tipped back his beer, and Nate's gaze lingered on the bob of his Adam's apple. "You're more than welcome to one." Linc gestured to the six-pack on the ground beside him. "I just needed a refresher after a long day, and Beckett's crashed out."

"Please," Nate said, dipping down to snag the neck of one of the wheat beers in the pack. His relief at the gesture washed over him, the way Linc invited him to join rather than keeping him at a distance. He clenched the cool bottle tight, the condensation imprinting on his palms. "How is Beckett doing? After…" Nate trailed off.

Linc's gaze darkened, and he took another swig of his beer.

Crap. Two seconds into being invited to share a drink and he already screwed things up. He couldn't help but care, even though he'd learned years ago that attitude wasn't always welcome.

"I'm sorry," Nate apologized, the frantic nerves rising again as he shifted his stance. He always seemed to fuck up around this guy. "I wasn't trying to pry. It's just… hey, I dealt with that sort of thing plenty as a kid, and I know how much it sucks."

"He's a strong kid," Linc murmured, his voice scraping low. "Way stronger than his dad. His sunshine attitude hasn't changed, even after a bad day."

"Is the school handling the other kids?" Nate asked, letting out a soft exhale. He hadn't ruined the night. Linc shook his head, his jaw tightening. "Fuck," Nate breathed. "I'm sorry. The situation must make you feel so helpless." He tried to twist the bottle cap off and failed, the edges scraping his fingers.

Linc offered a hand, and Nate passed it over. A second later, he popped the top with the opener attached to his keys, a hiss echoing through the air. "Not twist-off," he mentioned with a ghost of a smile. "And yeah, I can't just stand around his school and loom menacingly to keep the other kids from being assholes. I'm tempted though."

"Hey, I wish I had a dad who cared that much when I was bullied," Nate said, taking a swig of the wheat beer. The sweet liquid washed down his throat, the first bit of comfort he'd grasped onto today. "Not like my parents were terrible or anything, but my dad was always more of a man's man, tough-it-out type of guy."

"Yeah, that wouldn't work for Beckett," Linc responded. "Kid's way too sweet for that approach, and I don't want to see him change."

The look on Linc's face held such a fierce tenderness that Nate's heart squeezed tight. The man was obviously a good father—anyone could see that from talking to him for a second about his son, and the fact did not help diminish his crush in the slightest.

Nate shook his head. "From someone who always grew up an optimistic sucker, I can tell you even though the world tries, some things can't get beaten out of you."

Linc looked at him, the arch of his thick brow inquisitive.

"That's meant to be reassuring," Nate added. "Though based on my current track record in this town, who knows."

"Already feeding the rumor mills?" Linc asked, taking another swig from his beer. The movement was so graceful, his neck bobbing, arm flexing with the motion, and Nate couldn't tear his gaze away. Heat rose to his cheeks.

He scratched the back of his head. "Just completely changing my uncle's store and making an ass of myself a dozen times over in front of my neighbor-slash-hired-contractor. Nothing crazy. I've barely had the time to meet anyone in the town to even start any rumors."

Linc leaned back in his seat, the porch light highlighting his messy dark curls and the defined edge of his jawline. He gripped the neck of the beer bottle with a few fingers, swishing it back and forth. "Haven't gone out in town at all?"

Nate gave him a pointed stare. "What about all this fumbling suggests I'd know where to meet people around here? Chances are, I'd show up at the only biker bar in town thinking it was the place to mingle."

Linc pursed his lips, attempting to hide his grin. The way his eyes danced gave him away regardless. "Mighty big assumption that we'd have a biker bar in town. Maybe a knitting circle."

A laugh escaped him, the surprised sort that lightened the weight that had settled over him after days of stressing if he'd made the right choice in leaving everything behind to move here. "I don't suppose you'd be willing to go out with me to wherever the hell anyone under fifty hangs?" Nate blurted out. Linc watched him, his gaze questioning. Crap, his wording, again. He batted a thousand with Linc so far. "I mean, not go out, go out, as in a date—I know we're working together. But just… fuck, I don't have any friends here."

The admission felt a little like relief and a little like shame at the same time.

Linc shook his head, a wry grin spreading on his features. Nate breathed a sigh of relief. Something about this man got him tongue-tied. Maybe a little because of the rampant fantasies rushing through his head every time they were in the same vicinity—because, fuck, the guy was gorgeous—but maybe a lot because the guy's quiet intensity was the exact opposite of him.

"We've got two main bars in town—Port of Call and Harbor Pointe. Out of the two, Port of Call's the place to go, and not just because my best friend's the owner," Linc responded, flashing him one of those grins that made him weak in the knees.

Nate let the words sink in. That wasn't accepting the invitation, so he must've been letting him down gently. Not like he could expect anything more—he worked with Linc, that was all. Disappointment filtered through his veins, but he kept his smile steady regardless.

Linc shook his head, amusement crinkling the corners of his eyes. "You can't hide anything, can you? If you've got time this weekend, Beckett's going to his grandparents', so we can head there then."

Nate stared at Linc, in shock that the guy had offered to go out to the bars with him. He began to lift his beer to his lips when the nerves set in and he missed his mouth, the top of the bottle brushing against his chin. He made a quick swerve in the hopes Linc hadn't noticed, but once he took a swig and glanced over, he caught Linc's eyes twinkling.

He chugged the rest of his beer, his pulse picking up like he'd begun a sprint.

"I think I can shelve the big plans of Netflix, bourbon, and anxiety attacks for a night," Nate responded. He fought with a smile as anticipation welled inside him. How the hell he would manage to spend an evening with Linc without combusting on the spot was another challenge altogether, but he'd grasp the kindness the man offered.

"Right, Saturday then," Linc said, warmth in his tone. "It's a not-date."

Nate's grin widened as he gave up restraint. He dropped the empty bottle in the six-pack holder and slipped his hands into his pockets again. "Port of Call on Saturday. I'll be there." He took a few steps backward to the steps. "Thanks for the beer. I owe you."

Linc nodded, his gaze lingering in a way that made Nate shiver. Jesus, Mary, and Joseph, the man was like a Molotov cocktail of sexuality. Everything he did turned Nate on. Nate hopped down the steps and began to stride along the sidewalk again to his house three down. In the brief span of time, his troubles had melted away.

He might've declared Saturday a not-date, but he'd just wait and see what happened. For the first time all day, hope unfurled in his heart again, hesitant and wildly unreliable, but always waiting.

CHAPTER 6

Saturday arrived in a blink.

Linc had been busy with jobs all week, including the remodel at Chesapeake Brew with Nate. Even though their night at Port of Call wasn't a date, it sure felt like one. Though, that could be the fuck-me eyes Nate kept giving him every time they interacted. Hell, he'd spent several shower sessions working out the sexual frustration after the guy continued to blurt out things that sounded like come-ons just to fumble over them a moment later.

Linc stood in front of his bathroom mirror and splashed on some sandalwood cologne. Samwise hung out on the floor beside him, lounging like he had nothing better to do with his time. Linc had already combed his curls and threw some product in to tame them after his shower, so he came off somewhat presentable. He opted for simple—jeans and a black T-shirt, because he wasn't great with dressing up to begin with. Marissa had always helped him with outfits for more formal occasions. The twist in his stomach followed, the ever-present tinge of guilt that arose any time he went on a date.

Even though this wasn't one.

He'd already warned Nico he'd be coming to visit Port of Call, so they might get a chance to catch up. Apart from their monthly board game night they now included Beckett in, he hadn't spent much quality time with his best friend in the past few years, which made him feel like garbage when he got a second to think about it.

A knock pounded on his door, snapping him to the present. Nate had arrived.

He strode through his house, which felt quieter and emptier without Beckett's loud presence. Any time his son stayed over his parents' house, the house was deafening in its quiet, as if all the grief and memories might threaten to smother him. Beckett was the bastion that held them at bay. All the better he got out tonight.

Linc grabbed his keys and wallet before he tossed on his leather jacket. The spring air still cast a slight chill. When he swung the front door open, Nate stood before him. Linc's breath hitched as he soaked in the sight. Nate had slicked his hair to the side, and the fitted tee and dark jeans he wore showcased his slender frame and compact muscles. He tugged at the edges of his navy blue blazer, a mix of casual and elegant that fit him perfectly. Those blue eyes flared as he glanced to Linc.

"Are we driving or walking?" Nate asked, tweaking several strands of hair.

Linc pointed to the right. "It's about a two-minute walk, so you tell me. If we were heading to Harbor Pointe, it'd be a different story since we'd have to go across the bridge, but I owe my allegiance to Nico's place."

"I'm just excited to be going somewhere other than the coffee shop and my house," Nate admitted as Linc locked up and stepped out with him. "Not like I was insanely social in Boston. Sam was the reason I went out most times, since he loved to hit the clubs." His gaze darkened.

Linc took the lead to the sidewalk. "Sam an ex?" He recognized the past tense and had grown all too aware most folks referred to breakups, not deaths. A slight chill in the breeze caressed him, and the indigo hues of night crept across the asphalt.

"Five-year relationship down the drain," Nate said, a tinge of bitterness in his tone. "We met in college, and I figured, hey, this is endgame, right?

Turns out, he thought he never got the chance to play the field and explore, so he left late last year." Their footsteps thumped against the concrete, lonely echoes on the quiet streets. While Saturday might be hopping at the restaurants, most of the town only bustled during the daytime.

"What about you?" Nate asked, turning those baby blues on him. Fuck, the man was so damn pretty that the question caught him off guard.

"Exes?" Linc asked, trying to stall for time. Whenever he dropped the dead wife card, things got incredibly uncomfortable. He'd been able to avoid that when he went on dates with folks who grew up here, but then came the elephant in the room as well, because they always danced around the subject of Marissa.

Nate glanced at him, an inquisitive look in his eyes. Of course, Linc had dragged out the silence long enough to make it clear his past held a couple of landmines.

"If I brought up a sore subject, you don't have to talk about it," Nate offered. The lamp from the streetlight highlighted the cleft in his chin, the square jaw, and midnight eyelashes.

Linc shook his head. He needed to rip the Band-Aid off. "My wife died in childbirth six years ago." The words came out stale and clinical, the standard response he gave. Voicing it aloud wasn't what hurt —it was the unsuspecting way grief still crash-collided with him even after all these years.

Nate's expression fell, as expected, and Linc sucked in a breath, preparing for damage control. Whenever he broke the news, they treated it as fresh, whereas he'd had years to process these jagged wounds.

Nate glanced his way. "So who did Beckett get the unbridled optimism from? I'm hazarding a guess it wasn't you, Mr. Pragmatist."

Linc's jaw dropped for a second before he scraped his composure together. Out of all the responses he'd expected, that hadn't been one.

Nate offered a wry grin. "I figured you were 'sorried' out."

A raw laugh escaped Linc's throat. "Every time someone says 'I'm sorry' in response, I get a reflex twitch at this point, like I need to go punch something." His chest grew lighter as they strode closer to Port of Call at the end of the block. The lights were aglow, gliding over the cars crowding the parking lot. Murmurs already filtered their way from the busy bar. "Marissa was all that sweetness. Definitely not me."

Nate's lips curled in a smirk that looked fucking adorable on him. Under the streetlight, his elegant nose appeared even sharper. "I don't know. You look like you've got a bit of sweetness buried under there."

"You must be mistaking me for some other guy," Linc responded, amused despite his hesitations. He hadn't enjoyed himself like this on a date—not-date —for years. Something about Nate felt easy in a way other folks were hard. In the short time he'd known Nate, the man coaxed more words out of him than most of the people in this town had in years.

As they neared Port of Call, the breezes picked up, carrying the crispness of the nearby water. Port of Call was the perfect waterside bar, a large deck spanning out along the water with places along the edge for small boats to dock. Around this time of year, the deck would be getting utilized again, and once summer hit, the place would be packed every weekend. For the time being, everyone veered toward the white multilevel building with plenty of seating on both floors. When Nico had bought the business, he transformed it from a dumpy older bar with ugly linoleum floors into this beautiful landmark of Chesapeake City. That fresh energy was exactly what Nate would bring to Chesapeake Brew too.

"I've got first round tonight," Nate said, his thumb hooked into the pocket of his blazer. "As a thank you for the beer the other night. I needed the unwind."

"Did your uncle's mess finally overwhelm you?" Linc asked. He hadn't inquired the other night, but he didn't make a habit of prying into people's business. If they wanted to tell him, they would.

Nate shook his head. "Just unexpected stressors with the coffee shop. This outing went a long way in helping shift my mood though. It's a relief to socialize again. I'm guessing you know most of the folks in town—mind warning me if I start talking to anyone with too many red flags?"

Right, this wasn't a date. Linc tried to ignore the sinking in his chest. If he'd just nutted up and asked Nate, it probably could be, but instead, he'd hid behind the easy excuse. They worked together.

Linc nodded. "I'll give you a warning." Or he'd watch like a coward as one of his single friends swooped in and offered what he could never. Nate deserved more than a few dates and then a soft let down, which had become Linc's MO ever since he returned to the dating scene a few years ago.

Linc walked to the door and held it open, gesturing for Nate to step inside. The flash of warmth in those gorgeous eyes had his pulse picking up. The moment he entered behind Nate, the loud chatter washed over him in waves, along with the heat in the air, so different from the slight bite of a spring night.

The polished oak tables and chairs scattered through the place were all mostly full, but they weren't heading there. The best place to run into folks and strike up a conversation at Port of Call was the second level, which was also usually where he found Nico, behind the bar.

"How come I haven't been here yet?" Nate said, soaking in everything with wide-open eyes. "This place is awesome."

"Maybe because you just moved here," Linc responded. He tried to follow Nate's gaze, as if he could see this place with new eyes. The bar was filled with wooden décor, all matching shades of polished oak, brass fixtures buffed until they glowed, and hazy globe lights stationed throughout to cast the place in the perfect sort of soft ambiance. Nico had created an inviting atmosphere, and the loud chatter echoed—nice enough for a good night out, but not so fancy that folks felt the need to speak in hushed voices.

He wound his way to the steep staircase leading to the second floor. Nate strode close enough to him that he caught the scent of him, fresh and clean, like spring rain. Linc couldn't help the flare of his libido, the way his cock came to life during most of their run-ins. Nate stumbled a pace, and Linc's arms shot out on instinct. His hands rested on Nate's shoulders as he helped him balance.

Nate glanced at him, lush lips opened in surprise and those gorgeous blues widened. Linc could feel the heat radiating off the man beneath his palms, and the temptation reared to find the bathroom and strip him down. It had been ages since he'd gotten laid. Linc realized with a start his hands hadn't budged from Nate's shoulders. Their eyes met, and the air between them grew saturated with tension. He sucked in a sharp breath and took a step away.

"Graceful as always, I see," Linc teased as he took the lead again.

"The day's not complete if I don't almost run into a brick wall," Nate responded cheerily. "Though shockingly, I get steadier the more I drink."

"This, I need to see," Linc said as he strode up the wooden stairs, their steps echoing through the narrow corridor. The orange-hued lights glowed from the top, and he emerged to the second floor, which didn't look as busy at the tables, but more people clustered around the barstools. He spotted Nico sitting alongside the bar this time rather than behind the long oaken expanse. Jeremy tended bar on this floor tonight, flashing charming grins and moving with a fluid grace that begged to be watched.

"Want to meet the owner?" Linc asked as he headed in Nico's direction. He couldn't get away with visiting and not saying hey.

Nico was in the middle of a conversation with Deb, one of the regulars, as they approached. His friend possessed the sort of stunning features and bright, clever personality that made it a mystery why he was still single, but Nico tended to go through guys too fast for anyone to keep track. With his natural good looks—thick black hair, smooth sepia skin, and sharp cheekbones—the dude could always find a hot hookup, and that had been his MO even back in high school. Linc had always been the opposite—find "the one" and stick with them forever.

Obviously, that had worked out well for him.

"Linc, I was beginning to think you hated me," Nico called. "No game night last week, and I haven't seen you here in ages. How will I survive without my fix of Settlers?"

"He's been working hard on my remodel," Nate jumped in, coming to his aid even though Nico just liked giving Linc shit any day of the week. Still, Linc couldn't help how the corners of his mouth twitched into a grin.

"Yeah, Nic," Linc responded, his tone dry. "I'm working hard."

A startled laugh slipped from Nico. He glanced in

Nate's direction. "I'm guessing you're the new owner of Chesapeake Brew?"

Nate lifted a brow. "Does gossip really spread so fast around here?"

Nico grinned. "Of course. Small towns and all that. But I also make it my business to know what's going on with the other shops in town. We all try to work together here. At least, most of us do."

"Ignore him," Linc murmured to Nate. "He just has a vendetta against the owner of Harbor Pointe." Linc took a seat next to Nico, and Nate snagged the one beside him. Jeremy had spotted their arrival and wandered in their direction, handling refills along the way.

"I'm already working with Cozy Corner," Nate responded to Nico, "but I'm happy to help out with the other businesses any way I can."

Nico's grin turned feline. Oh fuck.

Linc caught Nico's gaze and gave him a frank look. No way would he let someone as sweet as Nate wander into Nico's dine-and-ditch den. Nico pouted at him, and Linc glowered.

"So are the two of you…?" Nico said pointedly, offering him a challenging glance. Linc bit back the sigh. Of course. He should've expected that one. Before he could say anything, Nate jumped in.

"No, no, no. Linc agreed to take me here out of

pity. I don't know anyone in town and was hoping to meet people," Nate filled in.

Linc wanted to correct him—no pity was involved in the decision—but he kept his mouth shut. He'd earned as much of a no-commitment rap as Nico. Time after time, he indulged in his attraction, realized there wasn't the depth he had with Marissa there, and then he moved on. He still hadn't introduced Beckett to a single person he dated.

After Nate's response, Nico had given Linc an arched eyebrow. Guaranteed, he'd be demanding an explanation sooner rather than later.

"I need a drink," Linc announced, trying to regain control of the situation. With his best friend around, the chances were unlikely.

"We can help with that, handsome," Jeremy responded, appearing on the opposite side of the bar. "Getting your usual?"

Linc nodded. Maybe he should hate that everyone knew his orders because he never changed them, but he liked what he liked. It didn't make sense to leap off into uncharted territory because something new and shiny entered the field.

Nate leaned in. "I've got his drink. I owe him one —and not just for doing an amazing job on the remodel."

Jeremy's eyes lit up as he scanned over Nate. The

guy was shameless, like half of Linc's friends, which had made him easy to date when Linc entered the field again. He didn't have to make any guesses or play any games, and just as easily, their handful of dates and hookups transitioned to friendship.

"And what can I get you?" Jer asked, his voice dripping with intent. He offered a crooked smile which worked perfectly with his all-American looks: tanned skin, blond hair, and deep brown eyes.

Nate blinked in surprise, as if he couldn't believe someone was flirting with him. Linc wanted to slam his head against the wall. Had the guy not realized that was what he'd been doing since they met? He tried to avert his gaze, because he was pretty sure he'd started glaring at Jer.

"I'll take a Jack and ginger," Nate said, chewing on his lower lip, which didn't just draw Linc's attention but Jer's too. Unlike with Nico, he couldn't will Jer off with a look either. A piranha was circling, and Nate was fresh meat.

"Sure thing, gorgeous," Jer purred, and a blush spread on Nate's cheeks.

Goddamn. The man's reactions were so genuine. If he flushed like that from a compliment, he probably looked stunning when he came. The image traveled south quick, stirring other parts to life. Thoughts like that one would get him in trouble. He was no better than these other guys circling around the hot new guy in town. Linc speared his fingers through his curls, trying to calm his pulse.

Nate glanced to him. "Does everyone know everyone around here?"

Linc couldn't help his wry smile. "When you've grown up in a small town? That's a guarantee. Can't walk five feet without running into someone you know."

"I don't know if that's terrifying or a comfort," Nate responded, tapping his fingertips along the surface of the bar.

"A bit of both," Linc responded. Going out like this felt easy and natural in a way nothing had for a long time. He didn't know if it was because they weren't on a date or just the spell Nate cast, but he found himself relaxing for once. He caught the way Nate's gaze lingered, which stoked the hunger that flared to life in his chest.

Focus. He went through the rolodex of excuses— work together, Beckett, Marissa, wanting to leave....

Jeremy swung back over with their drinks, placing the pint of whatever they had on tap from Charm City Brewing in front of Linc and then the Jack and ginger in front of Nate. Instead of jetting off like usual, Jer decided to linger. Fucking great.

"So, how long have you been in town?" Jer asked, fixing his gaze on Nate.

"Just long enough to become the talk around here," Nate responded with an effortless grin. "Because everyone seems to know I'm from Boston and arrived to renovate my uncle's old business."

"Word spreads like a wildfire." Jer flashed his charmer grin again. "Especially when you're that damn good-looking."

Nate blushed again, and Linc's chest flared with a cinnamon heat, one he hadn't experienced in a long, long while. Yet it emerged with every slick line Jeremy tossed out to Nate, every flirty glance.

Fuck. If he was getting jealous, tonight would be hell.

CHAPTER 7

Two Jack and gingers in, and Nate was feeling toasty.

He hadn't gotten drunk since his going-away party in Boston—drinking by himself made him feel like crap—but this seemed to be the perfect opportunity. Already, not only had Linc introduced him to a few of the bar regulars and the Port of Call owner, but the bartender, Jeremy, had been flirting with him most of the night.

Nate stared at the surface of his mostly empty Jack and ginger. He should be leaping at the attention from Jeremy—the guy was Grade A gorgeous. However, he couldn't help but gravitate back to Linc every time. Given his circumstances—kid, widowed, and probably still dealing with the grief—he wouldn't be available. Besides, he currently worked for Nate. But Linc had captured his eye from the second they met, and the more he got to know him, the more he liked the guy's quietness, his dry humor, and his grounding presence. Combined with those dark and delicious good looks and a body that demanded attention, Nate was a goner.

"Want another?" Jeremy asked, eyeing his drink. "It's on the house."

Nate lifted the drink and eyed the dregs. "If I drink any more, someone's going to need to carry me home. I'm good."

"That's a shame. I'd volunteer," Jer said, hunger flaring in his gaze.

Linc had been chatting with Nico beside him, but he turned around. "No worries, I promised to get Nate home in one piece." The way he said it held a note of finality, and he met Jer's eyes with a stubborn look that warmed Nate throughout.

Even though Linc could talk to plenty of folks here, he hadn't budged from Nate's side all night, something he'd appreciated. Not like he couldn't float on his own, but he noticed the more Jer flirted, the closer Linc inched to him, and Nate would gladly welcome the gorgeous man in his proximity.

"That mean you're carrying me?" slipped from his lips before he could help himself. *Thanks, drunk Nate. Great job at keeping things casual.*

Linc's gaze flared. "Think I can't?"

Oh, hell. The look alone had him half hard, and the idea of Linc lifting him up did the rest. Nate shifted in his seat, trying to readjust himself without anyone noticing. He slammed back the rest of his Jack and ginger, the cool liquid traveling down his throat, even though it did little to help with the heat scorching him from the inside out. A pleasant buzz filtered through his veins, on the precarious ledge before he slammed into drunk.

"Don't start challenging him to feats of strength," Nico warned, leaning past Linc. "The bastard is so stubborn he'd try and then throw something in his back. Someone keeps forgetting he's not a teenager anymore."

Linc gave Nico a lazy shove. "Spending a day lifting pavers would've knocked teenage me out too. And I kept up with Beckett regardless."

"He was the only reason any of us knew you were hobbling around at home. 'Daddy walks crooked,'" Nico teased, his eyes glittering with amusement.

Nate's chest warmed at the stories of Linc. Piece by piece, he was getting more of the puzzle of Lincoln Lane, and the bigger picture made him even more interested.

"Thank fuck for Beckett," Sarah chimed in. Another regular here, she worked at the bank in town, which he would've never expected from first sight of her. Her look was a splash of sophistigoth, with silver pendants around her neck, a black dress fringed with lace, and dark red lipstick. The second she opened her mouth, she swore like a sailor and reminded him so much of Laura that he knew they'd get along.

Tonight had been a rousing success in the socializing department. He'd met so many more folks than if he'd come here on his own, all thanks to Linc.

"You look light enough to pick up though," Jer commented innocently, even though the man seemed anything but.

Nate shook his head. "I mean, I know I'm not jacked or anything, but I'm not rail thin either. I don't want to go throwing out anyone's back."

"Come on," Jer said, leaning against the bar. The guy's eyes twinkled as he skimmed him over again. "You wouldn't throw out mine."

Nate chewed on his lip. He was being stupid, shooting doe eyes at Linc all night when Jer stood right in front of him, clearly hitting on him. The guy was hot as hell too—it wasn't his fault Nate had gotten fixated on someone else. Laura would tell him to go for a spin in the sheets with Jer if she were here, but he'd always been more of a serial monogamist than a sleep-around type.

"I'll feel terrible if I do though," Nate said, placing his glass on the bartop.

"It's okay," Jer responded. "You can nurse me back to health." Their gazes met, and Nate could see the questioning in Jer's eyes. The invitation was there if he wanted it. Yet, he'd just arrived in town, his whole life was spiraling into disarray, and his boxes weren't even unpacked. Adding a one-night stand to the mix would complicate things further if he caught a case of the feels afterwards. Which inevitably would happen, because Nate attached himself to people more easily than a puppy at the pet store.

From the moment Jer flirted with him, he could read loud and clear that the guy went for one-night stands.

"Fuck, it's already past midnight?" Linc said, loud enough to draw attention.

"Yeah, Grandpa," Nico shot back. "Way past your bedtime."

"You finished your drink?" Linc asked, meeting Nate's eyes.

Nate nodded. The hours had passed quickly, but future him would be grateful for stopping here and getting the extra sleep if they left now. "I'm ready to go if you are."

"Laaaaame," Sarah called, pounding the bar counter with her fist. "Nate, you better come out more often. We need more of us transplants amidst all these fuckers who've lived here their entire lives."

"Definitely." Nate flashed a genuine grin. He tipped his two fingers in a salute to Jer. "Thanks for the drinks, man."

Linc stood, and Nate took that as his cue, rising beside him. A second later, Linc slid in front of him and glanced back. The corner of his mouth quirked in the faintest grin.

"Hop on," he said, gesturing to his back. "I've got something to prove at this point."

Nate's mouth dried with want, even as his nerves took over. "No way, I'm not going to be responsible for wrecking your back. I need you to do the remodel on my business, remember?"

"Do it, do it," Nico chanted behind him, like the devil incarnate.

Linc leaned forward a bit, knees bent at the ready. Goddamn, the man looked delicious, his defined arms as biteable as ever. Nate glanced over to Sarah, who offered a thumbs-up with a cheeky grin, and he rolled his eyes at her.

"Fine," he murmured and placed his hands on Linc's shoulders. Within seconds, the man grabbed his legs and hoisted him up. The strong grip around his thighs felt even better than he'd fantasized. Hoots and hollers sounded from the bar as he leaned in, his chest pressed against Linc's back. The two drinks had nothing to do with the way his mind dizzied right now.

Linc began to carry him out, moving forward with steady strength he should've expected, given the man's livelihood. Nate settled against him, his body lined flush against Linc's, thighs wrapped around his hips. He dug his fingers in a little tighter as Linc hoofed down the stairs with him on his back. The bumpy way his crotch brushed against Linc's back had his cock growing hard, something he'd be more mortified about if he didn't have the pleasant buzz of alcohol numbing him. Nate let out a helpless laugh at the ridiculousness. He'd never expected the spontaneous move from Linc, but damn was it hot.

"You can let me down," Nate protested. "I weigh way too much to get hoisted around."

"Nonsense," Linc responded. "You're no competition for the shit I normally haul at work." He headed for the door, a few folks looking their way. Nate flushed. Next, talk about them would be circulating in the gossip mill of this town, and chances were, Linc would go racing the other way. Heat emanated from the gorgeous man carrying him, and Nate drank in the earthy scent of him, all sandalwood and musk.

Linc pushed his way out the front door and out

into the brisk spring night. He glanced back. "Think you can manage to hoof it the rest of the way?"

"I was fine to walk out of Port of Call on my own in the first place," Nate mumbled, sliding to the ground. His feet rested on the concrete, but his legs might as well have been jelly after all that close contact. The guy had been on his mind from the second he'd arrived in town.

"True, but I had a point to prove," Linc said, raising his hands behind his head. He strode a couple of paces faster while Nate found his footing. He was okay with the space—not like he wanted Linc to see just how flustered he made him. Overhead, the silver moon looked almost full in the sky, glowing with pearly promise. The stars studded the glorious expanse, more visible out here than in Boston, which was too filled with neon lights.

"It was either me, or Jer would've when his shift ended." Linc glanced back. "Unless that was something you wanted?"

The edge to his voice had Nate curious. Was he imagining all the heated glances, the way Linc glued himself to his side all night and literally swept him off his feet?

If he'd misread him, he was going to feel like a complete moron, and he'd already made an idiot out of himself around this guy a thousand times over.

Nate shook his head. "Jeremy's hot, don't get me wrong, but he seems like he's looking for a hookup. That's not my scene."

Linc's lips quirked, but Nate, for the life of him, couldn't tell if that was in relief. Still, he couldn't help but hope.

"And what is your scene, Nate McAllister?" Linc asked, his voice a deep rumble that would feel like sin against his skin. He needed to get his mind out of the gutter when it came to Linc, even if the man continued to feed his fantasies every time they hung out. Their houses stood out at the end of the street, a short walk away, though Nate wished their time together could stretch a little longer.

He chewed on his lip, unsure if he wanted to dive so deep. The alcohol decided for him, moving his lips before he gave permission. "I want something permanent, something real. Don't get me wrong, I've had a few random flings, but I've been looking for someone who makes me see the future. Who can quiet my mind and tether me to the ground, because I tend to run away with myself otherwise."

His chest ached. He'd known for the last year or two with Sam that their relationship wasn't the pinnacle in his mind. Yet, he couldn't help but hope it would turn into something better, that all his time wouldn't be wasted.

Instead, he'd come home one evening to see apartment listings up on Sam's computer... only to discover the man had already found one and planned to move. Once he broke up with Nate, at least.

His palm went to his chest, and he absentmindedly rubbed it, as if he could erase all the pain. The concrete beneath held cracks he avoided as he kept his gaze down.

A warm, large hand clapped on his shoulder, stopping him midstride.

Nate glanced up to see Linc beside him, those dark eyes serious. He swallowed, hard.

"There's nothing embarrassing about that," Linc murmured, his voice a bit rough. "It's a beautiful dream, Nate."

Those words socked him in the chest. Voicing them aloud, having someone acknowledge them—damn, he didn't know how much he'd needed that. Nate shook his head. "You know, for as distant as you try to seem, you're a softie, Linc."

Linc's lips slid into a half smile, and his dark eyes twinkled under the pale light from the streetlamps. "Don't tell anyone."

Nate's heart did a swan dive. The unexpected hint of softness from Linc surprised him, as did most of the facets he'd witnessed tonight. This man would be all too easy to fall for, which was insane. They'd just met a few weeks ago.

"Secret's safe with me," Nate responded, gliding his fingers through his hair. His heart pounded a little faster as they approached Linc's house first. He didn't want this night to end.

After months of monochrome since his breakup, after his entire life shifted into terrifying new terrain when he took the chance and moved down here, and after the loneliness of feeling like an outsider had begun to creep in, this night offered a slice of light at the end of a long, long tunnel. For the first time since he'd arrived, he felt like he might genuinely make a home for himself. Even though he was away from his family and friends, this town offered a warm embrace he hadn't realized he'd been missing at his apartment in brisk Boston.

"Looks like my stop's arrived," Linc said, hands in his pockets as he tilted his head toward his place. His lips pursed, as if he wrestled with something, but then he took a step in that direction.

"Hey Linc?" Nate said, his voice echoing in the quiet around them. Linc stopped midstride and turned to look at him. With the moonlight sharpening his graceful jaw and proud nose, the man was more beautiful than ever. Those brown eyes appeared liquid in the night as he stared at him with enough intensity to banish the thoughts from his brain. Nate forged on anyway. "Thank you."

"For what?" Linc asked with a shrug. "Stop acting like it was a chore to go to Port of Call with you. I had just as much fun tonight."

"Yeah, but not everyone is willing to take a chance on a stranger, and you did," Nate murmured. "I won't forget that."

When their eyes met, Nate found himself unable to move. The tension between them crackled through the air, the electric sort that held his heart in suspension. Linc stood mere feet away, but the way his gaze caressed over the length of Nate's body, he might as well have been pressed against him. The spring breeze filtered through, causing a fluid shiver to course down his spine. Nate couldn't help but linger on the man's lush lips, desperate for the invitation to brush against them. Still, his feet were frozen in place.

A car wound down the street, the bright headlights slicing through the space between them.

With that, the spell broke.

"I... better get going," Nate murmured, even though he wished he could stay here in this moment for far, far longer.

"Sweet dreams, Nate." Linc flashed him a

crooked smile that all but stopped his heart before he turned on his heel and headed toward his door.

Nate took the cue and began to walk the short distance to his own house. His pulse pounded in his ears as he approached his front door, key in hand. He paused to look at the sky, all-encompassing and aching with promise. The stars twinkled out of reach, but for a brief, flickering moment he felt like he could reach out and grasp one in his palm. He slid the key into the lock and turned, tugging the door open to enter his house.

For the first time since he'd moved here, his heart grew full, and his horizon opened with the same promise he'd felt when he drove across the bridge to Chesapeake City. This was where he'd make himself a home, come hell or high water.

CHAPTER 8

LINC PAUSED TO TAKE A SWIG FROM HIS WATER BOTTLE. Sweat dripped down his forehead and coursed down his back. He'd been working on the teardown all morning, and he'd made a solid dent in the front counter and the lights. Of course, that also meant tarp covered most of the place, broken pieces of wood were piled in the corner, and old track lighting fixtures were scattered across the ground. The new items had begun arriving, and hopefully by the end of the day he'd at least have the new lights installed overhead.

From the back, he could hear Nate rustling around.

Ever since their not-date at Port of Call last weekend, the tension between them had multiplied by a thousand. He'd been tempted to kiss him right outside his house, but Nate had walked away before he'd gotten the chance. Linc had hoped the impulse would fade through the week, but instead the urge grew.

The whole thing was his fault anyway, after he'd gotten jealous and competitive at Port of Call when Jer started flirting with Nate. Already, Nico was giving him shit about Nate, and Abby Porter had seen him carrying Nate out of the bar and had *questions*. Fuck him sideways. He didn't have answers even if he wanted to seek them out—which, he didn't.

Daria stepped out of the back room. "How's the progress coming?" she asked, casting a critical eye over his work.

Linc frowned. Nate was the one who'd hired him, yet Daria seemed to have an opinion on everything he did, which he ignored. If the directive didn't come from Nate himself, he assumed Daria was weighing in where it wasn't wanted. Thank god he wasn't doing the job for her, anyway. The woman's criticisms ranged from occasionally valid to so nitpicky that she'd be a nightmare client.

"Solid for the day. What does Nate have you doing?" Linc asked, his phrasing chosen on purpose.

Daria glared. "I'm here to work on the new inventory Nate ordered in, including those bean samples.

If you ask me though, we should've stuck with the coffee Harold used to order. He had a great relationship with the old vendor."

Linc bobbed his head, not really nodding in response. He hadn't asked for her opinion in the first place, but even if he had, he didn't agree in the slightest. Chesapeake Brew hadn't been thriving, and the coffee was better at Cozy Corner—just less convenient. The fact Nate planned on ordering somewhere new was a blessing, and based on the guy's meticulousness and savvy mind for business, he'd probably picked a fantastic new roaster.

Daria leaned against the wall, her arms crossed. "I don't see why the remodel was necessary. Harold should've left the business to me. I wouldn't have ruined the legacy he created here."

Linc cast a glance to the back. "Like it or not, Nate's the owner now. Might want to watch how you talk about your boss." He bit back the other things he wanted to say—that she was an ungrateful shrew and would've done a miserable job at running this business. He'd worked with folks long enough to know when to speak up and when to stay silent. She clearly hadn't learned the same lesson.

"He can't get rid of me," Daria responded, a smug-as-hell expression on her face. "How would he be able to navigate the place? Guaranteed, the guy hasn't dealt with the day-to-day of a coffee shop before."

Linc lifted his brows. Apparently, she didn't know Nate had plenty of experience in that department from his college days. The choices he made lent insight to that—economical decisions on certain items like basic wholesale to-go cups while he leaned toward spending more money on the important aspects, like the beans themselves.

Linc just shook his head. He wasn't here to educate her. He sucked down some more water from his bottle and surveyed what he had left. "Better get to work on the fixtures if I want to leave at a decent time."

"I'm out for the day. Looking forward to seeing what you've done," Daria said as she strolled toward the door, her tone less than convincing.

Nate had a loaded time bomb on his hands with that one, but Linc didn't have the right to interfere there. It was his business and his choice of employees.

He approached the back room where they'd been storing the fixtures and just about everything else to keep the front clear while he did this teardown and remodel. The front door creaked and settled as Daria exited, which left him with the intimate knowledge that only the two of them were in the building again.

A thump came from the back, followed by a "Fuck, fuck, fuck" from Nate.

Linc ducked into the room to see Nate standing in front of a rack that had collapsed. One of the open five-pound bags of coffee had slipped to the ground, and beans spilled all over the tiled floor. Nate gripped the steel beam of the rack, his gaze glued to the ground as he stared at the mess helplessly.

"That's an easy fix," Linc offered as he headed in Nate's direction, past the fixtures he should've been carrying up front. "I can repair the beams tomorrow, and we'll get it in shape."

"What am I even doing here?" Nate asked, his voice hollow and his grip tightening on the beam as he set it down.

Nate's tone snapped his attention at once. His heart twisted at the sheer emotion leaking out of that phrase. Linc walked a few steps closer until they stood mere feet apart. "I'm guessing this is about more than spilled beans."

Nate let out a ragged breath. "My best friend let slip that my ex isn't just in a new relationship—he's engaged. After six months."

Linc winced. That wasn't the sort of news anyone liked getting, and given how much Nate had clearly put into the relationship, finding out must've stung.

"But of course, today had to keep snowballing

downhill. The second I got here, I went to make coffee—and the water heater broke, which is going to be yet another expense stacked on the heaping ones to turn this place around, something Daria clearly doesn't want me to do. But she's my uncle's manager, and I'd be the biggest dick in the universe to find a replacement for her." Nate was rambling at this point, his devastating blue eyes wide and helpless.

Linc stepped in a few paces closer, not sure what he could do. The man was spiraling into a full breakdown, and he was standing witness. Not like he could pull away though.

"Then she brought up the fact that I'd missed a bunch of things on my inventory order, because of course I did, since I need more places I'm failing. I don't know why I thought I could do this in the first place. Sam was right—I'm aimless, and no one's going to stick around to deal with that. Why I figured I could make things work down here is a mystery—"

Linc's feet moved before he was fully aware. All he could register was Nate crumbling to pieces before him, and he needed to help, somehow. In whatever way he could.

He closed the space between them in a few long strides until they stood inches apart, and his lips descended to Nate's, stopping him midramble.

Those lips were impossibly soft, and the way they

pressed against his felt so right. For a second Nate stiffened, and then the man softened against his mouth. All the excuses exited stage right as Linc sank deeper into the kiss, reaching around to weave his fingers through Nate's thick hair. He gave the silken strands a gentle tug as he swept his tongue into the man's mouth. Nate let out a sinful moan that traveled straight to Linc's cock.

His other hand circled around Nate's waist as he brought the man's hips flush against his. Heat crackled between them, and Linc sank into the taste of Nate, all coffee and cream. With their bodies pressed together, he couldn't ignore how his length pressed against the confines of his jeans, nor could he miss Nate's hardness and how it nudged against his leg. Linc stole a breath of the charged air before he dove back in to possess his mouth.

While the kiss might've been gentle at first, all too fast he grew ravenous. Their mouths clashed in a frenzy of lips, of tongues, of teeth, and he sank into the delirious bliss that coursed through him. Nate swayed for a moment. Linc tightened his grip on him and kissed him harder, needing this man more than his next breath. This close, he drew in the fresh, clean scent that had lured him in the other night, tempting him closer.

All of the charged glances, flirty comments, and

the slight touches exploded into this as Linc lost himself in those plush lips, the hot, willing mouth. Nate panted for the seconds they broke apart, his gaze glassy and feverish. Linc plunged back in with even more fervor, dragging his tongue along Nate's desperately, as if the moment they broke apart everything would shatter.

With his hand braced on Nate's hips, he guided him the few steps back, their shoes crunching on some of the spilled coffee beans. Nate's back thudded against the wall, and Linc slid his palm against the cool, hard surface as he continued to devour this beautiful man. Nate tilted his head up as he hungrily met him for kiss after kiss, their mouths crashing together, their tongues gliding against each other. Linc sank into the headiness of it in a way he hadn't for ages, in the sheer thrill of each loaded breath and each brush of their limbs.

They continued to kiss for an eternity, minutes melting away. Linc lost himself in the way Nate melted for him, sweetness evident in every facet of the man. Nate's total surrender to his touch had his cock hard and his mind reeling—everything about Nate McAllister felt right, something he hadn't experienced in a long, long while. Beyond chemistry, his chest grew warm with a possessiveness that spread the longer their lips memorized each other's again and again and again.

Eventually, the fevered kisses grew slower, a little less desperate. He could taste a slight tang on Nate's swollen lips from how he bit and nipped them. Linc finally pulled back, the quiet interrupted by the ragged sound of their breaths. His shoulders heaved, and he realized he was still covered in sweat and dust from working on the remodel—which he should be doing right now, not kissing the hell out of the guy hiring him for the job.

Nate looked at him with those stunning blue eyes, his face flushed and his lips glossed from the way they'd just made out. His hair was ruffled from where Linc had run his fingers through it to grip his nape, which he currently still held. Linc swallowed, his throat bobbing as he released his hold on the back of Nate's neck and the wall, pushing himself upright, even though his world had become tilted.

Nate's mouth opened and then shut again. His brows drew together as he stared at Linc, a questioning look in his eyes.

Linc's tongue traced his lips as his brain reeled for an answer. Not like he had a convenient one beyond the fact that Nate had been stressed as anything and he'd just wanted to take it away in that moment. If he dug any deeper, the truth was this kiss had been inevitable from the day they'd first met. Every interaction had been building toward this, small steps in a direction he wasn't prepared to comprehend quite yet.

Nate broke the silence first. "I'm not going to lie, I'm suddenly forgetting why this was such a terrible day in the first place."

Linc couldn't help the grin that broke onto his face. "Good."

Nate chewed on his lower lip as his gaze scanned the floor. "Right, so... I should handle the water heater situation."

Linc grabbed onto the life raft Nate tossed him. "If you order one, I can install it. It'll be cheaper than bringing in someone new for the whole repair."

"Pulling me out of trouble yet again, Lane?" Nate responded, a little breathless. Hunger roared anew in Linc, and he needed to take a step back to resist the urge to press this man against the wall and have his way with him.

"Any time you need it," he responded, his voice a little hoarse. He glanced toward the front of house. "I better get back to work. I promised those fixtures would be up before the end of the day."

Nate just nodded, absentmindedly gliding his thumb over that full lower lip. Fuck, he needed to remove himself from the room. The man was too damn tempting.

Linc turned around and headed past the racks toward the door, even though it felt a little like running away. He didn't have the slightest clue how to explain any of what he'd done to Nate. He rarely acted on impulse, yet the more time he spent around this man, the more he found himself succumbing to it. He rifled his hand through his hair, his heart still pounding like he'd just raced his truck down 95.

He was attracted to Nate. That was all. His pace quickened as if he could escape the throb of guilt that followed.

The front of the coffee shop stretched out before him, a mess of sawdust and old fixtures gracing the tables that would also get discarded or donated before the week's end. He needed the physical work right now—he could throw himself into it and try to ignore the pulse of his erection or the thousands of questions ballooning in his mind. Linc sucked down another swig of water, even though it did little to cool his scorching insides.

They might've been dancing around this for weeks now, but Linc was the one who'd gone and crossed right over the line.

Even though he'd have to talk about it eventually —they still had weeks of working together—right now he'd push it off for as long as he could. Despite the chaos of his mind, the way his chest twisted like filament relayed a truth he wasn't ready to acknowledge.

Not like he should be getting involved with anyone right now, with the Baltimore job on the horizon and the temptation to wander away from this town rising with every passing day.

Nate was a slice of sweetness in a world that should've stamped it out, his bright nature the exact sort of pure most had crushed out of them at an early age. He deserved kindness, he deserved love, and he deserved his dream coming true.

He deserved far more than the husk Linc had become.

CHAPTER 9

NATE HAD THROWN HIMSELF INTO WORK EVEN MORE THE past few days, ever since that mind-melting, unforgettable kiss.

He'd seen Linc at the shop and around town, and by some miracle they managed to banter and chat like normal, yet the tension of what lay unsaid weighted the air between them, threatening to emerge.

He tugged his canvas jacket a little tighter as he stepped into Pell Gardens Park, a beautiful stretch of green right along the water. Already, boats chugged through the canal, picturesque with their bleach-white hulls that mirrored the puffy clouds in the sky. Even though he loved being by the waterfront in Boston, there it felt like a breath amidst the chaos, whereas here in Chesapeake City, the entire place emanated a serenity he'd been searching for.

With all his internal turmoil, he'd needed a slice of quiet. He wandered over to the edge of the grass where it sloped into the muddy banks of the river. He'd just come from a business meeting with Nico at Port of Call before it opened for the day—they'd figured out an arrangement to help promote each other, a drink punch card that worked at both Chesapeake Brew and Port of Call. Talking with another young business owner had given him a necessary confidence boost.

Ever since he'd arrived here, Daria had fought him on most of his decisions, and the constant conflict chipped away at him more and more each day.

"Hey, Nate," a familiar voice called out. Sarah jogged up to him, her little corgi waddling behind her. She still clung to her all-black attire, though this time jogging pants and a tee.

"You always walk him around here?" Nate asked as he bent to pet her corgi, Max. The pup soaked up the attention, lifting his snout and brushing his head against Nate's hand.

Sarah lifted a brow. "Does it look like there's anywhere else to walk dogs around here? This town's the size of a peanut."

"It's a nice change of pace," Nate said, running his hands through Max's warm fur.

"But...," Sarah continued, her eyes twinkling. She tugged on the hem of her loose T-shirt—black with rainbow stars scattered across the front.

He shook his head, a grin forming. "Sometimes I miss Boston's gay scene. The folks I've met around our age have been open, but it's definitely a limited pool." One he'd already dipped into with the scorching kiss from Linc, but he still didn't have a clue what that meant or if it had a hope in hell of going anywhere.

"Nico and I drive to Baltimore for that. There are some great clubs we can check out, doll. My favorite is Club Apollo—they've got a killer goth industrial night," Sarah offered. The wind rustled, sending some of her dark strands tumbling across her forehead. Max began prancing back and forth. "Though, I'm surprised no one in the pool here's caught your eye." She lifted one of her lined brows with intent.

"Even as the new kid, I know Linc is complicated," Nate said, not bothering to beat around the bush with her. Nico had made a few comments as well, since everyone happened to be in everyone's business around here. Besides, Nico was Linc's best friend, so if anyone would notice, it'd be him.

Go figure. The first person to catch his interest

after the breakup with Sam happened to have a repu-tation as perpetually unavailable.

Sarah shrugged. "Yeah, I've seen him go on a few dates since I've been here—Jer, this chick Ana who was on vacation here for the summer, and a couple others, but none of them would be what anyone could call serious."

"So, pretty much bad news for someone who happens to be a serial monogamist," Nate said, pointing to himself. His chest sank, those fragile hopes threatening to suffocate.

Sarah offered a lopsided grin and tugged at Max's leash before casting a glance to her right. "Why don't you ask him yourself?"

Nate followed her gaze to spot Linc walking over in smooth, powerful strides. The white T-shirt he wore placed those broad shoulders on clear display, melding over defined pecs and abs Nate wanted to lick. The mere sight of Linc had Nate's heart pounding harder, and he brushed his hands through his hair as if he might be able to tame the windswept strands.

Both of Sarah's brows rose with her smug look. "I'll leave you two. Don't be a stranger, Nate."

"We can get dinner sometime this week if you want," he offered. They'd exchanged numbers at Port of Call, and already they'd been texting back and forth a bit. Sarah not only had a biting wit but as much of a penchant for baby animal pictures as he did.

"I'm holding you to that one," she called as she headed the opposite direction of Linc, tugging Max along with her.

Nate turned toward Linc and offered a half-hearted wave. Linc nodded in response, cutting the distance between them quick until he stood feet away. Mud splattered his steel-toed boots, and he had a smudge on his cheek of something, probably from whatever job he'd been on. Nate fought the temptation to reach up and brush it off. Linc was due to Chesapeake Brew later, where they'd continue their awkward dance.

"I was parked right along the road and happened to see you here," Linc offered, hooking his thumbs into his front pockets. The motion brought his shoulders forward into a hunch, and he cast a hesitant glance in Nate's direction that made his heart hiccup.

"You caught me—I was playing hooky after the meeting with Nico before heading over to my prison, the coffee shop." Nate tried to offer a cheerful smile, even though he might as well be a rowboat on the water with how much his confidence rocked back and forth.

"Look, I figured we could talk," Linc murmured,

those dark eyes arresting Nate. Those were the words he'd wanted to hear ever since the kiss, but now that they'd arrived, the nerves swept through. What if this was Linc telling him the whole thing had been a mistake? That he was shit at kissing or the experience had been enough to send Linc running in the opposite direction?

Nate shrugged. "If you want to. I'm not one for pushing."

"I noticed." Linc eyed him, a soft grin creeping to his features. "And I'm not one for impulsive actions."

Nate arched a brow. "Could've fooled me."

Linc stretched his arms overhead, fingertips laced together as he averted his gaze. "I do owe you a talk though. I don't go randomly kissing people."

Nate's pulse sped. If this was the point where Linc crushed his tentative hopes, he wanted to skip right past to the devastation. After the funk the breakup with Sam had put him in, he wasn't sure how bad he'd spiral if the first guy who genuinely interested him rejected him too.

"Look, I don't have any expectations." Nate hurried out with the declaration, as if he could somehow protect himself. "If it was an impulse, just tell me, and we can move forward."

Linc glanced to him, their gazes snagging again.

STRONGER THAN HOPE   113

"The action might've been impulsive, but I've been wanting to kiss you for a while now."

Nate's mouth dropped open, and then he shut it again. "Oh." He raked fingers through his hair, a flush rising to his cheeks as warmth spread inside him like hot tea.

A while.

The idea dizzied his mind.

"I could lie to you and tell you I held off because we work together, but the truth was, I didn't want to hurt you. I'm sure you've heard my reputation around town." Linc shoved his hands into his pockets and cast an irritated glance behind him, as if he were cursing the entirety of Chesapeake City.

"That you don't do serious relationships," Nate filled in, his heart sinking. Not like he'd expected after a single kiss they'd be rushing off to get married, but he'd be lying if he said a secret part of him hadn't been hoping this would turn into something more. Linc might not be one for relationships, but Nate didn't do one-night stands. He needed to know the person he was with, to trust them.

"This is the problem with hearsay," Linc said with a sigh, scuffing his boot against the muddy ground beneath him. "They miss the nuance. I've always done serious relationships, but the last serious relationship was my wife. It's only been dates since then."

Nate let his words sink in. None of that spelled out that he was only in for one-and-dones or quick flings. Linc pursed his lips as he stared at the ground, a slight vulnerability evident in those gorgeous brown eyes.

Understanding crystallized. "You haven't found anyone you've connected with like you did your wife," Nate murmured.

Linc's head whipped up as he looked at him. "Yeah...," he said slowly, as if digesting what Nate had said, the wrinkles in his forehead smoothing with his surprise. "That's the problem."

Nate's lips quirked as hope flowered anew in his chest. "What I haven't heard in all that is a rejection though."

"I can't promise this won't end like the others—a few dates and then me calling it quits. I make it a policy to be honest. I don't want to lead anyone on," Linc responded. The air thickened between them as they both moved forward with their words, like learning new steps to a dance.

Linc was risky. He'd flat-out admitted Nate's chances were terrible and anything between them would most likely end. After the heartbreak with

Sam, Nate shouldn't be throwing himself into something so shaky, so unsteady.

Yet, Linc was the first person who'd made his heart flare to life again since his breakup. And if Nate could do anything, it was dream, even when things seemed bleak.

Nate took one step forward, then another, resolve settling inside him as he stood right in front of Linc. The man's gaze was magnetic, neither of them willing to look away, and the air grew so tense that even the freshwater breezes couldn't slice through. This time, he closed the distance between them.

His lips brushed against Linc's, soft and exploring. The first kiss had taken him by surprise, erasing all thought from his mind, and he'd just surrendered. To the heat, to the relief, to the thrill. Yet this one held an intention he needed to communicate the one way he knew how.

The moment their mouths met was electric, as intoxicating as the warm sun on his skin or the first scent of spring in the breeze. Linc didn't hesitate to take control. His callused hand wrapped around Nate's nape as he devoured with his kiss. Within seconds, the kiss went from tentative to scorching under Linc's steady guidance. Nate's legs turned to jelly at the stroke of Linc's tongue against his, at the tight grip at his neck, and the steady heat stoked between them.

Nate wanted to drown in the swirl of the fragrant gardenias mixed with Linc's earthy scent, all musk. He leaned against him until their bodies were flush against each other, until he was impervious to the gentle chill brought on by the breeze. Linc kissed with a reassurance he couldn't help but fall into, a confidence that contradicted everything he'd said. He could lose himself in this kiss, the sheer strength carrying him away.

Nate sucked on his lower lip, kissing back with the same intensity. He loved the taste of this man, and the more their mouths met, the more he was dying to lick and suck his skin from head to toe. Linc pulled away for a breath, the hot puff tingling against his lips. Before he could get carried away with kissing this man for the rest of eternity, Nate stepped away as well.

Linc's lips quirked in a half smile as their eyes met. The man's curls were tousled, his lush lips inviting, and those thick brows accented the seriousness in his deep brown eyes. His hand still rested on the back of Nate's neck, a steadying force that bolstered his courage.

"We haven't even gone on a single date yet, so I'm

willing to gamble," Nate murmured. "Why don't we start there?"

Linc licked his lips, the motion sending a shiver down Nate's spine. The hunger in his expression made him want to take this somewhere private, and fast. That sort of hunger demanded he forget every red flag or warning in his mind that he might break his heart, just for the chance to experience something so intense.

"You want a date?" Linc said, his eyes crinkling with his grin. "I think I can handle that." The guy was so gorgeous, Nate's breath hitched in his throat. From Linc's bronze skin gleaming in the sun to the proud slope of his nose, the firm arch of his brows, Nate found he couldn't look away.

"Good." Nate let out a laugh, all nerves. "Because I'm garbage at planning them."

Linc let his hand drop to his side, even though Nate could still feel the phantom weight of his palm on the back of his neck, pinning him in place. If not for that, he might just float away on the giddiness swirling through him. He hadn't dared allow those hopes burst free that Linc might be half as interested.

"So, we're dating. Going on dates, that is." Nate hesitated, the other question bubbling in the back of his throat and threatening to erupt. Linc cast a curious look to him, and it exploded out. "Look, I'm not here to dictate anything, but if this is a... seeing multiple people sort of thing..."

"I'm one-track, McAllister." Linc clapped a hand on his shoulder. "I can only handle going on dates with one person at a time."

A knot in his chest released. Nate nodded in response. "Me too." Not like he got a player vibe from Linc, but he was already taking a chance here. The last thing he needed to add to his pile of anxieties was the thought of the man hooking up with someone else.

Linc took a step forward, a gleam in his eye. "I'd better get going though. I've got a job to get to, and the boss is a real hardass."

Nate rolled his eyes as he nudged Linc in the side. "Yeah, huge disciplinarian, that one. Especially when he lets his one inherited employee walk all over him."

"No one said you have to keep her," Linc offered, those words mirroring what Laura had said.

"Yeah, yeah," Nate deflected, not wanting the raincloud of his Daria problem to dampen this bit of reprieve he'd found. "I've got a back room I need to lock myself into, anyway. Better join you."

Linc smirked as he ran his thumb over Nate's lower lip. A sinful shudder rolled through him. Jesus, Mary, and Joseph, this man was sun in the middle of

August hot. "Come on then," he said, turning on his heel and taking the lead. "Let's go."

Nate cast one last look toward the glittering river before he followed a step or two behind. His heart hoped, and his mind reeled, yet those fears percolated beneath the gilt surface of all those amazing feelings.

Linc hadn't made any promises—they might go on a few dates and then he'd be dismissed like the others. This could ruin him, could set him back from all the progress he'd made post-Sam.

Yet, he couldn't silence the small voice deep inside him, the one that asked—what if it didn't?

Nate followed that voice every time.

CHAPTER 10

LINC SETTLED INTO THE BOOTH SEAT, AN UNFORGIVING cracked red vinyl. Maverick Diner might not be the most elegant place, but despite the need for a fresh coat of paint and some new seating, it remained consistent with a delicious meal. Beckett hummed next to him at the window spot, the diner mat turned into his latest work of art as he applied cobalt blue to the blank backside. He'd already tuned the world out, based on the purse of his lips as he concentrated. Linc shook his head, biting back his grin.

"What are you working on, Beck?" Dad asked, leaning in. Beck didn't answer for a second as he furiously scribbled an extra line here or there.

He blinked up for a second. "I'm almost done, Grampa. Then I'll show you!"

Mom gave him an indulgent grin. Beck always got like this when he was working hard on a piece, just lost in his own world.

She glanced up to Linc. "You've been keeping busy with work, right?" Her brows were knitted in the constant concern that had arisen after Marissa's death. As if any hiccup or difficult patch might send him teetering off into oblivion. Dad propped the big plastic-coated menu up, scanning for dessert options, since they'd just polished off breakfast.

"Finishing up the remodel for Chesapeake Brew," Linc said, unable to squash down the barrage of images that stirred—none of them having to do with the building and all centered around the owner. Ever since he and Nate had their talk, they'd stolen at least three more scorching make-out sessions in the back room when Daria wasn't there. He had a plan in mind for their date, but that wasn't until next week when his folks were taking Beck for his Saturday-night sleepover.

"What do you have lined up after?" Dad asked, folding the menu and placing it down.

Before Linc could answer, Beck thrust his artwork in his face. "Look, Daddy, I made a swamp monster."

Linc plucked the drawing from his son and spread it out in front of them, scanning over the broad swirling lines of his mostly blue swamp monster. He glanced to his father. "I've got a job in Baltimore," he admitted. "I was going to ask if you could take Beck for the couple of days I'm going to be on-site." He turned to look at Beck, who stared up at him, eyes wide and eagerly waiting for an answer. "Your swamp monster looks great, kiddo. Are you going to draw him a friend?"

Beck's eyes grew a little dimmer as he shook his head. "No, the swamp monster doesn't have any friends."

Linc swallowed hard. He knew Beck was the "weird kid" at school. He knew even though more incidents hadn't been reported, that didn't mean the other kids weren't hurting him with their words. Fuck, he was failing at this.

His mom passed a sympathetic glance at him, both of his parents letting him take the reins on this one.

He rested a hand on Beck's shoulder. "How about you draw the swamp monster's daddy?"

Beck pursed his lips, but he snatched back his paper and nodded, pulling out an orange crayon this time. Where this kid had gotten his idea of swamp colors, he had no clue.

"Why are you taking an out-of-town job?" Mom asked, her tone sharpening. He'd expected this—they'd pick up on the subtle shift in his thoughts of leaving, simply because he hadn't taken a single job that took him too far from Chesapeake City since Mar died.

"I was recommended for it, and I figured I might as well scope out the area and see what the work is like there," Linc murmured. His stomach twisted with nerves. He hadn't broached this conversation with Beck yet or even the idea of moving, and he sure as hell didn't want to do it here.

Mom's brows drew together in her patented disapproving look. "In Baltimore? It's dangerous there, and not close in the slightest."

"The city's an hour and some change away, Ma," Linc countered. He'd grown up forever hearing how the Lanes had always lived in this town, how his grandfather had helped build and keep it alive. His grandpa was how he'd gotten into construction work in the first place when the old man took him under his wing and taught him the basics.

Still, this town had also been where Marissa grew up. She'd made her imprints all around it, and they continued to haunt him, lingering reminders of the depths of blissful happiness he'd never reach again.

"I'm just looking," Linc said, his voice firm. "It can't hurt to expand the business, in any case."

"We'll watch Beckett." Dad stepped in at this

point. "Though, I can speak for both me and your mother in saying we hope your jobs stay local."

Linc nodded. Tension creased the air between them. They weren't going to get into this argument here, especially when he was so unsure. But Beck wouldn't even be leaving friends behind—just a school filled with shitty bullies who picked on him. And the idea of letting go of their house felt a little like grief, but also a little like salvation. He'd be able to start fresh, somewhere that wasn't haunted by the whispers of his marriage at every corner.

"Thanks," he offered. "You know I appreciate it."

"We're always happy to see our Beckett," Mom said. "Right, sweetie?" She reached over to muss Beck's hair. He looked up and offered a bright smile. A worried line formed between her brows, one Linc put there. If they moved, Marissa's parents wouldn't be thrilled either, though they weren't as involved in Beckett's life. He noticed the tinge of melancholy whenever they had Beckett, like he was the remaining fragment of their daughter they had to grasp onto.

He understood how that felt.

"All right, kiddo, pack away the crayons," Linc said. "We'd better be getting home."

"And here your father hasn't even picked out

dessert yet." Mom grinned, the mood lightening, since this happened every time.

"I'm waiting for the day he does," Linc responded, tension leaching from the air. Beck still doodled on the page, as usual ignoring what Linc had said while he was wrapped up in his creative space. Linc gave him a few minutes, sipping the dregs of the coffee in his cup—the kid was clearly putting on the final details to his picture. When Beck paused, Linc stepped in again. "Now it's time to put the crayons away."

Beck blinked at him as if this was the first time he'd mentioned it. "Oh, okay." Beck began to shove the crayons into the zippered bag he carried around —Linc had long since given up on organized boxes.

Linc rose at the same time as his parents—he'd already paid the bill for breakfast—leaving Beck fussing over his crayons in the booth. The world could be ending, and Beck would still be lagging behind. The kid couldn't help that his head floated forever in the clouds. He reached over to give his folks hugs goodbye, and all three of them shared a grin as Beck finally made his way out of the booth to throw his arms around his grandparents in an excited hug.

"Love you, munchkin," Mom said, squeezing him tight.

"All right, kiddo, let's head home," Linc said, reaching his hand down to hold Beckett's. His kid's other hand gripped tight to his new drawing, which would join the stacks and stacks of them in the house. Linc had bought a filing cabinet, but he'd mostly just put the stacks inside there without rhyme or reason.

Linc bobbed his head in acknowledgement to the hostess in the front of Maverick Diner before they stepped out onto the main stretch of Chesapeake City. The sun shone warm even in the early morning, spring beginning to overtake the city with every unfurled green bud they passed. Beck waved to half of the folks they walked by, whether he knew them or not. Linc's heart squeezed tight at the way the kid remained so open to the world.

The more he was bullied or ostracized here, that might change, and he couldn't bear to see his son's light snuffed out.

He turned the corner onto their street, their small two-story house standing out like always at the end. Beck scampered faster down the sidewalk, to the point Linc was sure the kid would trip. Thank god for long legs—he kept up with ease.

His gaze wandered as they approached Nate's house with the cranberry shutters. He couldn't help himself. The guy had been on his mind more than he cared to admit of late. Even though they'd made no promises—his fault—he couldn't help but notice the differences between every interaction with this man and the past dates he'd been on. Where he'd lacked chemistry with the others beyond the superficial, he enjoyed peeling back every layer of Nate McAllister.

And by the time their first date arrived, he'd hopefully be peeling off other layers.

"Come out, dammit," a voice shouted from the front of Nate's yard. Linc's gaze traveled to the source. Nate squatted in front of the line of hawthorn hedges, tugging on a long weed that had sprouted up.

Beck looked at Linc with big eyes. "Daddy, he said a bad word."

Linc bit back his laugh, forcing a serious tone. "Yes, he did." Before he could stop Beck, the kid bolted in the direction of Nate, probably to communicate his indiscretions. His stomach flipped. He liked to keep the men and women he was interested in away from Beckett, but since Nate was his neighbor, he couldn't do that. One thing he'd never done was introduce them to his son as someone he dated. The mere idea sent an undercurrent of panic coursing through him.

Nate stood from his crouch and brushed his knees off, stained with dirt from his valiant attempts at weeding. Beckett planted himself in front of him, and by the time Linc closed the distance, he could hear the admonishment for the "bad word."

Nate's head dipped, properly chastised. "Well, I'm sorry about that." He lowered to a crouch to put himself on a more even level with Beckett. "What's your name? I'm Nate."

Beck jerked a thumb at his chest. "I'm Beck, and that's my daddy." He turned toward Linc and waved at him. Linc shook his head, unable to restrain the grin on his face as he stepped up to the pair of them.

"Hey, Nate," Linc responded, rifling a hand through his hair. "I see you've met my son."

"He rightly pointed out my filthy language. I've seen the error of my ways." Nate grinned, still in his crouch, his eyes dancing as he glanced to Beckett.

"Are you the new neighbor?" Beck asked, interrupting them. "Do you have any kids? What's your favorite color?"

Linc watched in amusement. He was used to Beck steering the ship with conversations, because the kid could talk like no one's business.

"Well, I am the new neighbor," Nate said, placing his hands on his knees. The crouch had to be uncomfortable, but he maintained eye level with Beckett regardless. Linc tried to ignore the way his chest was suffused with warmth at the sight. "I don't have any kids for you to play with, but I like to play games too. And my favorite color is blue."

Beck's eyes widened, as if he'd reached some brilliant new insight, and he thrust his picture out in Nate's direction. "You have to take this then!"

Linc rolled his lips inside his mouth in an attempt not to laugh. Nate appeared equally as startled by the outburst and offering shoved in his face, but that was pure Beckett.

"He's blue," Beckett explained when Nate hadn't responded, as if they'd all missed the most obvious connection.

"Can you tell me a little more about him?" Nate asked, wiping his hands down on his jeans again before accepting the picture. Linc's heart thudded a little faster.

Beckett nodded. "He's a swamp monster who lives all alone except for his dad, who's right beside him there. He growls when people come too close and likes to swim a lot."

Nate looked up, his eyes meeting Linc's for a second. The flash of understanding struck Linc square in the chest, as if Nate had interpreted Beckett's drawing too. Nate turned his focus back to Beckett. "Can I be the swamp monster's friend?"

Well, shit. If he hadn't been interested in Nate before for a thousand and one reasons, that comment alone sank the final nail into his coffin. Linc's chest twisted tight with gratitude. Somehow Nate had gotten what Beckett was expressing on the page within seconds of meeting him, and he'd crossed the divide without even being asked.

Beckett's whole face lit up, those deep brown eyes filled with the same expressiveness as Marissa's. "He would love a friend!"

Linc swallowed hard.

Nate's eyes crinkled as his grin deepened. "Good, because the swamp monster seems pretty cool to me."

"I'm glad you're our new neighbor," Beck declared. "Mr. Nate is nice, isn't he, Daddy?"

Linc shook his head, a wry smile clinging to his face. "Mr. Nate is definitely nice." His gaze snared on Nate's, and he found he couldn't look away. The man beamed, as if he were just as excited as Beckett over making a new friend. That sort of unadulterated sweetness was his kryptonite every damn time. Linc sucked in a sharp breath. Any longer here and he would likely combust. "All right, kiddo. Why don't we wave goodbye to Mr. Nate and head on home?"

Nate pushed up from his crouch and lifted the drawing Beck had given him. "Thank you for this," he said to Beck. "I needed new art for my walls since I just moved here."

Beck brightened. "I can make you more pictures!"

Linc shook his head. "You have no idea what you've unleashed." Still, the kindness toward his son made his heart melt. Beck took any excuse to draw, and this would fuel him for weeks. "I'll see you around, Nate."

Nate offered a lopsided grin and a wave in response.

"Bye, Mr. Nate," Beck called before he scampered in the direction of their house. Linc cast one more lingering look to Nate. The man's thick hair was a mess, and the sun brought out the firm lines of his nose, his chin—pure gorgeousness. They shared a smile that felt more intimate than any so far, one that settled in his bones. Linc sucked in a breath to steady himself.

He slipped his hands in his pockets as he trailed after Beckett, who hopped and skipped his way to their front porch, a ball of vibrant energy. Nate had known just what to say to his son, and he hadn't missed the fact. In a way, he was envious of Nate's immediate understanding and ease, but in another way, the situation struck such intense longing that he almost forgot how to breathe.

That was something to analyze on another day.

Linc passed Beck, messing up his son's hair as he went, and slipped the key into the door. Right now, he needed to focus on giving Beck a chance to unwind, since school had been stressful of late. Approaching his house brought the echo of guilt he should be feeling far more strongly right now. He'd have all the time in the world to obsess over Nate—at work, in the shower, or on their date next week.

CHAPTER 11

NATE LEANED AT THE SECOND-FLOOR BAR OF PORT OF Call, which was empty of most folks apart from the early birds for dinner, who ranged in the sixties and over crowd. He and Nico had been hashing out plans for everything from their joint drink card to a collaborative coffee and alcohol booth at Chesapeake Days, the town's big yearly festival.

Nico swung around the opposite side of the bar and began pouring himself a gin and tonic. The slender man moved with a natural grace that fit his sleek appearance—slicked-back inky hair, a tight, well-fitted button-down, and a pair of gray Oxfords without a blemish. "Now that we've gone through most of the business talk, can I get you a drink?"

Nate tapped his fingers along the surface of the bar. "Just a cider, if that's okay."

Nico lifted a brow, a charming grin sliding onto his face. "I wouldn't have asked if it wasn't." Glasses clinked as Nico flowed like the liquid he poured. He assembled his own drink and then filled a pint of cider from one of the taps. Even though Nate had shown up for work talk, he brimmed with curiosity at what Nico might be able to tell him about Linc. Not like Linc kept his life a secret from him, but the man only said what was necessary, and when it came to him, Nate wanted to learn everything.

Nico slid the honey-colored cider across the counter and then sauntered on out to take the seat beside him. "Cheers," he said, taking a sip of his drink. "Hope this venture helps the both of us."

"I'm indebted to you," Nate admitted. "I'm just starting out in town, and you're already so well-established here."

"This is where I'd normally make a flirty comment or a pass, you know," Nico responded. "But I'd never do my boy Linc dirty like that."

A flush rose on Nate's cheeks. Maybe the pool was much smaller in Chesapeake City than Boston, but he hadn't been hit on this much in ages. Nico was a beautiful man too, way out of his league, so the ego stroke didn't rate as a bad thing. "Has he said anything about me?"

Nico arched his defined brow. "Apart from

warning me off when we all hung out the other week, no. But based on the look in your baby blues, there's something I should know."

Nate threw his hands up. "No, no, nothing to mention." Apart from the date they had tomorrow and the fact he'd been burning up all week at the idea of potentially spending the night with Linc.

Nico snorted. "Anyone ever tell you that you're a garbage liar? I need to demand some answers from Linc."

Nate took a gulp of his cider in an effort to keep himself from giving anything else away. He chugged a bit more than anticipated and spluttered on it. "Nah, they all tell me I'm great at hiding things," he attempted midcough. Nico let out a bark of a laugh.

"Look, I don't know if you guys are involved or if you're looking to get involved with him, but I'll give the obligatory best friend warning." Nico leaned back, his hand wrapped tight around the gin and tonic. His tone lowered to serious for the first time since they'd met. "Ever since he lost Marissa, he's kept folks at a distance, but I know he's still hurting. If things ever get serious between the two of you, if he lets that happen, just be willing to push with him. The guy is stubborn as anything and sometimes needs to be smacked over the head to understand."

Nate swallowed hard. Despite all the excitement

jittering through his veins at the idea of tomorrow, he knew the massive hurdle that lay between them. He couldn't imagine shouldering grief while trying to raise a kid, yet the man did it by his lonesome. The idea of trying to compete with the memory of Linc's dead wife felt insurmountable, but he couldn't help but fumble forward anyway.

"You're a good friend, Nico," Nate said, warmth welling in his chest. It was clear how much the man cared, and that touched Nate in a way he hadn't expected. Not like he didn't have close friends of his own—Laura and Rex back home sprung to mind—but he'd also lost a lot of them in Boston with the breakup. Most folks ditched him for Sam, and he'd be lying if he said those departures hadn't left a mark.

Nico shook his head. "None of the sentimental junk or I'll puke," he said, lifting his drink. Nate clinked his half-finished cider with Nico's. "To a flourishing partnership," Nico toasted. "And the hope my best friend can take the hint and scoop you up before someone else does."

Nate's heart pounded a little faster. As if he'd be so lucky. Those moments when Linc focused his whole attention on him—that sort of intensity was like standing in the middle of a blizzard and watching the snow overwhelm everything. And he just wanted to let it overtake him. Tomorrow he'd have Linc all to himself, something that both terrified and thrilled him.

"Here's to hoping." Nate lifted his cider in salute before he tipped the rest of the smooth, honeyed liquid back. "Now, unfortunately I've got to go finish the system update on the computer I got installed in the back. Once I get everything upgraded to the modern era, I'm torching Uncle Harold's filing cabinet."

"Good damn luck," Nico said, leaning against the bar as he surveyed the tables, which were beginning to see a slight uptick in patrons. "It was a hellacious process when I took over this place."

Nate pushed up from his seat and left the empty glass on the bar. "See you around," he said before he strode in the direction of the steps leading to the bottom level. The nautical theme permeated every inch of this place, even along the walls as he descended the staircase. Portholes hung up there, along with decorative ship's wheels. If he could manage to transform the coffee shop like Nico had this restaurant, he'd be in great shape. He'd seen the old pictures of what Port of Call used to be, and it had sorely needed an update.

He stepped out from the stairwell and headed toward the door. Nate bit his bottom lip. Just the other week, Linc was carrying him down those steps. Heat welled deep inside him, threatening to send him into total combustion.

Before he'd reached the door, a voice called out behind him. "Nate McAllister?"

He stopped midstride and turned around to see an older woman, probably midseventies, with short whorls of white hair, a nose that protruded a bit further than normal, and makeup painted on as heavily as her wrinkles. She wore gaudy blue earrings, a checkered scarf, and a shapeless navy dress. Even though she seemed to know who he was, he'd never met the woman in his life.

"You're Harold's nephew, aren't you?" she crooned.

He nodded and offered a hand to shake. "Yeah, I moved down here from Boston to take over the coffee shop after he passed. And you are?"

She looked at his hand and lifted her nose, not meeting the gesture.

Nate lowered his hand and took a step back. He'd assumed she wanted to reminisce over his uncle or something of the sort, but she stared at him with a hard, unforgiving gleam in her eyes.

"Shame on you," she said, loud enough to startle him, even if the words hadn't.

"Excuse me?" Nate responded, unable to figure

out what on earth he'd done to warrant this reaction from a stranger. Was she a Bible thumper who wanted to lecture him on the sin of his ways? Not like he had gay stamped on his forehead, but he hadn't made it some secret.

"Chesapeake Brew was an institution in this town, one your Uncle Harold spent his entire life making a welcome place. Raising the prices like the folks here can afford those big city numbers? You should be ashamed." The woman scowled at him, censure dripping from her words.

Nate's jaw dropped.

What the hell?

He hadn't released those numbers to the public yet—hell, he hadn't even finalized them, with the amount of resistance Daria gave him every time he made mention. Had she gone and badmouthed him around town? How else could this old lady have found out they were raising the prices when they opened?

Out of the corner of his eye, he caught stares from some of the other patrons on the lower floor of the restaurant. This was bad for his business, and he hadn't even opened yet.

He slipped his hands into his pockets, not knowing what to do with them at this point. Nate sucked in a slight breath, trying to hold onto his deteriorating composure. "Look, I don't know what you've been told, but the prices aren't finalized yet. And I promise you, while they might be different from what they were, I'm making sure they're fair."

The woman shook her head, still refusing to introduce herself. This wasn't going anywhere good.

"Right," Nate murmured, his stomach churning like he'd swallowed cement. "Well, I won't try to sell you on change—it's hard when an institution you've known your whole life transforms into something different." He glanced around Port of Call. "But this place wouldn't exist if someone hadn't come in and shaken things up a little. I hope you'll give the new Chesapeake Brew a try before you write us off completely."

With that, he turned on his heel and exited.

He hadn't made it several paces outside the door before shakes traveled from his feet all the way up his body. Breaths exploded out of him as if he'd been in a knock-down, drag-out fight. The woman's accusation had been the equivalent of a slap to the face. Nate forced his feet forward, even though his steps were shaky and his mind off-kilter, like he'd just stepped off a Tilt-A-Whirl. The late afternoon sun gleamed golden around him, sharpening the cracks in the concrete as he followed the sidewalk back in the direction of his house.

To be honest, he was half afraid if he looked up, someone else would accost him in the street.

The farther he walked, the longer the shadows stretched, until he realized he'd passed his house. Still, he couldn't bring himself to stop moving, his arms and legs firing with aftershocks from the way the woman had snapped at him out of the blue. His breaths came out shaky, uncertain, like someone had taken the card tower he'd spent weeks assembling and smacked the structure down with a single, decisive strike.

Sure, maybe he shouldn't give a damn what some random old biddy had to say.

Yet, he couldn't help but care.

That impulse got him into trouble in the first place, the need to understand everyone, to try and make them happy. The reality that had been lingering in the back of his mind settled like sediment in a disturbed puddle.

After the ire he'd experienced today, he saw not everyone would be warm and welcoming like Eliza and Nico. The unknown was what would happen once he opened—whether this town would help him succeed or ultimately sentence him. However, one thing was for sure.

Daria was becoming a huge problem, one he would eventually have to deal with.

CHAPTER 12

Even though Linc had worked hard on the remodel at Chesapeake Brew all week, the rest of the time there was spent flirting, and once Daria left, making out with Nate in the back room.

Still, the day of their date arrived, and Linc couldn't deny the shiver of anticipation or the nerves that accompanied it. He normally floated through his dates, feeling more sick than anything and unable to enjoy them half the time. Self-recrimination took up an unwelcome seat at those dates, souring things before they could begin.

He tugged on the backpack over his shoulder as he approached Nate's house. Linc had debated on doing the traditional date—restaurant and a movie—but something about Nate made him want to try harder. As if it might mean more than his average first date. Truth be told, the way they were going into this contradicted every date he'd been on since Marissa died. After all, they'd gotten to know each other and kissed first. Completely backwards.

Yet, it felt right, when nothing had for a long, long while. Linc wasn't ready to dwell though—he was taking this one day at a time.

Linc strode to Nate's door and knocked. He hooked a thumb in his belt loop as he waited. A moment later, a rustling sounded from inside and the door swung open. Nate stood in the frame, looking gorgeous enough that Linc flat-out stared. Unlike the night they went on their not-date to Port of Call, today he'd dressed for their adventure in jeans showcasing what spectacular long legs the man had as well as an olive-green T-shirt that made his eyes pop even more. That goddamn chin dimple was beyond adorable, more noticeable with his fresh shave.

Nate's gaze landed on Linc's backpack. "Is this a more serious outdoor excursion than I thought? Do I need to bring something?"

Linc shook his head and tilted it in the direction of his Toyota, parked along the side of the road. "I've got everything we need."

"Plan on telling me where we're going now?" Nate asked, slipping out of his house and locking the door behind him. He offered a grin, the radiant, unguarded sort Linc could look at for hours. Ever since their talk the other week, Nate didn't bother hiding his open affection, even though his blushes still emerged just as often. Someone like him was as rare as hitting every green light when you were in a hurry or finding the hidden trail at the state park that led to the best view of the water. The more Linc got to know him, the more he found to appreciate.

Linc flashed him a grin. "Where's the fun in that?"

"The fun is me not making an ass of myself at a brand-new place," Nate said. "Though I suppose I'd do that whether I knew where we were going or not."

Linc swung the driver-side door open and climbed into his truck, Nate following suit on the passenger side. He tossed his pack into the back seat before peeling out of the parking spot and heading down the street. When they reached the bridge leading out of the town, Nate started looking back toward Chesapeake City.

"We're heading out of here?" he asked. In the car together like this, the man's fresh, clean scent permeated the space between them, more delicious than ever.

"I'm betting you haven't gotten much of a chance to explore the area." Linc tapped his fingers along the top of the steering wheel as he sped along the bridge, heading toward one of the best gems near Chesapeake City.

"What gave me away?" Nate asked. "The interminable hours I've spent cloistered away in Chesapeake Brew or the fact that I had to beg you to introduce me to people?"

"Let's be honest—I had my own motives in wanting to spend time at the bar with you," Linc admitted. His chest thrummed at the memory of their night at Port of Call. Despite this being their first official date, all those tiny footprints along the way made this feel inevitable, like there would've never been another destination. "Which was apparently a good thing, since half the men in this town seemed to want to take you home."

"Is this a small-town thing?" Nate asked. "Because I'll be honest, I've never been that lucky in my life."

The car zoomed along the highway, and something loosened in Linc's chest at the freeing feeling of racing across asphalt. When things got too confining, too oppressive, he always took to the road.

"That's a you thing," Linc responded when he realized the conversation had lapsed between them. "Nico and Jer don't go after anything that moves— just anyone hot enough to catch their eye. And I play both sides of the field, so I'm not wanting for choice." He spared a quick glance to the side and was rewarded by the bright blush gracing Nate's cheeks. Fuck, the man was gorgeous.

"Does being beautiful earn me answers of what we're doing besides 'outdoor things?'" Nate asked, a teasing tone returning to his voice.

Linc snorted. "What are you worried about? That I'll be dragging you to free climb on cliffs for a first date?"

"Well, now I am," Nate responded.

"We'll be there before you know it," Linc assured him. He drove a little faster across the asphalt, as if he could catch up with the way his heart raced. This wasn't the type of date he usually went on, or the normal feelings that arose—chill, pleasant, under-whelming.

Talking with Nate was easy—too easy—when it was difficult with everyone else. The man offered the comfort he'd been missing from every single person he'd gone out with since, well, since Marissa. It didn't hurt that between his thick brows, expressive eyes, and slender frame, the guy was far too good-looking.

Linc's throat tightened as he waited for the tidal wave of guilt to sweep in and saturate him to the bone. He'd been bracing for the blow from the moment he took interest in Nate and then dove in to pursue him. Yet, it hadn't arrived. Which meant for these blessed few moments, he'd remain in the present to enjoy his time with the stupidly pretty man he'd come to appreciate more and more each day.

Tonight, he wouldn't be drifting toward the past, and if he was lucky, he wouldn't be sleeping in his own bed either, haunted by too many memories. Maybe tonight, he'd be finding a new sort of bliss, here, with Nate.

ELK NECK STATE PARK MIGHT GET CROWDED IN THE summertime, but barely anyone visited the beach area in the spring. Linc had decided to capitalize on that, because the views were some of his favorite as far as nearby escapes went.

"When you mentioned outdoors, I didn't think we'd be doing anything like this," Nate mentioned as he strode down the walkway with him toward the beach.

"Disappointed?" Linc asked. Not like he worried too much, with the way the breezes swept by, carrying the crisp scent of the water. The driftwood cast longer shadows along the pale sand in the late afternoon. The mixture of tangled trees looming close to the shoreline and the scattered stones leading to the water made a gorgeous contrast. Sawed-off stumps and planks of wood sat at the fringes of the forest, offering a perfect vantage point to just watch the coast. He couldn't imagine someone not appreciating the beauty this place had to offer.

"Relieved," Nate said, swinging his arms by his sides as they walked, the effervescent playfulness oozing out of the man. "Given the fact you're ridiculously in shape and I'm more the 'TV marathons' kind of guy than 5Ks, I was worried we'd be doing some strenuous hike."

"We can save the tougher hikes for later down the road," Linc said, before realizing his mind already leapt toward the future. He swallowed hard, trying to ignore the flare of surprise in Nate's eyes and the hope gleaming there. As much as Linc had longed to move forward for a long while now, it hadn't been possible. Chances were, Nate would end up hurt sooner rather than later, and he'd be the asshole who broke the man's heart.

Linc swerved past some of the skeletal limbs of driftwood washed up onto shore, structures he would need to climb rather than hop over. The sun gleamed on the crests of the rippling water, the liquid turning to pure gold under the desperate light of late afternoon.

He led them farther away from the water, which would be pure ice this time of year. Instead, he headed closer to the woods fringing the shore, the view of the nearby cliffs beautiful from here. A hush settled between them as they walked, but it was far from awkward. A calm threaded through the currents, the sort he'd been longing to grasp for so, so long.

Once he reached the stumps that had been turned into stools straddling the line between the beach and the woods, he slid the straps of his pack off his shoulders and dropped it to the ground. "I'll give you fair warning," he said as he unzipped the pack. "I'm not a great cook, so don't expect anything fantastic."

Nate's brows lifted. "The fact you brought me food is by far enough. I'm easy."

"Good to know," Linc responded, unable to help the husky rasp in his voice when he scanned over Nate from head to toe. The man's cheeks lit up again, emphasizing the brightness of his blue eyes fringed with dark, dark lashes and the lines of his square jaw and cleft chin. Linc pulled out a blanket and spread it across the ground. He took a seat and patted beside him.

Nate sat in the spot, close enough their legs

brushed together. When he looked like he might move his, Linc nudged his leg closer. Nate's lips turned up in a soft grin that struck Linc square in the chest. Hunger crept in, the way it always did around this man.

Before he could change his mind and claim Nate's lips, Linc forced himself back on task. He pulled out the sandwiches and salt and vinegar chips he'd packed, as well as the cans of cola. "Hope you're okay with ham and cheese."

Nate shook his head, his eyes sparkling with his grin. "This is just about the most dad meal you could've made. It's pretty adorable, to be honest."

Linc's cheeks heated at the comment. He hadn't realized, but for the past six years, he'd been so zeroed in on Beckett that not much else crept into the picture. "Welcome to the extent of my skills—cooking for children."

"Don't downplay it," Nate responded, leaning back onto his elbows. "I happen to find the fact you're a great dad terribly attractive."

"Is this where I find out you have a lengthy history of chasing after guys with kids?" Linc joked.

Nate snorted and jostled his leg against Linc's. "Never have in the past. Sam hated kids, and I didn't have a lot of committed relationships before him.

Must be why he got sick of me after all that time. I can't say I ever grew up."

Linc lifted a brow. "You're selling yourself short there. You've got a sharp mind for business, and you're able to take care of your essentials. Being an adult doesn't mean you have to become serious."

"Like you, you mean," Nate teased.

"Guilty," Linc responded, turning toward Nate.

The man's eyes twinkled as he stared at him, a light in them that brought out every protective bone in Linc's body. Nate looked delicious spread out on the plaid blanket there, all lanky limbs and corded muscle, making Linc hungrier than ever. The wind swept the thick strands of Nate's chestnut hair back, and his jeans may as well have been spray painted on his legs with the way they highlighted his thighs. The sun's last beams of the late afternoon painted Nate's skin golden, and Linc wanted to taste it more than ever.

Linc leaned in, tilting Nate's chin up as he brushed his thumb across the man's lush lower lip. "You look fucking mouthwatering."

He could feel Nate's slight shift of breath at the statement, could see how his pupils dilated with full-blown lust. Linc slipped his thumb between those parted lips. The way the tip of Nate's tongue traveled along his thumb as he sucked it in got Linc's cock rising to attention. His hot, wet mouth had been all he could think about for days now. Linc withdrew his finger and closed the rest of the space between them to kiss Nate.

Shivers rolled down his spine at the contact, the brush of their lips together igniting something deep inside him. The urge to possess, to claim grew stronger with every stroke of his tongue against Nate's, every crush of their mouths together.

He climbed over the man, his forearms sinking into the blanket on either side as he continued to kiss the ever-loving hell out of him. His thighs bracketed Nate's, and with the way they pressed together, it was impossible to miss Nate's hard length testing the constraints of his jeans. His own erection had stiffened to the point he was tempted to toss out restraint and fuck him here in this public park. He continued to devour the man's mouth, lush and inviting as he lost himself in the sweet taste of this kiss. Linc had made out with him multiple times this week, but honestly, he hadn't tired of it in the slightest. Nate explored his mouth with a vibrant energy that mesmerized him, like every time they kissed was the first.

Linc broke from the kiss to press his lips along the light stubble of Nate's jaw, in the crook beneath his ear, and along the defined column of his neck. The sound of Nate's throaty moan brought him right to attention, and he resisted the urge to grind his hips against Nate's.

Linc pushed up with his palms to force some space between them before he stripped the man down and got them both into trouble.

"Right," he murmured, Nate's lips inches from his. "We should eat."

Nate licked his kiss-swollen lips, which did not help in the slightest. "Hey, you're the one who happened to climb on me. I was perfectly fine eating my ham and cheese sandwich." Even as he said the words, his chest still heaved. Linc didn't want to pull away, but he forced himself to get up. When he reached down to readjust himself in his jeans, he didn't miss how Nate's gaze traced the movement with ample hunger.

"You keep looking at me like that, and we'll be back where we were five seconds ago." Linc grabbed his sandwich as if it might form some defense to keep him from jumping on Nate again.

"You don't see me complaining. Like I said, I'm easy." Nate grinned, a few teeth peeking out. He reached for the can of Coke, cracking the tab open and taking a sip. "So easy in fact that if you don't have anything planned after this, I'm tempted to invite you back to my place tonight."

Relief saturated Linc's chest. He hadn't wanted to invite himself over to Nate's—if they'd been horny and desperate enough, he'd considered fucking him in the car. His place was off-limits. He'd never brought a date or a hookup there, because it had always felt uncomfortable or wrong, like they trespassed. He took another bite of the sandwich and met Nate's eyes, drawing himself to the present.

"Good," Linc responded, unable to contain the heat in his voice. "I've wanted to strip you down all week."

A beautiful flush rose to the apples of Nate's cheeks again. "Noted."

Linc couldn't help the way his lips lifted. He hadn't smiled this much in years, yet every time he was around Nate, the man coaxed them out of him. His heart quickened at the realization, but he pushed it aside.

Tonight, he'd just live in the here and now.

CHAPTER 13

THE EVENING AT ELK NECK STATE PARK HAD BEEN perfect. One of the things Nate appreciated the most was how easily the conversation flowed between them, like the gentle breeze that whipped by without a care. Yet now they were heading up the walk to his house, nerves set in.

He hadn't been in Chesapeake City long enough to make the place truly feel like his, and Linc happened to be his first visitor. Even still, that wasn't the source of his anxieties. Nate chewed on his lower lip as he slid the key into the lock on his front door. He could feel Linc's presence behind him, his tall, broad figure the sort Nate was dying to wrap himself around. Every other time they'd stolen a few moments to make out, they'd risked the chance of someone walking in—whether at his work or out in a park.

Tonight, he had Lincoln Lane all to himself, and that both thrilled and terrified him.

"Is old man Fletcher still living in the upstairs apartment?" Linc asked as they entered his place.

Nate flicked on the lights and nodded. "Though I've seen him a whopping once since I've been here. Apparently, the old man doesn't leave his place much." The pale lighting stained his barren walls— he'd been way too busy to decorate.

Linc let out a snort behind him. "The man's been a recluse for years. It's a matter of time before his daughter makes him leave the place and move to a retirement community."

Nate strode past the foyer and into the kitchen. It was in the center of his floor of the house, the two hallways that ran parallel leading to the couple of rooms. Linc had left his pack in the truck when he'd parked along the street, right between their houses. Both of them seemed to understand the trajectory of this night implicitly, and if the scorching kiss Linc had sprung on him earlier gave any indicator, he had a feeling the experience would leave a mark.

"I suppose this is the point where I offer you something to drink, right?" Nate joked. He'd never been great at initiating, too awkward and stuck inside his anxiety most of the time.

"I think we're well past pretenses, don't you?" Linc responded. He prowled toward Nate, the hunger clear in his dark velvet eyes. Linc eyed him up like a meal, and hell, it turned Nate on more than anything. Nate's tongue slipped out to wet his lips, and Linc stopped right before collision, their bodies mere inches away.

Ever since their first kiss, there'd been a natural ending point to their make-out sessions, whether a package got delivered at the shop—oh the irony there —or the eventual realization they weren't in the right place to go further. In a way, Nate had been relieved by it. Not like he wasn't burning up inside for Linc, because he'd rubbed far too many out in the shower while thinking of the sexy contractor, but he didn't want to feel like a one-night stand. Part of him was terrified that once they slept together, the allure would die.

That Linc would lose interest and walk away.

"What's going on in your head?" Linc murmured, his mouth close enough that Nate felt the puff of his breath against his lips.

"Am I that transparent?" Nate responded, biting his lower lip. He didn't miss the way Linc's eyes traced the motion. Nate inhaled. "Just the usual fears of being ghosted or dumped after. Nothing crazy."

Linc slowly nodded, as if he soaked in the knowledge. "Ghosting isn't a possibility, so let's gloss over that one." His finger skated under Nate's chin, tilting it up so their eyes met. "While I can't make any promises for the future—hell, I can't even make them for myself—I can say you aren't a random fling for me. I'm not going to cold shoulder you tomorrow, if that's what you're worried about."

Nate's heart stumbled at those words, ones he'd needed to hear. While the fears still fluttered around in his chest, knowing Linc wasn't just toying with him gave the comfort he'd needed. He leaned in to close the mere inches between them and pressed his lips to Linc's.

Once their mouths met, a switch flipped, and any hesitation vanished. Linc wrapped his hands around Nate's hips, gripping tight, and he walked him a few paces backward until his back thudded against the cabinet. Pinned there against the wooden cabinet and Linc's hard, defined chest, Nate felt like he would combust. Their lips met with a newfound ferocity, like each kiss led to a destination, each one with an intent purpose.

Nate slid one of his hands down to grip Linc's belt, surrendering to the fierce way the man kissed.

Linc pulled back to kiss along Nate's nape like he had earlier, and a loud, throaty moan erupted from Nate. Shivers exploded through him at the way Linc sucked at the tender area, and his cock stiffened, testing the strength of his boxers and his jeans. Linc's hips pressed against Nate's, his erection thrust up against his inner thigh in a way that made him ache.

Nate's fingers fumbled with the latch on Linc's belt, opening it with a *snick*, and then he managed to undo the button and zipper of his jeans next. All the while, Linc continued to nip and suck along the side of his neck, followed by sinking his teeth into his shoulders in a possessive gesture that almost made him come right then and there. Heat blossomed in the air between them, to the point Nate's breath hitched in his throat. With Linc's tight grip on his hips, his back against the wall, he was utterly possessed, and it sent a silent thrill through him.

Nate managed to tug Linc's jeans and boxer briefs down and dropped to his knees. Linc's impressive length stretched out in the space between them, long enough to make him salivate, with a thick cockhead, cut like him. Nate leaned in and licked the slit along his tip, lapping up the salty drops of precum that dribbled from it. Linc let out a low grunt and threaded his fingers through Nate's hair, giving a slight tug. The linoleum floor felt cool against his knees as he took more of Linc's length into his mouth.

His lips strained around Linc's cock, and the tip bumped the back of his throat. His own erection throbbed in the confines of his pants. He was turned on beyond reason. He looked up at Linc as he bobbed forward and back, beginning to find a rhythm. The man's eyes darkened, gleaming like blown glass, and the way he loomed over him sent Nate's heart pounding in double time.

Nate sucked him even deeper, continuing at a desperate pace as he tasted the salt of Linc's precum and drank in the musky scent of him. Linc's grip on his hair tightened, the slight sting sending a thrill down his spine. He deep throated Linc's cock, savoring every grunt and groan from the man. He wanted to feel that powerful chest pressing him down, those arms snaring him in place. Nate's cock ached, but he didn't touch it as he focused his entire attention on taking Linc's erection down his throat.

Linc jerked harder on his hair, enough to pull his cock out of Nate's mouth with a wet pop. "If you keep up like that, sweetheart, I'm going to explode," he murmured. "And if I'm going to come, it'll be inside you."

Nate sucked on his lower lip, so damn turned on by Linc's filthy mouth. Linc reached down and offered a hand, one Nate accepted as the man yanked him to standing again.

"Let's take this to a better place then." Nate slipped his hand in Linc's and began the trek toward his bedroom. Each step pounded louder in his ears, which were thumping from the intense desire swirling through him. Even the shift of fabric against his cock had him close, needing release more than ever. He stepped inside his bedroom, glad he'd made up the bed earlier, since the blankets had been a mess. Not like they'd remain pristine once he and Linc crashed onto them.

Nate thumped down to take a seat on the mattress. Linc stood in front of him, kicking off his boots first, and then dropping his pants and boxer briefs. A moment later, he flung his shirt to the floor as well. Nate's mouth parted with want as he soaked in the vision of the man before him, all sculpted tan muscles and big enough to push him against the wall or toss him around.

"One of us is severely overdressed," Linc murmured, closing the space between them. Nate helped as first his shirt hit the floor, and then Linc's hands attacked his belt and his zipper, until his jeans were sliding down his legs too. Nate was tempted to cover himself up again—compared to how well-defined and in shape Linc was, he just looked slender, his muscles pretty useless. Before he could get too caught up in his head, Linc climbed onto the bed beside him and captured his lips again.

This time, they sank down together as they made out, the glide of skin against skin enough to make him delirious. Their cocks brushed against each other, the silken feel causing his breath to hitch in his throat.

"You're goddamn beautiful," Linc whispered as his lips brushed against the line of his jaw and down his neck. Those words plucked at something deep inside him, quieting the voices in his mind. Linc had a simple, definitive way of speaking that reached him like nothing else. The man didn't parse words.

"For someone who's quiet, you're pretty talkative in bed," Nate murmured, unable to help his smile as he pressed his hips closer to Linc's, luxuriating in the velvet feel of their cocks brushing together. "It's ridiculously sexy."

"You have no idea how much I've been thinking of this," Linc responded, his thick, hoarse voice like a shot of adrenaline.

Nate traced the lines of Linc's abs with his fingertips as he leaned in to press a kiss against those lush lips. The sheer thrill of being with him here, completely stripped down, was intoxicating. He could lose himself in the sensations of their skin brushing together, their lips meeting for hours.

Yet, the ache in his cock grew, and based on the hungry look in Linc's eyes, the man wasn't planning on just rolling around and touching. Nate shivered under the weight of Linc's intense focus. The man made him feel like he saw his wide forehead, his too-skinny arms, and not only accepted them but found them beautiful. Nate's heart pounded hard enough he could hear the throb in his ears.

Linc reached down to cup and squeeze his ass, causing Nate to thrust his cock against him. Fuck, those callused palms got him hot.

"Please," Nate begged, delirious with the idea of Linc plunging inside him.

"Please what?" Linc asked, a deep rumble vibrating across his skin as he bit Nate's shoulder.

"Please, fuck me," Nate let out breathlessly. He thrust against Linc again, their cocks brushing in the process, which sent another sinful shudder down his spine.

"Thought you'd never ask," Linc murmured, teasing Nate's nipple with the tip of his tongue. The sensations exploded through him, and Nate let out a low curse.

"Lube and condoms are in the top drawer," he forced out.

The rasp of the wooden drawer sounded, followed by the creak of the bedsprings as Linc returned to his side. Nate watched as Linc rolled the condom down his delicious length before slicking a liberal amount of lube over it. He pushed Nate onto his back and hovered over him. Nate sank into the mattress, the jersey knit sheets soft against his skin.

"How long has it been?" Linc asked.

"Not since Sam," Nate breathed, desire making him delirious with want. "But that doesn't mean I haven't fingered myself since."

"Fuck." Linc's voice came out in a low rasp. "Show me."

A flush rolled through Nate from head to toe. Linc sat back as Nate grabbed the lube and slicked up his fingers. His gaze met Linc's as he circled his fingers around his hole before easing them inside. Linc didn't break eye contact once as Nate began to pump them in and out, the wet sound echoing in the room. A moan slipped past his lips as he hit his prostate, sparks flaring through him. Still, he couldn't bring himself to close his eyes, not with Linc looking at him like that.

He upped the rhythm, and his cock ached with the need for release, his moans growing louder.

"I can't take it anymore," Linc growled, looming over him. "I need inside you, now."

Nate pulled his fingers out, leaving his legs wide open while he lay sprawled on his back. Linc slid between his legs, brushing the tip of his cock against Nate's hole. The sensation had him spreading his legs a little wider, desperate to feel the thick, hot length inside him. Linc began to inch in, bit by bit. Nate threw his head back in surrender as the man took control with a steadiness that didn't surprise him in the slightest.

There was a slight stretch and burn as Linc pushed deeper in, and Nate sucked in his breath. Yet then Linc sank all the way inside, the tip of his cock brushing against the sensitive bundle of nerves, and pleasure shuddered through him. Nate let out a long, lusty moan. Linc gripped his hip in one hand, and he pressed the other into the mattress by Nate's head. Braced like that, Linc rocked inside him with an increasing intensity Nate just surrendered to.

Linc pulled back only to slam in harder, each stroke causing electricity to course through his veins. Nate tilted his hips up to accept him, precum dribbling from the tip of his cock as the need for release mounted each and every time Linc plunged into him. The man began to pick up his pace, those thick brows pulled together in concentration and his lush lower lip jutted out. Sweat beaded on Nate's brow as he gave himself over to the sensations short-circuiting his thoughts. They carried him away until all that existed was the fevered breaths between them, the slap of skin to skin, and the squeeze of his tight ring of muscles around that hard cock as it tunneled into him again and again.

His hips moved automatically as his desperation grew for the feel of Linc deep inside him. Moans flew from his lips every time Linc thrust, and Nate drank in each breath, the scent of sweat, musk, and the earthiness unique to the man caressing him. Linc grabbed his thighs, hooking Nate's ankles at his shoulders. The increased angle brought Nate even closer to the brink. Each time Linc slammed inside him, Nate saw stars.

This was the culmination of so many hot looks, scorching make-out sessions, and an insane sort of tension that exploded between them. And Nate couldn't help but just melt in the face of the man's competence, those callused palms, and that steadiness that made him feel grounded, even when he was soaring higher than ever. Sweat pricked on Nate's forehead, and his breaths came out quicker.

The low moans coming from Linc's lips were a melody he wanted to memorize as they collided together again and again and again. His heels dug into Linc's shoulders as the pressure mounted, his cock begging for release.

"I'm going to…," Nate breathed out, barely able to form words, let alone coherent thoughts. Before he could reach down and grab his erection, Linc wrapped his hand around it. The man set a furious pace at this point, one that had his legs trembling in anticipation. Linc's thick brows furrowed, his lips set in concentration as he thrust in over and over.

"Come with me," Linc ordered, those husky words reaching him.

The second Linc began stroking Nate's cock, he couldn't hold on anymore.

Linc sank in deep, hitting the blinding spot right as Nate's length started to pulse. Nate tipped his head back, Linc's name escaping his lips. His world zeroed in on the mind- and body-numbing bliss claiming him in one fierce sweep. Nate's eyes closed as he surrendered to the pleasure wrung from him as he came and came and came.

Hot, wet cum streaked up his chest, and a moment later, Linc thrust in again, staying there this time as his body shook and his cock pulsed. Linc's grip tightened, his nails biting into Nate's thighs as he finished inside him. Silence spread through the room, punctuated by their sharp breaths. Nate's chest heaved as he slowly opened his eyes to look at Linc.

The man hovered above him, knees dug into the mattress and his eyes shut in the sort of pristine bliss that softened his features. Like this, he looked penitent, reverent, and gorgeous in a way that caused the breath to snag in Nate's throat. Even as Linc's length softened inside him, Nate didn't want them to separate. The feeling of being filled by this man, possessed by him, claimed by him was one he'd been chasing for a long, long while.

Linc leaned down to brush his lips against Nate's as he pulled out. Their soft, sweet kiss left Nate even more breathless. His heart careened, as if he ever had a chance of guarding it against Lincoln Lane.

"Let me grab something to clean up with," Linc murmured, pushing himself off the bed. He tied the condom off and threw it in the trash can.

"Bathroom. Next one over," Nate responded, barely able to form sentences let alone process getting up. Linc loped out the door and a heartbeat later came back with a wet washcloth. The mattress creaked as he sank onto it and wiped the streak of cum from Nate's chest. Nate's heart thundered at the soft ministrations, how this man emanated care from every pore in his body. Nate plucked the washcloth from Linc's hands and tossed it over to the hamper. When their eyes met, Nate pushed through his hesitance.

"You know, it's an awfully long way back to your

place," Nate said, trying to keep his voice nonchalant.

Linc grinned. "Oh yeah, that three-house stretch is killer."

"I couldn't put you through that," Nate responded. "Guess you'll just have to crash here tonight."

"Why do I get the feeling this was your plan all along?" Linc murmured, leaning back on his elbows in the bed. All his glorious, tanned skin and those swoon-worthy muscles were splayed out before him. Nate might be damn exhausted, but the sight sparked his libido as if he hadn't just come harder than he had in years.

"You caught me. Devious mastermind here," Nate teased. He didn't miss the ravenous sweep of Linc's gaze as the man soaked him in from head to toe. With his limbs all loose and languid from the mind-blowing sex between them, he couldn't summon his normal anxieties.

Linc slipped closer to him, and they shifted so his chest pressed against Nate's back. Those muscular arms wrapped around him, and fuck, it felt like heaven.

Here in this man's arms, Nate felt safe, warm, and grounded in a way he hadn't for such a long time. For once, Nate was glad he wasn't facing Linc, because he wouldn't be able to hide the softness in his expression for anything. His heart lurched with the realization that in a few short weeks he had well and truly fallen for Linc.

"Guess I'll just have to stay," Linc murmured.

If only.

CHAPTER 14

"I'm pretty sure the Dinobots can wait a second, kiddo," Linc said, pulling the plate of pancakes in front of Beckett. The rich scent of them wafted his way, Eliza's family recipe that had been passed down for generations. Quiet chatter flowed in the packed vinyl booths around them, the lazy Saturday morning murmurs he expected.

Beckett continued to play with his half dino, half robot toys, making them stampede across the table with little clickety-clacks. When Beck was little, Linc had gotten the kiddo's hearing checked, because he wasn't sure if the kid couldn't hear him, but he was fine. Beck just got so lost in his imagination and daydreams that he forgot to respond sometimes.

"Guess I'll have to eat them myself. Can't let them go to waste." Linc grabbed a fork and plunged it into the pancakes, drawing Beck's wide-eyed attention at once.

"No," Beck exclaimed, scrambling for his own fork, as if the pancakes were going to disappear before his eyes. "I'll eat them!"

Linc bit back his amusement as he lowered the fork and passed the plate over to Beck, who began dumping packet after packet of maple syrup over the pancakes until they drowned. The sweet scent drifted through the air, battling with rich coffee for dominance. Cozy Corner always lived up to its name in the mornings, casting a quiet, comfortable spell over everyone who wandered inside.

Linc leaned back in the brown vinyl booth, pushing around a few of the uneaten hash browns still on his plate from his omelet meal. He'd devoured the bacon and cheese omelet pretty quickly while Beck still played with his toys, ignoring his own breakfast. He tapped the tines of the fork against the ceramic plate, listening to the *tink, tink, tink*. Without realizing, he caught himself scanning Cozy Corner, as if he might spot Nate at any moment.

A week had passed since their night together, and he'd be lying if he said he could get it out of his mind. The connection between them had grown powerful enough to make him wonder, the sort of experience that promised to imprint on his memories for good. And between the date, the conversations, the sex—*goddamn*, the sex—Linc's mind had been in tangles ever since. Even when they didn't see each other during the week at work, they'd been texting, the constant conversation soothing an ache he hadn't even been aware of.

One date in, and they'd waded into far deeper territory than anyone had breached in a long time. Not since… well, Marissa.

Beck's chomping noises snapped him out of the mental panic he teetered into. He'd always been able to walk away from the people he'd seen since her because none of them took a socket wrench to his chest and cranked it right open. None of them made him feel the inexorable mixture of attraction and ease that made him think of the future.

At least, not until Nate.

He'd always told himself once he found someone like that, it'd be a snap to move forward. Yet, bile rose in his throat at the idea of picturing a future without Marissa there. As much as she haunted the house, an ever-present reminder of his loneliness, he still couldn't imagine moving on without her presence. Even if he needed to—for his sake, for Beck's.

"Hey, keep chewing with your mouth open and someone's going to steal your food," Linc murmured, reaching over to ruffle Beck's thick curls. He took a sip of coffee, enjoying the dark, rich flavor. These morning rituals with his son were one of the highlights of his week, something he wouldn't replace for the world. But even if they didn't take place at Cozy Corner, he could always start them somewhere else.

It was this town, that house, keeping him mired in memories of his wife, unable to move forward.

Beck zipped his mouth shut as he continued to chew, already one pancake down. Once his kid set to it, he had a fantastic appetite.

Linc glanced up again to spot the door to Cozy Corner swinging open.

Nate strolled inside. Linc soaked in the tamed deep brown hair, those bright, bright blue eyes, and the comfortable stance. The man had a way of looking like he belonged anywhere he went, even if he was filled to the brim with anxieties—there was just something too damn likeable about Nate McAllister. Hunger coiled in his gut at the sight of the gorgeous guy he couldn't get enough of. He'd been thinking about the next time they'd be able to sleep together ever since the first occurrence.

Then the nerves slammed in full force with the realization this wasn't just him and Nate.

He was here with Beckett today. No matter what dates Linc went on, he always, always, always kept his dating life separate from his kid, who needed constants more than ever. He and Nate hadn't discussed this, especially after Beck had met him at random when they'd been walking home. But "Nate the neighbor" and "Nate the guy Daddy was seeing" were two different things, ones he should keep separate.

Nate strode up to the counter where Eliza bustled back and forth, topping off coffee for her regulars or bringing out dishes from the back. Linc couldn't help but track where he went, even though he should be averting his gaze.

Like he could ever manage the feat. Ever since Nate arrived in town, Linc had been unable to keep his eyes off him.

After Nate handed a box over the counter to Eliza, his gaze skimmed across the room. The moment he glanced in Linc's direction, their eyes locked. Fuck. No way he could hide his presence now—not like he'd done a great job to begin with.

"Daddy, my pancakes are all gone," Beck announced, lifting his fork in triumph.

"Good job, kiddo," Linc said, his voice remaining calm even as his mind sent out panicked signals. "We should get ready to go."

Was running cowardly? Absolutely. However, he didn't know how to merge the two worlds without hurting Nate or his son in the process.

Beck frowned and his feet kicked faster beneath the table. "But I'm not finished playing with Commander Rex and Sergeant Raptor."

Linc sucked in a long, slow breath to control the spike of his nerves. He should've expected this, since Beck didn't do anything fast. The building could be on fire, and Beck would still be taking his time, either collecting his crayons or trying to find some toy that slipped onto the floor while he'd been playing. Linc let out the exhale. He couldn't get out of this.

Nate wove his way in their direction, a bright smile on his face that any other time would have Linc's heart pumping faster. The man was like sunshine incarnate, which made Linc feel even shittier for not being able to get over his issues. How many times had folks around town told him he needed to just move on past Marissa by now? Too bad his heart never took the memo.

Beck looked up right as Nate stepped into view. "Mr. Nate!"

Nate's smile brightened to staring-directly-at-the-sun caliber, if that was possible. "Hey, Beckett," he said, sliding into the seat opposite them. "I just stopped by to drop off merchandise with Eliza and figured I'd say hi." His gaze switched to Linc, filled with hope, promise, and all the sorts of things he should be leaping for. If only Linc wasn't so fucked in the head.

"We can stay longer, right, Daddy?" Beck asked, looking at him with those big brown eyes. "Mr. Nate, will you play Dinobots with me?"

Linc bit back a sigh. Not like he could explain to Beck that this was moving way too fast for him. Beyond brief interactions, he couldn't reconcile the idea of the person he was seeing spending time with his son. Sure, Beck had met some of his former flings like Jer and Layla, the florist in town, before, but those situations were more of a passing "hey" than any sort of real interaction. Beck didn't know them as people his father had been seeing, and Linc preferred it that way.

"We can't stay longer, buddy," Linc reminded him, hoping they could get out of here without any further complications. "Remember, we got invited to the barbecue later, and we have to save time to get ready."

"We can always play Dinobots some other time." Nate focused his gaze on Beckett, the way he had when they first met. If Linc were honest, the mere sight of that kindness aimed at his kid caused his chest to warm. "You're always welcome over," Nate continued.

Linc's throat constricted. Beckett would be

thrilled. He hadn't stopped talking about Mr. Nate for an entire day after they'd met. But Linc had seen how his son got firsthand with attachments. He might be more of a loner, but once he glued himself to someone, it was for good. If Beckett got attached to Nate and his dad fucked up yet another potential relationship because he couldn't move on... well, shit.

"We've bothered Mr. Nate enough," Linc said, his tone a little sterner than intended. "Let's get going."

Nate tilted his head to the side, obviously confused at Linc's insistence on leaving. It wasn't that Linc didn't trust Nate around his son. If anything, Nate seemed to reach Beck in a way not everyone did.

He just couldn't bear to pick up the fragments of both his and his son's hearts if things didn't pan out.

"Is it Sarah's barbecue you're going to later?" Nate asked, a hesitance to his voice that hadn't been there when he approached. Linc withheld a groan. Of course Sarah would've invited her new best friend. The two of them had bonded almost at once, because Nate was so damn lovable no one could resist him.

"We can play Dinobots there," Beckett interrupted, clearly pleased with his problem-solving skills. Any other time, Linc would be too. But, hell, this was moving too damn fast. Watching Beck interact with Nate, the heat welling in his chest mingled with a cavity ache—old and painful. A memory popped into his head, one he hadn't allowed in for a long time. The glow on his wife's face when she'd been pregnant, cradling her stomach, and the joy in her eyes when she talked about her Beckett.

The son she never got to meet.

His skin prickled, and nausea rolled over him again. Maybe he needed to return to the grief counselor.

"I'm pretty sure Mr. Nate's going to want to be talking to the adults there," Linc said, hating the words even as he said them. "Miss Sarah's friend Everly has a little girl around your age who'd love to meet you, though."

Beck's face fell, and Linc's chest dropped too. He was an asshole. He didn't miss how Nate stared at him, those expressive eyes not hiding an ounce of his confusion.

Nate pursed his lips and ignored Linc, looking to Beck again. "If the little girl doesn't want to play Dinobots though, come find me, and we will."

The streak of stubbornness sent a flare right through his heart. Goddamn, this man turned him upside down. At Nate's insistence, Beck brightened just as fast, the kid's emotions flowing like water through a freshly fixed faucet.

Linc speared his fingers through his hair. He couldn't talk about this with Beck here, but when the man's gaze returned to his, a hesitance existed there that he hated to see.

"Right," Linc said, placing a hand on Beck's shoulder. "Well, we've got to get out of here, or no one's playing Dinobots later."

Normally, Nate would crack a smile, but instead, he nodded. "I'll see you both at Sarah's later." He leaned forward for a second, as if he were going to reach out and place a hand over Linc's, but Linc's muscles tensed reflexively. Nate frowned for a flash, almost too fast to catch, but Linc did. After that, Nate pushed up from the seat and tossed his fingers in a wave before he headed in the direction of the door.

Beck finished up placing his Dinobots in his backpack while Linc cursed himself to hell and back.

Not only had he made his son feel like crap, but he'd hurt Nate.

Great job on his part.

Worst of all? No matter how he tried, the memory of Marissa, bright-eyed and full of joy, cycled in his mind, slicing away more and more of him until he barely knew what remained.

CHAPTER 15

Nate had been looking forward to Sarah's barbecue. It was one of the first events one of his new friends had invited him to, and on top of that, another excuse to see Linc and his son.

Everything this week since their date had been perfect. The conversation between them flowed nonstop, whether in person or text, and they'd shared some more searing kisses at Chesapeake Brew, which felt a whole lot like promise. Except, after all the awkwardness at Cozy Corner, he was closer to vomiting due to nerves than excitement.

Linc hadn't said anything, but he didn't need to—the way his expression powered off when Nate showed up and the hurry he'd been in to leave spelled it out for him. Did he already decide this relationship wasn't worth pursuing?

The lack of answers sat like a lump of iron in his stomach, and he couldn't bring himself to reach out and ask.

Maybe Linc just had an off morning.

Even as he fed himself the excuse, he barely believed it.

Nate shoved his hands into his pockets as he stalked down the sidewalk, almost at the end of the ten-minute walk between his place and Sarah's. The good and bad thing about Chesapeake City was how close everything and everyone was. Still, he couldn't skip. Sarah had invited him, and he was trying to build their friendship. As Nate turned onto the street, he checked the text she'd sent for the house number. Not like he couldn't hazard a guess by eyes alone. A bunch of cars clustered on the street in front of one house in particular, and even from here he could hear the shrieks of kids coming from the backyard.

Even with the slight briskness in the early May air, today was gorgeous, the perfect weather to grill outdoors. The plastic bag hooked around his arm swayed back and forth as he approached, because he couldn't show up empty-handed. His family had raised him better than that. The wind whistled through the trees overhead, new blooms sprouting on the dogwoods in the front yard of Sarah and her roommate Taran's place.

Nate couldn't quell the rapid beat of his heart. He didn't have the slightest clue as to who would be here, how big the party would be, anything, yet he'd tossed himself into this unknown. Perfect recipe for him to make more of an ass of himself. At least he was pretty sure there wouldn't be any old ladies here to yell at him for ruining the town with his newfangled ideas. That confrontation still left him on edge, like the old biddy might pop out of the bushes.

He was preparing to head up to the front door when he saw a gate on the side braced wide open. Given the hollers and laughs pouring from the backyard, he was most likely better off entering this route. The rich scent of grilled meat wafted his way, and his stomach rumbled, churning up the anxiety bubbling there. He hadn't gotten a few paces inside when he caught sight of Nico heading in his direction. Like always, the guy looked polished—Ray Bans propped up in his hair, a striped V-neck tee, and khakis that complemented his slim form.

"Looks like you made it," Nico said, offering a wave and slinging an arm around his shoulder. "Most folks are here, so I can introduce you. My little brother Taran's over manning the grill."

Nate almost gasped in relief at the friendly welcome. "Your brother is Sarah's roommate? Is everyone related here?"

"Fuck, I hope not," Nico responded with a charming grin. "Otherwise, I'd never get laid."

Nate snorted, even though his heart squeezed tight at the memory of him and Linc last week. Those worries were chased by the more immediate one of spotting the man himself standing beside Sarah, Jer, and another woman, beer in hand. The sun gleamed off his dark curls, and the black tank top he wore placed those gorgeous biceps on full display. His worn jeans were accented by a fuck-me black belt, and ugh, the man was so fucking hot it wasn't fair.

And now he needed to play cool and pretend he wasn't freaking out that everything had crashed and burned between them for good. Fun times.

Closer to the fence, Beckett crouched in the grass along with a little girl with braided hair about his age. When Beckett looked up and saw him, he gave a big smile and wave. Nate's chest warmed at the sight. At least one of the Lanes was happy to see him. The kid was one of the sweetest he'd ever met.

Nate followed Nico over to where the group of folks stood. Closer to the house, a young guy with similar dark hair, proud nose, and sepia skin to Nico manned the grill, flipping burgers. Taran, he guessed.

"Look who finally arrived." Nico jerked a thumb behind him at Nate.

"Is this it?" Nate asked, realizing his question sounded asshole-ish far too late.

Sarah grinned, and she closed the space between them to throw her arms around him in a hug. "What did you expect, city boy? A rave?"

"This is relief on my face, in case you couldn't tell," Nate responded. He took a step back and scanned over Sarah's outfit, a similar mix of goth-punk to when they'd first met—black dress that flared at the thighs and knee-high combat boots. The weirder look on her had been the first time he'd seen her at the bank in her pale white blouse and black slacks. "With the way everyone seems to know everyone around here, I wasn't sure if this would turn into a whole-town invite."

"Not when half the town is filled with assholes," Sarah responded. "I carefully curate my friends."

"Looking gorgeous, McAllister," Jer said as he stepped up to offer a hug.

Nate's heart twisted. Those were the words he wanted to hear from Linc, who thus far hadn't said anything, like some big, brooding statue. He'd known the situation with Linc would be complicated, and yet he dove in anyway. Someone like Jer would've at least been easy. Clear cut.

"Thanks," Nate murmured, unable to hide his

flush as he pulled back from the bear hug the other man offered him.

"Long time no see," Linc said, his lips quirking in a soft smile.

Nate wanted to be mad the man was keeping his distance on the PDA when mere days ago they'd been making out in his back room, but he wouldn't push. Before his stomach twisted up any further, Linc closed the distance between them and wrapped his arms around Nate in a hug as well, one that felt far more intimate than friendly. Nate swallowed hard. The earthy scent and the heat emanating from him soothed his shattered nerves, even if only for a moment.

"Yeah, it's been ages," Nate managed to force out, his throat dry. Intense desire surged for this man, all while he should be keeping his distance and guarding his heart. He took a step back, even though he just wanted to sink against Linc's chest, as if that might erase the discomfort from this morning.

"I'm Everly." The slender woman reached out to offer a hand, her soft features the exact opposite of Sarah's sharp ones. Her afro was beautifully styled with a purple-and-gold wrap woven through, and she wore a matching purple blouse. "And my daughter over there is Raven. We're planning on moving here in a few weeks."

Nate clapped his hand to hers, offering a huge grin. "You mean I won't be the new kid any longer? Great to meet you."

"Don't worry, you're still fresh meat around here," Jer teased, elbowing him in the side.

Nate snorted. "Good to know." At least someone here made him feel attractive and wanted. Linc stared between the two of them, a flash in his dark eyes that would look possessive and sexy on any other day. Today, Nate wanted to shake him and ask why he was getting iced out. Not that this was an appropriate time and place, surrounded by their friends and while Linc had his son with him.

"Fuck, I'm supposed to offer you beverages and shit," Sarah exclaimed, stepping beside him.

"You had one job," Taran called from over at the grill. He offered a wave. "Nice to meet you, Nate."

"Thanks for having me," Nate shouted back as Sarah steered him in the direction of the coolers lined along the side of the black fence separating their house from the neighbor's.

"Beer or cider?" Sarah asked, kicking open the cooler with the toe of her boot.

Nate thrust the tote bag toward her. "I brought a six-pack to contribute."

"Good man," Sarah said, clapping him on the back. He leaned down and snagged a cider, the cool drops imprinting on his fingers. He wrenched the cap open with a satisfying hiss and took a sip, as if that could settle him.

A wild scream sounded followed by the pound of footsteps as both Beckett and Raven came rushing in their direction. Both kids were laughing as they tore up grass in their wake. Nate couldn't help the wry grin that rose to his lips at the sight. That sort of carefree was something he couldn't help but love.

"Miss Sarah," Beckett called. "Don't close it! We're thirsty."

Sarah crooked an eyebrow at them. "Nice try. You two aren't getting any of the drinks in this cooler. The juice boxes are one over."

Beckett skidded to a stop, keeling over to slap his palms to his knees as he heaved for breath. He glanced up. "Hi, Mr. Nate."

Nate grinned, even though he could feel the pressure of Linc's gaze in their direction. "Hey, Beckett. Are you guys having fun?"

Beckett nodded before he plopped on the ground and set to prying open the kids' cooler. Nate allowed himself a glance to the rest of the group in time to catch Linc forcing his stare away. His stomach flip-flopped. He still couldn't figure out what the man's deal was today—chill and sweet one moment, and Mr. Damn Freeze the next.

Raven's braids bounced as she ran, and excitement gleamed in her eyes. "I want a juice box!"

Beckett thrust one in her direction and then pulled out one for himself. Raven sat beside him, kicking her feet out in front of her.

Sarah shook her head, a rueful grin on her face. "Don't get into too much trouble, munchkins."

The kids didn't bother responding, both too busy sipping their apple juice with gusto. Nate took the lead this time as they headed over toward the group of adults. On the positive, it wasn't an overwhelming crowd and he felt comfortable with everyone here. On the negative, he had no way to avoid Linc right now.

"Burgers are ready," Taran proclaimed, bringing a heaping plate of them over to the small picnic table covered in food. "If you want more, make them yourself."

"Beck, you hungry?" Linc called.

"I can nab him one," Sarah offered as she darted over, followed by Jer and Everly. Nate still wasn't hungry—he hadn't been ever since the weirdness at the café this morning.

"What kind of host are you?" Nico called over to his brother. "This is why you don't work for me."

Taran rolled his eyes before he doled a pointed look in the direction of his brother. "No, I don't work for you because I hate dealing with people and I'd rather spend my time with numbers."

"He's a programmer." Nico glanced to Nate. "Though that's no excuse for his horrible lack of social etiquette."

"What can I say, you bring out the best in me." Taran sidled next to his brother with a laden plate he began tearing into.

Linc snorted, drawing Nate's attention. At least here he looked far more relaxed than he had at Cozy Corner. Their gazes met, and Linc offered a small, private smile, one that made Nate's heart lift. He'd be lying if he said he wasn't confused by the guy's behavior today, but he'd happily accept a return to normal.

Jer returned with his plate, stepping between Nate and Linc. "Are you getting anything to eat?" he asked, tilting his head in concern.

Nate flashed him a smile. The guy might be a relentless flirt, but he was sweet and open, which Nate appreciated. He hadn't forgotten how Linc flinched this morning when Nate was about to reach out for him.

"Not hungry, but thanks for thinking of me," Nate said. Sarah and Everly strode over to the kids, bringing plates to them while they still sprawled out by the coolers.

"You sure?" Linc asked, an insistence in his voice that snared Nate's attention. "I can get you something."

Nate lifted a brow, not missing the way Linc had inserted himself into the conversation between him and Jeremy. "I'm good."

"Have you even been over to the table?" Linc asked. Those dark eyes looked a little pleading, and Nate caved. This was the closest they would get to a moment to themselves today. Linc hadn't had an issue with kissing him in public before, and Nico at the very least knew they were together. He just wanted some explanation, some clarity.

Because honestly, he'd been terrified this would happen after they hooked up. It wasn't the first time someone used the ruse of a relationship to get him to bed, though he'd thought more of Linc than that.

"I guess I better check the food out," Nate said, taking the first steps. Linc strode in time with him. Nate resisted the urge to reach out and slide his hand in Linc's. They might be dating, but Linc never said they were boyfriends. Maybe that was the distinction he'd missed. His stomach churned. He hated this uncertainty.

They reached the picnic table covered in a black tablecloth and a spread of creamy potato salad, nicely grilled burgers and hot dogs, plus a colorful fruit salad. Nate took a swig of his cider, as if the cool liquid might remedy the way his nerves sizzled.

"It looks pretty much the same as it did from over there," Nate said, attempting to keep his voice light.

Linc scratched his nape. "Look, tomorrow night my folks are bringing Beck to see a movie. Can I take you out to dinner?"

Normally, this would've been laden with flirty banter, but Nate had never been able to fake much. Still, Linc was trying here. Maybe if they went out together again, he could crack the guy open for an explanation on the weird behavior from today.

"I'm free," he said, hating the hesitance in his voice. Linc noticed too, based on the way the guy's gaze sank. "Let me know where and what time."

"That's date number two then," Linc said, attempting a grin. Still, the air grew charged between them, and not with the same electricity as before.

"Daaaaad," Beckett called out from his spot by the coolers.

Linc speared fingers through his hair and opened his mouth, looking torn, as if he wanted to say something more. Nate's heart lurched, just waiting, waiting, waiting.

"Raven told me I could eat this," Beckett called again. Linc blinked and whipped in the direction of his son.

He was already striding over as Sarah said, "That's a beetle. You can't eat a beetle."

Nate took another sip of his cider as he wandered back over to where Nico currently elbowed Taran in the side while Taran gave his brother a wan look. Jer laughed at the pair of them, the sound loud and easy. Nate swallowed the cool, sweet liquid.

If Linc hated him, he wouldn't be asking him on a second date.

Yet, those lingering doubts combined with their lack of labels tugged at his heels. He'd thought he'd be strong or patient enough to weather this "take each day at a time" thing.

Clearly, he'd been full of shit.

CHAPTER 16

LINC HAD ARRIVED TO HICKORY TAPROOM FIRST, AND honestly, he wasn't sure if Nate would show. After the way Linc fucked up both of their encounters the other day, he couldn't blame the man. Maybe they should've had the 'I'm a dad first' talk before they'd gotten so involved, but with Nate, things unfolded so naturally he'd barely been able to keep up.

Besides, he hadn't even been sure of what to say.

He still wasn't sure.

Tonight, he'd picked a bar that required driving at least, since he didn't want their date interrupted by a surprise drop by from Nico or even worse, Jer. His ex had flirted enough with Nate to make it clear that if Linc fucked this up, he'd be happy to sweep Nate off his feet.

Linc tapped his fingers across the surface of the

table and leaned back in the sturdy wooden chair. There wasn't much of a dinner crowd tonight, but then again, this was a restaurant off the main stretch on a Sunday evening. Hickory Taproom was all rich wooden interiors and thick etched windows—a classic pub vibe. Maybe not the best place for a dinner date, but it offered plenty of privacy with enough background chatter so they didn't need to whisper to avoid being overheard, unlike Primo Steakhouse in town.

Linc skimmed down the menu for the thousandth time, as if he didn't already know what he'd be ordering. At least, if Nate showed. So far, he was five minutes late, and Linc was sweating. The idea of not getting the chance to explain... damn, that socked him right in the gut.

The door swung open, and Linc's gaze followed like a Pavlovian response at this point.

Nate strode in through the door, looking like sex on a fucking stick. He'd tried to tame his thick chestnut strands that Linc remembered gripping tight on too many occasions, and the jeans he wore showcased his magnificent ass. His freshly shaved jawline was so clean that Linc wanted to lick it. Even as his libido revved at the sight of the man, he couldn't ignore the way his heart decided to plunge into a skydive too, which was the exact opposite of the light, breezy, and uncomplicated he went for.

"Sorry I'm late," Nate said as he plunked into the seat across from Linc. "The delivery guy showed up an hour behind schedule, which pushed everything off-kilter." Even as he offered an apologetic grin, distance remained in his eyes, a hesitance that hadn't been there before. One Linc had caused.

"Is Daria still dragging her heels about the new drinks on the menu?" Linc couldn't help but ask. If deliveries were coming in, Nate's shitty employee would be there, complaining and stirring up a whole lot of self-doubt for her boss. Frankly, Linc thought the man needed to fire her yesterday.

"Daria…" Nate trailed off, sending his gaze skyward. "Fuck, that'll unleash a whole slew of work talk, and I'm here to escape that. What do you recommend on the menu? I forgot to eat lunch, and I'm guessing you've been here before."

"They're known for having a great fish sandwich, but I always order the bacon cheeseburger," Linc said with a shrug, pushing his menu to the edge of the table.

"Why does that not surprise me," Nate murmured as he scanned over the menu. The faint grin on his face had Linc staring a second or two longer, wanting one of the full-blown smiles Nate had been giving him mere days before.

The waitress swung around, carrying both his beer and the cider he'd ordered for Nate.

Nate crooked a handsome brow as the waitress slid the cider in front of him, and he took a sip. "Good choice."

Once they placed their orders—Nate ended up going with the crispy fish sandwich—the waitress departed, and quiet settled across the table. Not the comfortable sort he'd gotten used to with Nate, but one loaded with the unasked questions in those April sky eyes. Linc took a long, deep swig of his pale ale, as if that might wash the awkwardness away. Oh, hell.

"The other day," Linc jumped in before he could talk himself out of it. He still wasn't quite sure what he would say even as the words bubbled to his lips, but he could at least be honest. Nate snapped to attention, a tensing to his shoulders that gave him away. "There's a conversation we should've had before the first date. I guess in the past no one's ever lasted long enough to come to this, so I didn't think of bringing it up."

Nate tipped his pint glass back, his Adam's apple bobbing as he swallowed down more cider. Tension crackled in the air between them, and Linc was well aware this could be the thing that caused Nate to walk away. Still, he needed to tell him.

"Beck's never met anyone I've dated," Linc said. When Nate's brows crinkled in confusion, Linc lifted a hand. "Let me clarify. It's impossible to avoid people in this town—that should be obvious at this point. He's never met them as someone I'm seeing—just another adult in the town his dad knows."

Nate didn't say anything, just tilted his head to the side as he listened. Linc didn't know what to make of that, but he continued.

"I'm guessing after meeting him for two seconds you've realized my kid will attach himself to anyone willing. And given the fact that I haven't been able to make any promises with anyone I've dated—well, hell. My boy's grown up without a mom, and I'm not going to have him getting attached to someone I'm seeing if he might get his heart broken a few months later." Linc forced the words out, even though his chest tightened. Truth be told, he might be the one more afraid of getting hurt.

Linc switched his focus to the trembling golden liquid inside his pint glass as if it held answers. After laying everything out, he didn't dare look up to see the potential rejection in Nate's eyes. For the first time in a long while, the emptiness in his life didn't feel as oppressive, and he knew who was behind the change.

An incredulous laugh sounded from opposite to him, drawing his attention back to Nate. The man shook his head, a half smile on his face.

"That's the reason you acted so weird the other day? Here I was thinking you'd gotten cold feet about us and wanted to call things off." He let out a snort. "My anxiety operated on cruise control as per usual, especially after our last date."

The knot in Linc's chest loosened. "You're not pissed?"

Nate's eyes crinkled with his smile. "At you for being a responsible father and not introducing your son to the guy you just started seeing? Not in the slightest. However, I am his neighbor, and I did make the kiddo a promise in friendship, which I don't take lightly. So, don't you dare try to act like I'm too busy for him again."

"You don't mind keeping things friendly around him?" Linc asked. Muscles he hadn't realized were tight unclenched.

Nate shrugged. "We are friends. And it's not like I'm about to dry hump you in front of your son."

A sharp laugh escaped him. Goddamn, this man. Nate had a way of making him smile no matter the situation. "Never change, gorgeous."

The blush on Nate's cheeks made the man look even more delicious. Linc took the chance to soak in the sight, relief saturating his veins. He couldn't wrap his mind around how easily they'd resolved that, how their communication flowed when with so many others his halted. Still, he swallowed down the hope that kept rising in his chest.

What the future held was an unpainted wall just waiting for the first strokes, especially if he followed through on the idea that infected him lately.

Of leaving Chesapeake City behind. Of starting over fresh.

That might just mean the end of this as well.

"You know, we never did any of those date-type questions," Nate broke through the silence. He swished around the liquid in his glass, a curious look in his eyes.

Linc glanced up, appreciating the break from his thoughts. "And what would be the point? I'm pretty sure I've got a fair estimation of you without them."

"Yeah?" Nate asked, crooking his brow.

Linc sat back in his seat, folding his arms. "I already know your favorite band's the Cure, that you take your coffee with milk and two raw sugars. I know you decided to boycott school musicals at the tender age of eight when they refused to let you audition for the role of Annie. I also know you've got a heart bigger than anyone I've met and take everyone's feelings into consideration, even those who don't deserve it."

Nate chewed on his lower lip, a gesture Linc noticed was his go-to when he got either nervous or overwhelmed. "Well, damn…," Nate said, his voice hushed. His smile spread like the sunrise, slowly overtaking his whole face with a rare, fleeting brightness that Linc would fight to keep there. "And here I was just wanting to know why you named your business Lamp Post Contractors."

The waitress made a timely interruption in bringing their food. Linc didn't get asked the question often, but every time he needed to take the breath to compose himself.

Nate lifted his sandwich, brows crinkling as he scrutinized the large slab of fried fish that dwarfed the round roll above and below it. "Did they just slaughter a whole fish and throw it on here?"

Linc chewed on one of his fries, crisp with the perfect amount of salt. "I named my business for Marissa. The Chronicles of Narnia were her favorite books, and when I was branching out on my own, fresh out of apprenticing and working for some of the older handymen who've long since retired, she made the suggestion." Linc swallowed, expecting the normal pity and slight discomfort he saw in people's eyes any time he talked about his dead wife.

"Marissa had excellent taste," Nate responded, his gaze warm. "I can see why you picked her."

This man never ceased to amaze him. Linc couldn't help the soft grin that slipped to his face. "I don't know—it's a bit questionable. She did marry me."

Nate's lips quirked to the side. "And what does that say about me?"

"Definitely questionable taste," Linc responded, his grin widening and his heart lighter than it had been in a long time. Nate stared at him long enough that Linc went to wipe at his cheek. "Do I have something on my face?"

Nate shook his head. "Nah, I was just wondering what a genuine smile looked like from you. It's breathtaking."

Those words lobbed hard into his chest, a tenderness to them that grew almost painful. Despite Nate's wry sense of humor that Linc found endlessly entertaining, the man's earnest statements disarmed him like nothing else. Heat rose to his cheeks this time, the tables turned for once. Linc took a bite of his burger while his mind reeled. Nate had rendered him speechless.

Nate's eyes glowed with humor. "Don't tell me

I've struck you mute," he teased. "You're already half there to begin with."

Linc finished chewing his bite and swallowed. "Thanks, wiseass."

"I'm stalling because I have no idea how to approach this 'sandwich.'" Nate offered air quotes before he lifted the big fish sandwich off his plate. "Do I just pull the buns off and eat the fish?"

Linc couldn't help his grin as he reached across for Nate's plate, took his knife, and sawed off the edges hanging over the sandwich bun on either side. "Why don't you try that?"

Nate's lips trembled with amusement. "Did you just 'dad' me?" Linc opened his mouth, but before he could make an adequate defense, Nate continued. "Because for some reason I find that ridiculously hot. Not like I'm looking for a daddy—that's so not my kink. But damn, man, warn a guy next time. Didn't realize you could get even hotter." He'd begun rambling in the adorable way that had driven Linc to cross the line between them in the first place.

Linc leaned forward, sliding his finger under Nate's chin to lift it up. His lips met Nate's in a searing kiss, the point of contact everything he'd been missing. Even though a hunger lit in his belly at the press of their mouths together, he kept the kiss chaste, long enough to swallow the man's words before he fretted himself into oblivion.

"You know, that's one impressive cure for anxiety-induced rambling. You should market it." Nate pursed his lips, a little glossier and even more inviting after the brief touch. "On second thought, I don't love the idea of you going and kissing everyone who's having a mental breakdown. Not on my behalf, of course. But I'm sure it'd get exhausting after a while. Chapped lips would be such a terrible job hazard."

A laugh erupted from deep in his stomach. "I think I'm doing well enough with the contracting. No need to add a side business."

"Right. Smart," Nate said, lifting his sandwich to his lips and taking the first bite.

Linc sat back in his seat, his legs brushing against Nate's in the process. Fuck, he was relieved the night had gone this way. That nervous buzz he'd arrived with had morphed into the thrum of anticipation. He took another couple of bites of his burger, enjoying the saltiness on his tongue. As they ate though, their gazes kept locking more and more over the meal. His leg remained pressed against Nate's, the contact stoking the flames burning inside him. A week had passed since they'd hooked up, and his libido had levied ridiculous demands ever since he met Nate.

All too fast, they finished their food, joking throughout the meal. Linc cast a glance to his phone. He still had a little time before he needed to leave to pick up Beck.

"Do you have to head out soon?" Nate asked, nodding to his phone.

"Half hour. Sorry," Linc apologized. "Beck has school in the morning."

Nate gave him a pointed look. "No apologies for being a responsible parent. However, there is a perk to both of us having driven here." He cast a heated glance toward the parking lot, and Linc's lips curved as the realization followed. "Last time I was in your truck, I'm pretty sure I saw a roomier-than-average back seat."

Lust punched through him. Linc sat up, flagging the waitress down. "I've got the bill."

The second he paid up, he slipped his hand across the table and interlaced his fingers with Nate's, whose eyes flashed with a brief moment of vulnerability. Linc squeezed their hands together. He might not be able to offer Nate everything the man wanted, but he'd give him as much as he was able right now.

"Let's get out of here."

CHAPTER 17

Nate waited in front of Chesapeake Brew, arms crossed and wanting more than a little to just step inside. His heart pounded fast, fast, faster at the idea of entering the building now. He chewed on his lower lip. Ever since his second date with Linc, things had been better than ever between them—scorching, even—but what he hadn't realized was how fast time flew by.

Linc had finished the remodel.

The exterior looked the same as before apart from the changed list of hours—he'd extended them into the evening with many, many plans including open mic, board game, and art show nights. Daria had insisted she wouldn't shift the hours she worked, which wasn't a great attitude for his main employee, but he didn't mind taking nights to start until they got busy enough to hire on more staff. Still, every time he clashed with Daria, Laura's words echoed in his mind. Nate tapped his foot on the concrete, squinting under the bright midday sun.

The door creaked open, and Linc stepped out.

His black tank top had gained streaks from the finishing touches he'd been working on all morning, but the grime and sweat made him look that much hotter. A curl stuck to his glistening forehead, and Nate couldn't help the pulse of attraction that zinged straight to his cock. When Nate met Linc's eyes, the guy's smug grin ensured he had the same filthy thoughts on his mind. Their last time together had been in the back seat of Linc's Toyota, a mess of tangled limbs, minimal space, and a hell of a lot of laughter as they tried to angle into positions, but goddamn, once they got into the groove it had been so hot the memory had been spank bank fodder all week.

"Ready to see the brand-new Chesapeake Brew?" Linc asked, a boyish glint in his eyes that had Nate's heart picking up speed. He'd been watching the transition occur over the past few weeks, but somehow seeing it all pieced together at last amped up his anticipation like nothing else. Linc had insisted on him staying out of the building this morning when he finished the last details so Nate could walk in and experience the final product.

Nate took the first steps forward, the reality settling into him as his hand rested on the door. The heaviness sank all the way to his feet, a grounding he hadn't felt in a long while. Linc ducked inside, gesturing him to follow. Nate sucked in a breath. This wasn't just a mess he'd inherited from Uncle Howard any longer. This was *his* coffee shop. His eyes fluttered shut for a moment as he took the final step over the threshold.

The scent of fresh paint and wood stain greeted him first, followed by the strong woodsy undernotes from all the oak surfaces they'd installed. Nate slowly blinked, opening his eyes. The lights were on, black pendant fixtures featuring Edison bulbs that cast a homey glow through the entire place. The oak countertop was stunning, the planks on display, the stain bringing out the whorls in the wood. The circular tables and chairs matched, all rustic oak that worked so well with the darker stained floorboards.

The back wall behind the countertop held a black chalkboard with a stainless steel backsplash beneath. The rest of the walls had been painted a creamy eggshell that soaked in all the warmth of the building. Standing here in the middle of all this, he could imagine the whirr of the machines, the low hum of chatter as folks sat relaxing at the tables, enjoying a foamy cappuccino or rich, dark mug of coffee. Everything looked exactly as he'd imagined when he first talked it out with Linc.

The man behind the magic leaned against the front counter, bracing himself there. Even though Linc exuded confidence, Nate didn't miss the hesitance in his expression, the slight lift of his brows as if he were waiting.

Ah, right. He still hadn't said anything, because the words had evaporated from his lips like morning dew under the sun. Nate took one step forward, then another, closing the distance between them. His hands wrapped around Linc's nape, and he brought his mouth crashing down on the man's as he communicated in the one way he knew how.

The attention to detail, the strong, sturdy lines, the genuine care poured into every aspect of the remodel—all of it radiated Lincoln Lane. He drank in the man's warm mouth, his intoxicating taste as he lingered in this soul-searing kiss. The man hadn't just left an imprint on his shop—in the process he'd branded every inch of his body and mind as well. Words bubbled up inside him, ones he longed to say —ones he kept close, secret.

He held onto the hope the time would come.

As he pulled back, Linc settled his palms around

Nate's waist, that firmness grounding him here even as he was tempted to float away.

"Thank you," Nate breathed, the words rising to his lips.

For being his first friend in this new town.

For showing him how to trust himself again.

For making him feel seen.

"Always," Linc murmured, a tenderness in his eyes that stroked Nate's heart. He didn't need to voice those words out loud, because Linc somehow had come to know him better than his closest friends.

"I can't believe the remodel is finished," Linc said, glancing around, the antique yellow gleam from the bulbs glinting off his eyes.

Finished. Which meant no more walking into his shop to find Linc hard at work, sweat glistening off his biceps. No more sneaking out front when he needed someone to vent to. No more excuses to see this man every damn day. His chest pinched a little tighter.

Linc's thumb brushed along his cheek. "Hey, handsome. Enough of that."

"That transparent, huh?" Nate responded, attempting a grin.

"It's one of your more charming qualities," Linc teased. "Just because I'm done with the remodel doesn't mean we'll never see each other again.

Unless you're planning on standing me up for our date next week?"

The reassurance thrummed through his chest, soothing the insecurities that bubbled up. Linc held all the cards here—he had from the beginning. And while Nate was willing to wait, because the man was beyond worth some patience, he couldn't help how past scars and future fears set root deep within him, growing a little stronger each day in this ambiguity, not knowing where they were headed or even if this relationship had a destination.

Hell, he'd thought his destination had been all mapped out with Sam back in Boston, until the man decided to dump him and move out in the same week. He'd been shattered.

Yet, he couldn't help but lose himself in the thrill of this, even if all he had was a flashlight in the dark.

Nate tilted his hips forward, grinding against Linc. Their chests pressed together, and their lips were a mere breath apart, the puff of heat making him delirious with lust. Linc's hand tightened on his hip in a possessive way that caused Nate to melt every damn time.

"A job completed deserves to be celebrated," he murmured, unable to help the quirk of his lips.

Linc's pupils darkened with desire. "Is that right? Sounds like you've got something in mind?"

Nate reached for Linc's hand, boldness licking him from head to toe. He pulled away, tugging Linc along with him as he began to lead them behind the counter. Linc arched one of his thick brows as a wicked grin transformed his features. Nate couldn't help but lick his lips in anticipation, well aware of the way Linc seized upon the movement.

"Well, this place is newly finished, but it hasn't been christened yet," he murmured.

"Goddamn, that's fucking hot," Linc growled, crowding him against the counter.

Nate glanced at the door. "Let me lock up."

His heart thumped in his ears as he jangled the keys in the lock and then took the steps back to Linc, tentative, as though approaching a wolf in the wild. When he slipped behind the counter, Linc's hands reached for his belt before he made it there, and the man brought him flush against his chest again. Nate reached into his pocket and dropped a condom and packet of lube on the counter in front of them. He'd taken to carrying them around with them all the time, just in case. He'd been hornier than he had in ages ever since he moved here.

Ever since he met Linc.

Nate tilted his head, about to speak, but Linc closed the space between them. Their hips pressed together, and the man claimed his mouth like he intended to devour it. Each stroke of their tongues in deeper and deeper kisses dizzied his mind. Fuck, Lincoln Lane ignited his system in a way no other man had. Nate leaned against the counter as his cock throbbed, trapped in the confines of his pants. Linc's hand wrapped around his nape as he ground against him, their lengths brushing, separated by far too many layers.

Nate reached down to tug open Linc's jeans, fumbling on the button and the zipper. He slipped his hand inside, past the elastic waistband to feel the silk of his hard cock beneath his boxer briefs. Goddamn. The jolt that traveled through him reduced him to jelly. He wanted to feel that hot length driving inside him again and again.

"I feel like I'm missing a thousand jokes with contractors and wood," Nate murmured, a smirk rising to his lips.

Linc fixed him a look. "If you're coherent enough to even formulate that terrible statement, I'm clearly not doing my job." He leaned in and licked the sensitive spot beneath his ear, and Nate let out a lusty moan. When the man's talented mouth continued to suck down the column of his neck, Nate tilted his head back in surrender.

"You win," Nate panted, rutting against Linc in desperation. Too many layers separated them. He just wanted skin against skin. "My mind's broken. Complete mush."

"Well, hell, I didn't expect it to be so easy," Linc responded, dragging his teeth over Nate's nipples, the fabric still between them.

"Easy's my middle name," Nate managed by some miracle.

Linc's hands landed on his belt, and Nate threatened to break out in a hallelujah. With a snick, Linc had the belt dropping to the floor and dragged Nate's khakis and boxers down moments later. Having his cock freed sent a thrill up his spine, especially when Linc then dragged down his own jeans.

When their lengths brushed together, Nate didn't bother restraining his moans. Linc reached down to draw both of their cocks in his hand and gave a few steady pumps. The edge of the counter bit into Nate's ass, but he didn't give a damn as he braced himself against the steady surface, letting Linc take control. The sparks gliding up his spine at the skin-to-skin sensation had his toes curling. If they kept up like this, he'd come embarrassingly early.

Linc let go, causing Nate to look up. That molten gaze seared through him, heavy with intent. "Turn around; hands on the counter."

"Bossy, aren't we," Nate sassed back, unable to help himself.

Linc smirked. "The only proper way to christen the place is by driving into you against this counter until you're screaming. So, I hope you're ready, sweetheart." Linc's husky voice could undo him any damn time.

Nate took his time pivoting around to face the counter, planting his palms on the cool, smooth surface. He thrust his ass back and glanced to where Linc stood behind him. "Like this?" If his voice came out coy, it was mostly due to desperate need.

Linc's sharp intake of breath split the space between them. "Fuck, you look edible." Desire hung heavy in the air, and Nate's legs trembled in anticipation. He was glad he was braced against the counter. Linc's callused palms settled around his hips, and he gave him a light tug. As the man's cock glided between his ass cheeks, brushing against his tight hole, Nate let out a moan.

"Need you inside" was all he managed, trying to fight the urge to thrust back.

"I aim to please," Linc responded, the cocky heat in his voice sending a new thrill rushing through him. Linc squeezed his hip with one hand as he pulled back. Nate glanced over in time to see Linc ripping the packet of the condom with his teeth, and how was that so hot? A shiver rolled down his spine, and he sucked in a sharp breath. Linc rolled the condom on with one hand, and a second later, he slicked his length with lube. He then dribbled the cool liquid between Nate's cheeks, and Nate chewed on his lip to bite back a moan.

Linc brushed the tip of his cock at Nate's hole, and Nate resisted the urge to thrust his erection against the nearest surface. The sensation was all electricity, running through his veins, sparking him up from the inside out. He kept his palms steady on the counter, even though drops of sweat beaded on them. Linc began to push inside him, and Nate forgot everything else. He took his time, working himself in slow, inch by careful inch, and Nate focused on his breath, on that feeling of fullness that he ached for. The slight burn was instantly forgiven once Linc slid all the way in and it gave way to pure ecstasy. Nate thrust his hips back, and Linc's cock thudded against the sensitive bundle of nerves that reduced him to a mumbling mess.

Linc pulled back before he sank deep again, starting to find a slow and steady rhythm. Nate leaned forward, surrendering himself to the sensations—the rough feel of Linc's callused hands at his hips, the smooth wood grain beneath his palms, and the prickle of sweat across his brow as Linc thrust into him over and over. Nate didn't bother restraining his moans, echoing in the fantastic acoustics of Chesapeake Brew as Linc pounded into him. Linc adjusted the angle until he hit Nate's prostate with every stroke.

Linc's hands around his hips were about the only thing keeping him upright as the man rammed into him again, blinding, searing bliss pulsing through him, threatening to bring him over the edge. His cock grew so hard it ached, and precum leaked at the tip. His breaths came out ragged, and his arms trembled with the effort to keep him upright. Drops of sweat dripped into his eyes, causing them to burn, but Nate didn't dare move, not while Linc pinned him like this. The man made him want to walk willingly into the flames.

"You're so damn tight," Linc murmured, his husky voice like a caress. All Nate could feel was the glorious slide of his cock inside him, all he could smell was the scent of fresh paint, sweat, and sex, and all he could see was the whorled wood grain of the counter beneath his palms. His throat squeezed tight before he let out another moan. His cock throbbed, the demand for release pushing him to the brink.

"Fuck," Nate moaned out, "Linc, I need…"

Before he could try to force out any more mush, Linc reached around and wrapped his careful, strong fingers around his erection. He stroked in time with his thrusts, turning Nate into an incoherent mess. The moment the man touched his cock, he knew he was done for. The pressure mounted inside him until he couldn't bear it anymore. Linc's hand ran along his length at the same time the man's cock hit the tender spot deep inside.

Nate let out a gasp, blinking back stars as his cock began to pulse. His cum splattered on the hardwood floor. The orgasm swept over him in shuddering waves, his palms still plastered to the counter. He rode that bliss, the intense sensations making him boneless. Linc continued to slam into him, their skin slapping together with a delicious sting until moments later, his length throbbed inside Nate and he let out a throaty groan as he came.

Linc slumped against him, his chest pressed against Nate's back as Nate continued to barely brace himself up along the counter. For a moment, they remained there together, their breaths harsh in the quiet of the storefront. Even as Linc began to soften, Nate didn't want him to pull out.

He didn't want this connection to end.

The realization settled bone deep as he stared at the polished surface of the counter that Linc himself had installed.

Nate wanted more than just day-to-day.

He wanted a future.

CHAPTER 18

Linc settled back in the booth, sinking into the soft vinyl. The fluorescent lighting in Champagne Diner blared down. His muscles burned and his stomach rumbled from the long days in construction. Not like he didn't have long days with his business, but he was used to taking breaks when he needed to and operating on his own schedule rather than the strict type at a site. One more day and he'd be heading home from Baltimore.

Rob plunked into the booth opposite him, passing a pint of pale ale over. "I've got to say, it's good to see you, man. It's been ages." Apart from a ruddier complexion and a few lines on his face, Rob looked the same as he had in high school, shaggy brown hair, lanky form, and an easy smile.

"How are Lynn and Melody doing?" Linc asked,

tipping back the pint. He enjoyed the smooth glide of the cool liquid. Lynn had grown up in the area too, but he had yet to meet Melody, Rob's seven-year-old.

"Mellie's currently obsessed with birds, so we've been going on bird-watching trips outside the city at Dan's Rock. Lynn's doing great, rising through the ranks at her marketing job," Rob said, running a hand through his sweaty strands. "How about Beckett?"

Linc didn't miss Rob's slight pause, probably to swallow back questions about Marissa. A lot of old friends had to do that, which made catching up awkward, always. Six years, and he still hadn't found a way to avoid the pauses, the cringes, and the pitying eyes.

"Kiddo has an artistic streak a mile wide, nothing like me," Linc said, trying to keep things light. "How's work been for you up here? Are most of your jobs for Millner, or do you have your own business running?"

Rob arched an eyebrow. "Why you asking? Thinking of taking a leap?"

Before Linc could answer, the waitress swung over with their burgers, placing the baskets in front of them. Linc took an immediate bite, savoring the rich taste as he tried to process the question. Was he thinking of moving? The idea had emerged so many times in his head over the past year that he couldn't deny it any longer.

"Business has been stagnant back home, so I wanted to put feelers out for other options, just in case," Linc murmured. Liar. He chewed on another bite, this one tasting a bit more like ash. How the fuck was he supposed to explain that he felt like he'd never be able to move on past Marissa and with every passing year the loss deadened him on the inside a little more?

Guilt coiled in his chest, followed by the flash of too-bright blue eyes.

"Of course, I'd want to know what the schools are like here too," Linc continued, trying to ignore the thoughts of Nate that kept bubbling to the surface. He'd never made the man any promises.

Rob nodded. "Mellie loves hers, and our district's solid. As for work, it'd be less local handyman and more high-paying, long-term projects. If you don't mind that sort of transition, I know you could get in here. Millner's liked your work so far."

Linc drummed his fingers on the surface of the table, wishing life was even a fraction simpler. "Thanks, man. I appreciate you vouching for me in the first place."

"Always. And if you're getting any hometown guilt for the idea of moving, fuck 'em. If I'd have listened to everyone, I never would've gotten out. Not like Chesapeake's shit or anything, but there's a whole big world out there." Rob took another swig of his beer and shrugged. "Besides, Mellie would always welcome a new friend, so you'll be starting out with someone for Beckett."

More than his son had now.

He'd checked in with Beck's teacher recently, and while they hadn't gotten more bullying incidents, Mrs. Carano had mentioned with a note of worry that Beckett spent most of his recesses drawing by himself rather than playing with the other kids. Fuck, it tore his insides apart.

"Yeah, the guilt's guaranteed," Linc replied, lifting his pint in acknowledgement. "Even if I moved an hour outside of Chesapeake City, my folks would treat it like I was packing up and heading to Australia. The amount of grief I've gotten for taking this job alone has been ridiculous."

Even as he made the complaints, he couldn't get rid of the guilt that pasted on his skin like the sweat from today's job.

"Tell me about it," Rob said, shaking his head. "My folks moved here to be closer to us, but every time we go to my aunt's for Christmas down there, she acts like we're strangers now. I do miss Eliza's breakfasts though. Please tell me Cozy Corner's still doing well."

"Eliza's slinging the same award-winning pancakes as ever," Linc responded, his chest warming at the thought of the weekend visits with Beck. Fuck, this should be simpler. He inhaled the rest of his burger in record time, if only to try and ignore the tug-of-war inside his chest. Still, Rob offered a surefire way out of the stuck feeling he'd been fighting for a while now.

The idea of heading back home made his stomach turn. Every time he stepped into the house, a blanket of subtle tension slipped over him, and he hated that. Hell, he couldn't even stand the idea of having Nate over in that place, which had once been filled with so many memories of Marissa, the home he'd fixed to her specifications as they'd started their life together.

His phone buzzed with a call. His folks.

"Let me take this," he said, hopping up from his seat. "Got to say good night to Beck."

Rob nodded, tipping two fingers in salute.

Linc answered the call as he loped toward the double glass doors, preferring to have a private conversation outside the diner. One more day on the job and he'd be home with his kiddo, who he'd missed the second he left.

Two more days until his date with Nate.

"Hey, Ma," he said the moment he stepped into the brisk spring air. Headlights glided by from the road in front of the diner from the few cars zipping by. The job was in Towson, the suburbs, which was where he'd end up if he and Beck moved. Even thinking in those terms made his gut clench.

"You have someone who wants to talk to you," she said, humor in her voice.

Rustling sounded, and before Linc could respond, Beck's voice blasted over the speaker. "Daddy!"

"Hey, kiddo," he murmured, relief washing through him at the joyful sound. "You behaving for Gran and Pop?"

"Yep, but they make me go to bed earlier than I do at home," Beck said. "Do I have to?"

"Their house, their rules," Linc responded, even though he bit back a grin. "I miss you. When I get home tomorrow, we can draw together, okay?"

Beck let out a squeal. "I miss you too, Daddy. Are you sure I have to go to bed?"

"Very," he responded, unable to hide the wry amusement in his voice. "Good night, kiddo. I love you."

"Love you toooo," Beck replied in his sing-song tone. More rustling sounded as Beck must've handed off the phone.

"Your mom's going to tuck him in," Dad said over the phone. "How is the job going?"

Linc's words stuck in his throat for a moment as he glanced to the entrance of Champagne Diner. He felt like a traitor for the topic of his conversation with Rob. Whatever he decided, his path wouldn't be easy. Either he stayed in stagnancy, unable to move past his wife, or he upset his friends and family by leaving town.

Liar. Liar. Liar.

Even here, he could recall the sound of Nate's bright laugh, the way everything just grew lighter around him.

"The job's going great, Dad," Linc said, leaning against the brick wall outside the building. The coolness seeped in past his thin shirt, the prickle of the brick biting into his skin. "Sounds like if I ever want to move up this way, I've got a job waiting for me."

Silence sounded in response.

Linc chewed on the inside of his cheek, needing to feel the sting. Of course this wouldn't go well.

A heavy sigh came over the phone, and Linc braced himself. "What's so terrible about Chesapeake City, son?"

Nothing. Nothing except the town had shattered his heart once, and he still hadn't forgiven the place.

"Beck's having a tough time at school, and the job

market's stagnant for me. It's not ridiculous to consider looking elsewhere, especially since Baltimore's not too far away."

"All right," his father responded, his tone heavy enough with resignation that Linc winced. "Your mother will argue something fierce on this, but I'm not going to dictate how you handle your life. I might be disappointed you don't want to stay and fight, but I've never been through your experience, so I won't cast stones."

Linc was glad he was leaning against the wall, because the floor fell out from under him at the statement. He worked his jaw for a few moments, not sure what to say. Fuck.

"Thanks, Dad" was all he said, gripping the phone a little tighter. He was shocked his voice remained steady. "Have a good night."

He ended the call and stared at the phone. His chest thumped hollow as he tilted his head to look at the velvety black sky. He'd take his mother's nagging any day over his father's disappointment. The man wasn't wrong either. He'd been trying to glue his pieces back together for years though, and nothing seemed to work.

A text lit his screen. Linc glanced down. Nate.

Giving a try at this whole 'planning a date' thing for

Friday. Bring a fire extinguisher in case it goes up in flames.

Linc snorted. Somehow, this man had wormed his way past his defenses, and he didn't know what to do about it. When he tried to picture a future with Nate, his limbs locked up, but he was too much of a selfish bastard to set him free. The past month he'd spent with Nate McAllister had been the best he'd experienced in years.

Yet, here he was, contemplating a move to Baltimore, one he hadn't even discussed with Beck yet. Guilt pounded in the back of his brain. Linc pushed off from the brick wall and strode toward the entrance of the diner. He stepped inside, casting a glance to where Rob sat waiting, sipping at his pint.

His father's words tugged at his heels with every step.

Was he moving forward or just running away?

CHAPTER 19

N ATE PULLED INTO A SPOT AT THE DINGY STRIP MALL that didn't look inviting in the slightest. Already, he was having second thoughts about his date idea, but it was too late now. Linc would be meeting him here any minute, and then they'd just have to bask in his terrible planning skills together.

He peered into the rearview mirror and ran his fingers through his thick hair for the thousandth time. His heart jackhammered in his chest at the idea of seeing Linc again for the first time in almost a week. Between the end of the remodel and ramping up for the opening, busy weekends, and then Linc's out-of-town job, it had felt like ages. They still texted every day, which was the reassurance he clung to, but damn. His heart had apparently missed the "don't get attached" memo.

Headlights flashed in the parking lot as another car turned in. Nate squinted out the window to see Linc's familiar Tacoma pull into view. He wiped his sweaty palms on his jeans, because this man turned him into a preteen going to his first winter formal. Jesus, Mary, and Joseph, he was doing great here.

He hopped out of the car and welcomed the brisk spring breezes for the pitiful attempts to cool his sweaty palms. The Tacoma settled into place in the spot beside him. Even though Nate wanted to rush up and greet him at the driver side, he attempted casual by leaning against the side of his car, arms folded. When Linc climbed out of his truck and strode around, the second the stretch of his shadow came around the bend of the car, Nate pushed up from his slouch.

Oh hell, he'd never been good at playing cool anyway.

Linc approached, looking as gorgeous as ever. His dark, glossy curls gleamed in the moonlight, and his whole leather jacket, white tank, and jeans ensemble got Nate's motor revving. Once their eyes met, Linc's lips quirked in a familiar half smile, and Nate gave up any pretense at hiding. He closed the distance between them in a few quick strides, his fingers wrapping around the lapels of Linc's jacket. Nate crushed his mouth to Linc's in a bruising kiss.

Nate drank in the taste of him, all coffee and man. The bristles of his stubble brushed against Nate's chin, and the coarse sensation caused desire to spike through him. Linc wrapped his arms around his waist, drawing their bodies flush together. The swift motion had Nate swooning, as if he'd stood a chance at resisting this man. Linc's earthy scent offered a welcome caress, one he'd missed in their days apart.

When they broke apart, their breaths cycled in the air between them.

Linc swiped his thumb against the side of his lips. "Well, that was one hell of a hello."

Nate couldn't help but beam. The way Linc made him feel was addictive. "Hope you can keep up that level of appreciation when I explain my shitty plans for the night."

Linc lifted a thick brow.

"I know you're a reader, so I thought this place sounded fun to check out. Look at some books and grab a coffee," Nate said, glancing to the red lit sign reading Book Attic in plain font. "But clearly, I don't know the area, so I probably picked one of the shit-tiest spots around."

Linc glanced over to the shop, and his Adam's apple bobbed with his swallow, his eyes unreadable.

Crap. He should've picked something outdoorsy. Hell, even just a restaurant in town would be better than dragging Linc to this podunk strip mall for the worst date in history.

"Or we could go somewhere else," Nate said, scratching the back of his neck. "I'm not married to the place or anything. And gauging by all this oppressive silence, I misread everything and this isn't your scene at all."

Linc shook his head, his lips quirking again in an offering. He slung an arm around Nate's shoulders, the gentle, solid touch silencing him at once.

"Nah, you read me right," he said, his husky voice a rumble against his chest that vibrated against Nate. "I... used to come here with Marissa. I've been here a few times since she passed, but not too often."

Oh. Damn.

Nate's chest sank. Of all the date plans he could've made, of course he picked out the place Linc frequented with his dead wife. Bully for him. Awards all around. "This is why I don't make plans," he mumbled, not even sure how to salvage the night from here.

Linc moved his arm away and instead reached down to thread his fingers through Nate's. "All it means is that you happen to know me damn well." He gave a tug and began taking the first steps toward the Book Attic. "This is one of the best bookstores in the area if you aren't looking for a big chain vibe."

"I figured since there was a café inside, books and coffee might be fun," Nate said, wishing his palm wasn't quite so sweaty. "I know we don't have all night."

"As much as I love Nico, I only trust him with my son for a few hours at a time. The man's powers of corruption know no bounds," Linc responded as they neared the entrance. "Last time he babysat, I came home to Beck learning how to mix a martini."

Nate squeezed his hand. "Hey, those are some quality life skills."

When they reached the entrance, Linc let go of his hand to grab the handle, and he swung the door open. He held it, sweeping his arm in a gesture. "After you."

Nate stepped inside, and the scent of weathered books greeted him at once. He took a deep inhale of the leather and old paper as the fluorescent lights cast yellowed beams onto him. The interior was all tall bookshelves lining the walls, a small coffee station in the back, and a large section of boxes in the middle filled with old comic books. An older man with an ever-expanding silver beard and thick glasses hunched over the register, reading a behemoth of a book. Nothing in the Book Attic preached of organization—instead, the shop was an explosion of colored spines, precarious stacks of books on tables, and random bookends placed as an afterthought.

Places like this reminded him of visiting his grandpa's house as a kid. The man encouraged imagination at all costs, and his house had been filled with enough odd, shiny knickknacks that he'd felt like Indiana Jones exploring for ancient artifacts. In a shop like this, a mystical sense of possibility bubbled through his veins.

"Since you've never experienced the Book Attic before, follow me," Linc said, flashing him a smile and taking the lead. "I'll show you the best corners of the store."

As they strode deeper into the Book Attic, Linc lifted a hand. "Evening, Ben."

The guy in the back looked up from over the edge of his book, blinking owlishly in surprise. "Is that Lincoln Lane? I figured you moved away."

"Nah, still here," Linc responded, a slight strain to his voice. Ben let out a grunt, a nod, and then lifted his book back up.

Nate couldn't help but bump shoulders with Linc. It couldn't be easy returning to places he'd shared with his dead wife. Christ, Nate couldn't even imagine loving someone so much to promise them forever and then losing them. Even the thought of the pain crushed his heart like aluminum foil.

Linc offered a grateful smile and slung an arm around Nate's shoulders, steering him to the right. "This area is a treasure trove." He brought them to a halt right in front of the sci-fi/fantasy section, far larger than most used bookstores. "It's where Marissa and I picked up a lot of old reads to stock our shelves when we moved into our house."

"What are your favorites?" Nate asked, leaning forward and drifting his fingertip along the spines sticking out from the shelves. "I'll be honest, I haven't read a lot of fantasy novels, so you're going to need to point out what's quality and not."

Linc leaned against the shelves, facing him. "At least tell me you've read Lord of the Rings."

Nate scratched his nape. "Does watching the movies count?"

Linc's brows lifted. "Not in the slightest. You never even get to meet Tom Bombadil in the movies."

Nate skimmed the shelves until he landed on Tolkien. "So, you're saying these should be my purchase of the night?"

Linc placed a hand over his and shook his head. "No need to buy them—I'll lend you my copies."

Nate chewed his lip, trying to hide the pleasant flush that rolled through him. He hadn't pushed Linc for any commitment, any talks of the future, yet he couldn't help but yearn. The fact Linc wanted to lend his favorite books was the sliver of hope he grabbed onto at claiming a more permanent status in Linc's life—that maybe Linc had started to reconsider his day-by-day stance.

That maybe he wanted more too.

"What's your go-to genre?" Linc asked. "I'm assuming you read, given the fact you chose a bookstore for our date."

Nate pursed his lips. "Toss up between thriller and romance."

Linc arched a brow. "You realize they're on extreme opposite ends of the spectrum, right?"

"Yet both make the heart pound faster." Nate continued to scan the books on the shelves, even though he noticed Linc in his periphery. It was impossible not to feel the presence beside him, and he resisted the urge to move closer and drape himself all over the man's ridiculously firm chest. "Though what I've read the most of over the years are comic books."

Linc grinned and took a step in closer to skim his fingers through Nate's hair. "Now, that's something we can agree on."

Nate bit back a shiver at the intimate touch, at the soft, amused look in Linc's eyes. He didn't have a hope in the universe at holding his heart back around this man. "How's the selection here?" he asked, glancing toward the center of the room dominated by comic book boxes.

Linc's grin widened, and he tilted his head in that direction. "You'll have to see for yourself."

———

"How is your favorite superhero Booster Gold?" Linc teased, leaning against the brick wall outside the building. "A random B-list hero?" They'd stayed until Ben was ready to close up and then brought their paper cups of coffee out with them. Yet Nate hadn't made a move toward his car, and neither had Linc.

"Don't get me wrong," Nate said, leaning against one of the pillars, the cold concrete soaking through his jeans where he sat. "I adore Green Lantern, the Flash, and Cap, but there's something to be said about the characters who take side-stage. He comes off all bluster and bravado, but the guy ends up having hidden depths. I just think his story proves we can't take people at face value."

Linc slid down to sit on the ground facing Nate, his back still pressed against the wall. "Well, when you put it like that, it's no surprise he's your favorite."

Nate took a sip of the crappy coffee, the tinny

taste rolling across his tongue along with a burst of heat. The paper bag of the couple of back issues Nate had picked up leaned against the pillar beside him. "With all your broody seriousness, I bet your favorite was Batman."

Linc's mouth gave a bitter twist. "And just like him, I can't seem to escape Gotham, no matter how much tragedy's happened."

Nate gripped his paper cup a little tighter. His lips pressed together for a moment but then he let out a small huff. "I think you're seeing it wrong," he murmured. Linc's brows lifted. "Batman's tied to Gotham, but he chooses to stay there despite the tragedy. To stand and fight. And more than all the fancy gadgets, that's what makes him a true hero. Because every night, he faces the streets that broke him."

Linc's intense gaze bored into him, and his jaw worked, but no words came out. He drew his knees in closer, resting his arms across them. "Every time I think I've got you figured out, you end up surprising me."

"Hope that's a good thing," Nate responded, his heart stepping in double time. He couldn't pull away from Linc's gaze, from the slightly awed way he looked at him like he was staring at the starry sky, the tides at night, or a sunrise. Those three words bubbled up in his throat again, but even though he wanted to say them, he tempered the urge. Not yet.

"You deserve the world," Linc murmured, his gaze dropping to the ground between them. His voice cracked. "You deserve so much more than this bullshit from a fucking guy too broken to make you the promises you need."

Nate's chest twisted. He stretched his legs out until his shoe bumped against Linc's. The sallow lighting reflected on them, sharpening the shadows of the man's features, haunted by his past.

"Hey," he said softly. "I'm the one who decides what I need. And none of this 'deserve' bullshit. Because this thing between us? It's not the sort of connection to pass up."

Even if he needed to be patient. Even if sometimes the lack of a label swallowed his nerves and spat them back out.

Linc's mouth wavered, and he looked at Nate with a soft glance that had him reeling. "I feel the same." This time he nudged his shoe against Nate's. "I'm glad you came to Chesapeake City, Nate McAllister."

Nate soared.

These moments were worth waiting for. This was worth fighting for.

Even if he was terrified every step of the way.

CHAPTER 20

THE ENTIRE DRIVE HOME FROM THE SCHOOL, LINC strangled the steering wheel, trying to contain his rage.

Again. He was picking up his son from getting attacked by bullies. Again.

His shoulders shook, the tremor traveling all the way down his arms. Beck sat in the back seat, staring out the window, the lost expression on his face scooping Linc hollow.

He was supposed to protect his son. Keep him safe. His throat spasmed, and his eyes burned.

Yet, he'd failed.

Beck's elbows and knees were scraped from getting shoved down at recess, and Linc didn't miss the tremble of his son's lower lip. He wanted to set the world on fire.

The drive wasn't nearly long enough. Maybe tearing down Route 1 might give him a little release for all this rage, but he needed to get Beck home. The school promised to do something more, since this was a second offense for these boys.

There shouldn't have been a second time. Linc worked his jaw.

The idea of picking up and moving to Baltimore sounded better and better.

At least there, Beck could start fresh, without this fear and sadness hanging over him. He wished with all his might Marissa was still here to talk to Beck, because right now, Linc was spiraling. He didn't know how to fix this, how to make it better, and that helplessness hurt so damn much. Beck didn't need him growling about the school or those cruel fucking kids.

He wouldn't trade raising his son for anything in the world, but some days, the burden of doing it by himself weighed so heavy he could barely breathe.

Linc pulled in front of his house and shut the engine off. He glanced to Beck, who stared up at him.

"Are you mad at me, Daddy?" Beck asked, his voice tinier than ever.

That smacked him straight in the chest. Apparently Linc hadn't done a good job hiding his temper. Fuck. Linc took a deep breath in through the nose, out through the mouth, trying to settle himself so he didn't upset Beck anymore.

"I'm not mad at you, kiddo," he murmured before turning back to look at Beck. He reached over and squeezed his son's knee. "Daddy's just…"

Confused.

Heartbroken.

So fucking alone.

Linc steadied himself and met Beck's eyes. "Daddy's just sad you got hurt."

Beck put his hand over Linc's, the motion so gentle and sympathetic that heat stung his eyes. This kid slayed him every time. The thought of someone hurting Beck, of pushing him down, of crushing the beautiful gentleness in his eyes—he wanted to scream.

"What do you want to do this afternoon?" Linc asked. "I'm all yours."

Beck tilted his head and tapped his chin. "Can we draw?"

Linc's soft grin threatened to break free. Of course that's what his kiddo wanted to do. "We can definitely draw together. Let's get inside."

Linc hopped out of his car and got the door for Beck. He slipped a hand in his son's as they headed toward their house. The second his porch came into view, Linc stopped. Nate paced back and forth in front of their house, staring at his phone.

Oh fuck, they were supposed to have lunch together. When the school had called, Linc phoned his next job and drove over to pick up Beck, and the blinding rage that followed scoured away any other thoughts. He slipped his phone out with his free hand and caught all the missed calls from Nate. His throat dried. He'd be such a dick to send him away now.

"Mr. Nate?" Beck's questioning voice broke through the air.

Nate whipped his head up, and when he spotted Beck, panic flared in his eyes. Guilt thudded through Linc, compounding all the other shitty feelings brewing around in his chest. He'd caused Nate to feel that way in his attempt to keep his dating life separate from his home life, even though more and more lately, he'd been fantasizing about the what-ifs.

"Daddy was supposed to have lunch with Mr. Nate," Linc explained as they approached the front porch.

"I'm so sorry," Nate said, his tone frantic. "When you didn't show and weren't answering your phone, I got worried and…"

"Can Mr. Nate have lunch with us?" Beck asked, tugging on his arm.

Linc hesitated, the "no" hovering on his lips. The idea of bringing Nate inside, sharing lunch with him in that house, soured his stomach. Nate must've noticed Linc's pause, and he lifted his hands, probably about to jet.

"Why don't I make us some sandwiches," Linc forced out. "We can eat and draw on the front porch, since it's a beautiful day out." Definitely not because the idea of bringing someone else into their home made him feel like he'd swallowed sawdust. "Does that sound good to both of you?"

Nate blinked in surprise. "Sounds perfect." His voice came out hushed and hopeful.

Beck nodded, a slight grin rising to his lips. Nate had already charmed his son, and after today, the last thing he needed was for Beck to feel like he didn't have any friends. He could shove away his own mental hang-ups.

"Stay here with Mr. Nate," Linc said as he wrestled for his keys. Beck let go and took a seat in one of the rocking chairs. "I'll be right back out with some snacks." He opened the door with a click. He could feel Nate's gaze press on him, but he wasn't at the point where they could have this discussion yet, not while his fingers were close to trembling. Hell, he didn't even know what it meant, just that his life wasn't the sort of tidy to make compartmentalizing possible.

He stepped into the house, the cool darkness washing over him. Just once, he wished returning to this place warmed his bones, but it offered tension, not relief. He quick-stepped over to the kitchen and whipped together turkey and swiss sandwiches, with mustard on his and Nate's and mayo for Beck, slicing them in half and piling them on a plate. Linc grabbed one of Beck's many pads of paper and his crayons, balancing them in one hand while he carried the plate of sandwiches in the other.

When he reached the front door, he paused, listening to the voices of his boyfriend and son. He peered through the glass to see them both rocking on chairs beside each other.

"They don't like me," Beck said, his voice quiet. "They said I'm weird cos I don't have any friends and I'm always drawing."

Nate glanced to Beck, stopping midcreak. "I used to get pushed around in grade school a lot too."

Linc paused, not wanting to intrude on this moment.

Beck looked up at him, wide-eyed. "You?"

"That's right," Nate said. "I would come home in tears almost every day, because there was a group of boys who'd shove me down and call me mean names all the time. I begged my parents to move. I just wanted to run away."

"Did you?" Beck asked. Linc's heart ached. He wanted to do the same for Beck so badly, to escape from all this pain.

"We couldn't," Nate said with a shrug. "My brothers and sister were at that school too, and they couldn't afford to pick up and leave. The bullying hurt a lot though. The day it started getting better was when I made friends with one of the other kids. The mean boys still tried to call me names and hurt my feelings, but I had friends who would stand up for me, and they took some of the hurt away."

Beck pressed his lips together, a very serious look on his face. "But how do you make friends?"

Nate broke into a beautiful grin. "You're already great at it, Beckett. The same way you made friends with me—by asking. Maybe the other kids might not want to draw with you yet, but you can see what they're having fun with and try to join that. And if all the kids in your class are being mean right now, then you hold on to the people you do have. A dad who loves you, grandparents who think the world of you, and as long as you need me, I'll be here."

Beck hopped out of his chair and walked right up to Nate to launch into a hug. Linc swallowed a lump in his throat at the sight. His chest was thumping out of control. Nate wrapped his arms around Beck and squeezed tight. The gentle, affectionate look Nate cast to his son had Linc careening. He'd already become smitten with the man over the past month and a half, but watching how easily he accepted the most important person in his life… goddamn.

Every time, Nate surprised him. This man made him want to hope that maybe… just maybe, he could move forward.

"The important thing is standing your ground," Nate murmured, stroking his fingers through Beck's thick hair. "You don't have to confront them or yell, but as silly as it sounds, the happier you are, the less power they'll have over you. If you run away, you might never learn to do that."

Linc took the moment to step onto the porch, unable to handle the rising tide of emotion threatening to crest and knock him down. Guilt dripped through him like paint. The conversation with his father blared with neon-light intensity, but he forced on a smile and lifted the plate of sandwiches.

"Who's hungry?" he asked, trying to keep the hoarseness out of his throat. He swept over to the small bistro table and placed the plate down.

"Food," Beck exclaimed, breaking free from the hug.

Nate glanced at Linc before rubbing the nape of

his neck, a sheepish hesitance in the motion. "Sorry," Nate mouthed.

Linc shook his head. "Thank you," he mouthed back. The man had comforted his son when he needed it the most, and if Linc was being honest, Nate had a better perspective than he ever could give. Linc had been on the soccer team as soon as he could start and had plenty of friends all through school, so he didn't possess a frame of reference for the pain Beck was going through.

Beck grabbed the paper and crayons out of Linc's hand and plopped onto the wooden planks of the porch. Linc lowered himself into the space opposite him.

"What are we drawing?" he asked, grabbing a handful of crayons. He'd do just about anything to coax more smiles from his son's face. He tried to avoid the Band-Aids on Beck's elbows from the scrapes he'd gotten after those kids shoved him down. Rage still simmered in his belly, but he contained it. Beck didn't need the burden of his feelings right now. He needed to express his own.

Nate slid off the seat to join them as Beck distributed paper and crayons. This was more than Linc would've ever dared before, yet he couldn't bring himself to break this tentative spell.

Beck lapsed into quiet as his dark eyes took on the

intense focus they always did when he was drawing. Linc swallowed hard. He was relieved to see such a familiar sight—far better than Beck's trembling lip and cast-down gaze when he'd come to pick him up.

Nate dragged a green crayon along the paper, lazy lines that didn't seem to be making any sort of picture. "Don't suppose you heard that Fletcher's selling the place."

Linc's brows lifted. "Did his daughter finally convince him to go to a nursing home?"

"Sounds like it," Nate murmured, grinding the crayon into the paper a little harder. "I'm just hoping I still have a place to live after he sells."

Linc wanted to reach out so badly that his hand twitched at his side. But if he started comforting Nate, taking his hand, planting a kiss on his lips, that would lead to questions from Beck he wasn't able to answer yet. Nate kept his gaze down at the paper.

"Even if there's a problem with keeping your place, we'll find you another one," Linc murmured. The idea of Nate not three houses away caused his chest to squeeze tight. Somehow, in the short time he'd known the man, he already made a significant mark.

Yet he was the asshole contemplating a move to Baltimore.

"I hope so, because with Chesapeake Brew

opening next month, I'm pretty rooted to the area,"
Nate responded. Guilt twisted in Linc's chest, but he
kept silent, listening as Nate continued. "We're going
to debut with our coffee cart in a week at the Chesapeake Days festival."

Beck's head whipped up at the word "festival."
"Daddy, can we go?" Lord, the selective hearing on
this child.

Chesapeake Days was the biggest yearly festival
in Chesapeake City, one that drew turnout from out-
of-town boaters as well as all the townies. The main
streets got shut down to traffic so everyone could
walk around, and between the food vendors with
their fresh wares, the boat parade, and the outdoor
games for families, it ended up being a colorful and
loud week. He'd loved going so much as a kid that
even though he'd gone with Marissa every year, the
festival didn't end up reminding him of her, unlike so
many other things.

"Sure thing, kiddo," he said, casting a sideways
glance to Nate. "We'll have to visit the coffee stand,
right?"

Beck's nose wrinkled. "That stuff is gross."

Nate let loose a hearty laugh. "No worries. We'll
have raspberry lemonades, and I've been working on
a sparkly blue iced tea."

Beck's eyes widened, and Linc bit back his laugh

at the sheer excitement painting the kid's features. "I can have a drink that sparkles?"

Nate's grin broadened. "You betcha."

Linc lifted a brow, casting Nate an amused look. "You'll create an addict out of this one."

Beck pointed a finger at the blank paper in front of him. "Daddy, you have to draw something. Mr. Nate already made a picture."

Nate lifted his paper of scribbles, all done with the same crayon. "I call it a study in green."

"Right, right," Linc responded, grabbing a crayon and beginning to follow a similar tactic. "Can't have Mr. Nate one-upping me." He tilted his head in Beck's direction and mouthed "tyrant" to Nate.

Nate balled his hand into a fist, pressing it in front of his mouth to keep from exploding in laughter. He failed a little, since his shoulders still shook and his eyes danced. The spring breeze wafted through the porch, bringing with it the scent of honeysuckle and the hope of long withered things beginning to come to life again. Linc shifted, the weathered planks groaning with his movement.

He couldn't help but soak in the scene before him, of Nate and Beck sketching away, the sun casting dappled beams across the porch. The warmth in the air permeated past his skin for once, settling deep inside him. This was good. This was right.

Yet why did the old, familiar terror still come climbing up his throat? Beck might've bounced back both times he was bullied, but Linc understood far too well how the world could shatter you. He refused to let that happen to his son.

Even if it meant turning tail and running.

Even if he ended up more ruined than before.

.

CHAPTER 21

NATE LEANED DOWN TO CATCH HIS BREATH, HIS PALMS resting on his thighs. A sheen of sweat coated his forehead, and the sun beat with the promise of a glorious day. Eliza's daughter Melody manned the booth across from them, selling loaded waffles, pancakes, or french toast—you picked the base and the topping. Eliza herself would be busy running Cozy Corner during this influx of people, a note Nate tucked into his back pocket for future years.

He scanned over the booth he shared with Nico. He and Daria would be taking alternate shifts throughout the days, while Nico would send over some of his bartenders to help sling drinks at the event while he drew folks over to Port of Call. Nate wished he'd been able to time the opening of Chesapeake Brew with this festival, but he hadn't found out about it until he'd arrived in town and talked to some of the other businesses.

Nate rolled his sleeves as he approached the industrial brewer he'd brought along. They were sticking to simple drinks—no espresso—in an attempt to feature the coffee they'd be using from the new roaster. He grabbed one of the paper cups from the stack and poured himself a cup, fixing it up. Before he stepped away, Nate skimmed the crowd and caught sight of Nico. He poured another cup of coffee.

Nico slipped under the tent, tipping his sunglasses down. Even though the man blinked groggily, his thick black hair was artfully styled, and like always, he looked sharp, this time in his salmon-colored polo with khaki slacks.

"Is that coffee?" he asked. "Because I'm dying here. Mornings are terrible, horrible things that shouldn't be wished upon anyone."

"Clearly why you run a bar, not a coffee shop," Nate responded with a grin. The atmosphere around town buzzed with a contagious energy and excitement for the festival. "I've been up for hours already."

Nico scanned over the setup. "I can see that. We're going to have to do a lot more events together, because none of my employees are good with morn- ings either. Hopefully these Irish coffees and rasp- berry-lemon mimosas are a hit." Nico took a long, slow sip of his coffee, as if he attempted to drown himself in the cup.

"Please, you're doing me the favor," Nate said, running a hand through his hair. "I don't know anyone here, and I'm only in the festival because you had the application completed." The heat from his cup of coffee imprinted on his palm, even though the bright sunlight promised a warm day ahead. Already, the scents of doughnuts, metal, and fresh water drifted his way, an interesting mix he knew he'd imprint on his memory. This might not come close to the celebrations he'd gone to in Boston, but this one felt more personal.

This time, he was part of representing the town itself.

Once he'd arrived here, he'd begun to feel his shoes stick a little more to this path, as if it was one worth remembering. As if this was a place worth staying. And the more he got to know the other busi- ness owners in the town, the friends he'd made like Sarah and Nico, the more attached he'd gotten. Linc… well, that opened up a whole different realm of possibility there.

Since the other day when he'd colored on the

porch with Linc and Beckett, he couldn't help the sharp yearning that rose in his chest. He wanted that. The warmth, the family, the simple moments on a sunny day.

He'd been searching for so long, only to realize he didn't long for the ambition or the big successes like Sam had wanted for them. Nate didn't need big cities, wild parties, or mingling with the upper tier of Boston. He needed hesitant spring days bursting at the seams with hope, outdoor barbecues warmed by laughter, and finding friendly faces as he walked around town.

"Mind if I refill?" Nico asked from behind, snapping him into focus.

"Help yourself," Nate said, taking a sip from the cup he still held in hand. The rich, piping hot liquid coated his tongue, all the delicate notes quality coffee contained leaping to the fore. This one was a medium roast with some berry notes and full-bodied. Uncle Harold's old vendor made crap coffee that tasted weak, and he'd been overcharging for the beans anyway. The customers would appreciate the change. He hoped.

Nate checked his watch. Chesapeake Days had officially begun. He scanned up and down the street, as if he expected a swarm to the booth.

Nico nudged him in the side. "Rushes aren't

going to hit until the weekend, when all the families arrive on the scene. We're looking at a slow trickle since it's only Thursday. Sit back and relax. When the customers arrive, we'll be able to give them plenty of quality time."

"I might be a *little* anxious," Nate admitted, rocking back and forth. "This is the first event I've ever worked. Plus, I'm terrified I'm going to get reamed out by more of the older folks in town for ruining things."

Nico popped open his folding chair and took a seat. "Trust me, I dealt with the same when I opened Port of Call. Every old geezer had some bitchy rant about ruining history, and you know what? They come to my bar every damn week regardless."

Nate took a seat beside Nico, the fabric creaking. "Well, that has me relieved."

A familiar figure strode toward them, her dark brown hair pulled into a bun, though unlike her normal khakis and hoodies she wore at the shop, today she was in a green shirt and jeans. Nate's brows drew together as she approached the booth.

"Daria?" Nate said aloud, pushing up from his seat. He placed his cup of coffee on the ground beside it and went to the front of the tent to meet her. His heart started pounding into overdrive. She wasn't supposed to work today. Had something happened at the shop?

She stopped in front of him with her arms folded. Nate swallowed. That couldn't be good.

"Is everything okay?" he asked.

"I saw the drink prices for the event," she said, her tone the annoyed one he'd begun to get used to. "They're outrageous. I thought you said you weren't coming in here to rob the town blind."

Nate shook his head. "Look, these are researched prices, and they're the ones we're using in the shop, so it's best to try it out now. If you've got some friends and family coming though, I'm fine with offering them a 15 percent discount."

Daria slammed her hands on the surface of the table, the loud smack making Nate take a step back. She'd been decent about these sorts of outbursts the past week, but the more her temper peeked out, the more uneasy he became. How had his uncle dealt with her attitude? She'd worked with him for over five years. Though, from the sounds of it, she'd been calling most of the shots during those waning years.

"I thought we were discussing the ones in the shop?" Her voice came out sharp and sour.

Nate sucked in a breath. Nothing killed a good mood like an argument. "I said we could discuss strategies for helping the customers who are having a tough time affording coffee, not that I'd bankrupt the business by criminally undercharging." He kept his voice level, even though he wanted to turn on his heel and walk the other way.

"Your uncle knew how to run a business just fine," Daria shot back. "The people here loved him. Think about how disappointed they're going to be to find out his nephew's a miser."

Nate ran his fingers through his hair. She was being terrible, and yet he could see how she'd been hurting during this transition. The more they'd worked together, the clearer it had become that she'd expected the business to go to her when Uncle Harold passed. So, instead of the retirement plan she'd worked toward, now she had to concede to him, this out-of-town guy she didn't know.

Yet there were lines you didn't cross, no matter how much you were hurting.

"They can think what they like," Nate said, drumming his fingers on the surface of the table to keep them from shaking. He needed to stand up to her. He knew that. "I'm still going to do what's necessary for this reopen, Daria. You may not like my choice, but I'm the owner, which means I make the final calls."

Daria's brows drew together, and her mouth pinched like she'd swallowed a grapefruit. For a moment, she stood there percolating, like at any moment she'd boil over.

Nate didn't back down though. He couldn't. Daria had every right to her feelings, but if she was going to work for him, she couldn't continue with these outbursts. He maintained eye contact. "Is this the only reason you came over to the booth?"

That seemed to snap Daria out of her headspace. "No. I saw you put me on Sunday night. I don't work nights."

"We agreed to trade off, remember?" He tried to keep his tone gentle, even though he wanted to scream. They'd had this conversation. She'd been with him when he made the schedule and agreed to it. Now, it just felt like she was being petulant on purpose.

"Well, I can't," she snapped. "And I'm not the boss here, so I'm not required to work outside of my availability."

He recognized the bitchy dig for what it was, one that didn't deserve a response.

"I'll be here tomorrow," Daria said, turning on her heel and heading back down the street, the stomp of her feet heavier as she left.

Nate watched until she disappeared down the road before he let out a sigh, his shoulders slumping. "Fuck."

A hand clapped on his shoulder, and Nico appeared beside him, thrusting his cup of coffee toward him. "I fixed it. You look like you need this."

Nate took a sip, the sweet warmth of the whisky, coffee, sugar, and cream melding in his mouth. At once, the drink coursed through him, like a warm blanket over his fritzing nerves. "Thanks," he said, glancing to Nico. A flush rose to his cheeks. "I'm embarrassed you saw that."

Nico shrugged. "No judgement here, though I definitely wondered why you kept Daria on when you took the place."

"Bleeding heart, I guess," Nate said. "She'd been working here when my uncle died, and I hated the idea of her losing him and then losing her job too."

"It's only fair to warn you, the way she acted with you right now? She pulled that attitude with customers when Chesapeake Brew was still open," Nico said. The man's tone was neutral, though the warning came across clear. Nate's stomach churned. The reopening was so close. Maybe once they started working together, she'd have a change of heart.

Yeah, right.

"Hey, boss," Nico called out, leaning past him to wave at someone out in the street.

Nate followed Nico's gaze to spot another familiar figure approaching. This one was far more welcome. His heart thudded faster as he soaked in the sight of Lincoln Lane, looking more gorgeous than ever in the early morning light. His black curls gleamed, and the bright sun brought out the deep notes of his tan. Linc cracked a grin, charming with white, slightly crooked teeth. Nate couldn't help but watch his approach, if only to appreciate the way those coiled muscles flexed. After feeling all his power up close and personal, the sight was dizzying.

Linc nodded to Nico, but he came to a stop right in front of Nate. "Think I could get a cup of coffee?" His eyes danced.

Nate couldn't stop staring as his palms pressed against the table's surface. A stupid, giddy smile rose to his lips.

"Hey, lover boy," Nico mock-whispered. "I'm pretty sure that's a customer asking for coffee. Whatever you're thinking of is definitely not on the menu here."

A fierce blush hit his cheeks, and he pivoted around to grab a paper cup and pour some coffee to save himself the embarrassment of looking back at Linc and Nico, who were both probably far too amused. "Right, coffee" was all he said out loud.

He came back to a pair of smirks. Nate rolled his eyes and thrust the cup of coffee in Linc's direction. "Here, on the house."

"Didn't realize free coffee was one of the perks of dating you," Linc murmured.

"Just about the only perk," Nate responded. "The rest is a cocktail of daydreams, klutziness, and anxiety."

"Sounds delicious," Linc responded, his husky voice *doing* things to him.

"You guys are disgusting," Nico complained, even though he had a grin on his face. "It's way too early in the morning for this kind of flirting."

Linc cast him the side-eye. "Like I haven't spent far too many bar nights being the third wheel to you shoving your tongue down some guy's throat."

"Well, when you put it like that…," Nico said, plopping down in his seat. "Go ahead. Flirt away. I'll just watch in lurid fascination."

Linc rolled his eyes. Warmth coiled in Nate's chest, watching the pair of them. They clearly shared a lot of history and a lot of love. Seeing Linc and the solid presence he was around his friends made Nate fall a little harder.

Linc tilted his head in Nate's direction, catching his eye. "I've got to get back to my job, but what are you doing Saturday?"

"I'm working the night shift here, but apart from that, nothing," Nate said, stealing another sip of the Irish coffee.

Linc met his gaze. "Want to explore the festival with me and Beck?"

Nate's chest exploded in butterflies. He swallowed back a squeal, because he'd already embarrassed himself enough, but he didn't hide his wide grin. "I'd love that."

Linc leaned in, brushing his lips over Nate's in a sweet kiss that dizzied his mind more than whisky. "See you then."

He pulled away and waved goodbye at both of them. Nate stood there clutching his coffee and watching Linc saunter off. Fuck, he was so smitten with this man it was ridiculous. Nate let out a wistful sigh, not caring if he sounded like a teenage girl. When it remained quiet, he glanced to Nico. He'd for sure been expecting a snarky comment on that one.

Instead, Nico stared at him, his head tilted to the side and a curious expression on his face.

"What's wrong?" Nate asked.

Nico shook his head. "Nothing, nothing. Just... surprised." The gently amused curl of Nico's lips offered a slight reassurance, but Nate wanted to know what he was referring to. Before he could ask him, Nico hopped up and waved to Sarah, who was walking to their booth, almost unrecognizable in her white blouse and black slacks. Not like Nate didn't notice an avoidance tactic when he saw one.

"Hey, party people," Sarah called out as she approached.

Nate sat back in his seat, his knees still delightfully unsteady from Linc's visit. He took another sip of his Irish coffee, letting that warmth linger. Inviting him to the festival with his son?

That felt a lot like progress.

.

CHAPTER 22

Saturday of the Chesapeake Day Festival and the town was *alive*.

"Make sure you keep a tight hold on my hand, kiddo," Linc warned Beck as they entered the main street, crowded with people. Given the way Beck's mind tended to wander and the sheer volume of the folks here every year, he kept a close eye on his son. The sound of a trumpet was followed by the robust noise of a French horn as the local high school band paraded through the streets with plenty of fanfare. Shouts and hollers came from the sidelines as the townies cheered. Linc shook his head, unable to help his grin.

That could be Beck and his friends someday.

Except, he'd started looking at places in Baltimore.

The grin fell from his face.

Beck tugged at his hand. "Daddy, I'm hungry."

"We'll get you food in a minute," he said, scanning in the direction of Pell Gardens Park, right off the main street. Plenty of families gathered in the distance, kids running and playing tag and folks setting out plaid picnic blankets in the park. Linc steered them toward the brick-and-metal archway, The Pell Gardens scrawled on the top.

A familiar figure stood right beside the archway in the exact place they were supposed to meet up. Nate waited there, his thick brown hair tamed with product, those blue eyes even brighter in the morning sun, and the cleft in his chin lickable. The maroon V-neck he wore highlighted those slender muscles Linc had memorized over the past month, and his snug black jeans placed his sexy ass on display. The man looked so good he could salivate, but beyond the dose of lust, Linc didn't miss how he fucking floated at the sheer sight of him.

Nate McAllister was trouble, and here he was welcoming him in through the door.

He'd *never* invited his dates out to a festival with his son. Yet, the way Nate was with Beckett had him melting, and before he could've reined himself in, he'd blurted out the invitation. Hopefully Beck wouldn't notice his daddy's palms sweating over this massive goddamn step he didn't think he'd ever take.

Nate caught sight of them and began his approach, carrying three checkered to-go containers in his hands. He muscled past a few guys to swerve in front of them, and Beck hopped up and down at the sight of his new friend, Mr. Nate. Linc swallowed a lump in his throat, trying to tamp down the sheer joy that bubbled up inside him at seeing the way his son reacted around Nate. He tried to ride that for as long as possible, because he was still waiting for the inevitable guilt to come crashing down.

"Swung by my stand to make sure Daria didn't burn it down," Nate joked, even though Linc caught the slight strain in his voice. Guaranteed, the hellish woman was still causing problems for Nate. "Figured you guys might be hungry, so I stopped at Eliza's booth."

Beck let out a squeal as Nate lowered a container of Cozy Corner pancake bites, these ones covered in chocolate syrup and strawberries. "My favorite," he exclaimed.

Linc arched a brow as he glanced to Nate. "How'd you know?"

A sweet smile spread on Nate's face. "Nico."

Linc let out a short breath, wanting to close the distance between them and kiss the hell out of Nate.

Yet the moment he moved toward him, his limbs locked up. One step at a time.

"It's okay," Nate mouthed, offering sympathy he didn't deserve. Nate should be with someone who could proudly declare him as their partner, someone who'd shout it from the rooftops. Not the painfully slow progress Linc attempted and the pitfalls he still stepped in.

Yet, somehow, the man chose him anyway.

Linc glanced to Beck, who'd smeared chocolate all over his face. Nate let out a snort he tried to hide fast with his hand, but Linc met his eyes, letting his own amusement shine through. They'd fucked each other on a regular basis for weeks now, yet this felt far more intimate.

"Waffle and syrup for you," Nate said, passing over another container. "And pancake strips with blueberries for me."

Linc stabbed his fork into the piece of waffle, cutting off a corner. "Thanks. You didn't need to do this though. I invited you here." He chewed on the waffle, the rich burst of maple syrup coating his tongue.

Nate fumbled with one of his blueberries as it almost escaped his mouth. Linc reached out, pushing it back in with the tip of his finger. He couldn't help but linger on the man's lush lower lip. Nate's eyes flared in surprise, and Linc pulled his finger away, even though he offered a scorching look in return. Just because he wasn't up to kissing the man in front of his son yet didn't mean he couldn't engage in some PDA.

It was okay. It would be okay.

His stomach twisted a little, and he buried the feeling. "So, what did you want to check out today?"

"I was hoping you guys would have an idea," Nate said between bites. "Despite having worked here for days now, I haven't scoped out the festival at all yet. I'm… just happy to spend time with you both."

"Thanks, Mr. Nate," Beck said in the middle of chewing.

"Mouth closed while you're eating, kiddo," Linc reminded him, resting a hand on his shoulder. Beck had finished the pancake strips in record time, leaving a significant trail of chocolate all over his face. "Maybe we can swing to one of the booths for napkins first."

"Trust me, I thought of that," Nate said, crouching in front of Beck. He tugged a wad of napkins out of his back pocket and brought them up to Beck who lifted his chin in encouragement. A gentle smile slipped onto Nate's face as he wiped up the mess along Linc's son's cheeks and the tip of his nose. Linc nearly swooned at the sight. Nate wasn't just good with kids—he was good with *his* kid, and that meant far more than he realized.

Nate straightened and focused on him again. "So where are we off to?"

Linc glanced to his watch. "The boat parade should be starting any minute now. Let's go check it out." By far, the boat parade was one of the more unique things about Chesapeake City's festival, and he couldn't help but want to show Nate. Besides, Beck loved to watch it every year, enjoying the closeness to the water.

"Will you hold my hand?" Beck asked, thrusting it up to Nate.

Nate chewed on his lip and nodded, the delight apparent in his expressive eyes. Linc could barely help the way his heart soared. Fuck, he was in far too deep. He took the lead toward the edge of the river, piercing his fork into the remaining waffle bites, a perfect mix of crisp batter and sticky maple syrup. Townsfolk and out-of-towners swarmed on either side of them as he carved through, glancing back every few feet to make sure Nate and his son hadn't gotten too far behind. Every time he looked, the sight made his chest squeeze tight.

This was what most days he refused to admit he wanted. A partner to share in the ups and downs of this parenting thing. Someone to make their family complete.

However, admitting it meant letting Marissa go.

It meant new memories in this town where they'd fallen in love and promised each other a lifetime.

Linc sucked in a shaky breath as he cast another glance to Beck and Nate walking hand in hand behind him. He wanted to take the leap so badly, even though it terrified him, both what he'd be leaving behind and the sheer promise of what might come from this.

One step at a time.

He slowed so they could catch up and elbowed his way to a spot under a tall, lush oak by the water. When they passed a trash can, he turned around to snag Nate and Beck's empty containers, tossing all of them in the trash, and then he led them to the area by the water he'd scoped out. The breeze was filled with honeysuckle and the clean crispness of the water, which banished the warring scents of sizzling hot dogs and burgers as well as the sweet waft of baked goods. The sun beat down on his bare arms, full of the promise spring in Maryland brought.

"Let's watch from here." Linc plopped onto a patch of flat earth and rumpled grass right by the edge of the water.

Beck sat beside him, leaning in. Linc wrapped an

arm around his son's shoulders, drawing the kid close. As long as he had Beck, he could survive anything. Truly, no matter how challenging life with a kid was, Beck had saved him. He leaned down to kiss the top of Beck's head, all thick, black hair just like him.

Nate settled next to them, stretching his long legs out. Linc couldn't help but follow the length of him, admiring the view. The man by his side wasn't just the hottest guy he'd seen in years, but he possessed dimensions Linc wanted to spend longer and longer uncovering.

One date hadn't been enough, one month wasn't enough, and the more time they spent together, the more he couldn't imagine an end in sight. If that didn't terrify him, nothing would. Nate caught him staring and offered a flirty wink.

A loud cheer rippled across the crowd as the first of the boats in the parade drifted down the canal. The opening one was the Chesapeake City float, filled with a beautiful display of flowers. The rippling flags behind it had Chesapeake City's name imprinted in white against blue. The water churned as the deck boat sailed on by, leading the way. Behind it, three sailboats in a row followed, the decorated sails rippling in the wind. These sails had been designed by artists to look like stained glass, the sunlight glittering through some of the translucent sections to cast colored panes onto the surrounding water.

"That's gorgeous," Nate murmured.

"I wanna draw those," Beck announced. He looked at him. "Daddy, can I paint that?"

Linc wrestled with his grin. "That depends, kiddo. Are you asking if you can draw boats on a piece of paper, or are you asking if you can paint on sails like they did?"

"The sails," Beck said, determination in his gaze. Of course.

"Why don't we practice on paper first," Linc responded.

Beck leaned forward, staring hard at the sight ahead of them, his palms pressed into the dirt. Linc took the opposite approach and sank back onto his elbows, angling a bit closer to Nate. A big barge headed through, this one featuring all sorts of metal contraptions on board, part of the Iron Workers' Union. The one following that had a bright rainbow flag waving back and forth, sponsored by the LGBTQIA Alliance at the local art college. He glanced over to Nate, whose grin widened at the sight.

The man leaned back, inches away from him, and in a burst of spontaneity, Linc reached out and closed the distance. He rested his fingertips over Nate's, Beck still hunched forward between them. His heart lurched. He hadn't held hands with anyone around his son, ever. Before his fears could cannonball out of control, he settled his gaze on Nate. Those bright blue eyes were radiant with a hope that made Linc choke up, and Nate beamed.

Fuck, he was gorgeous.

And fuck, he'd fallen hard.

The realization struck him right in the solar plexus.

Linc tilted his head back, closing his eyes for a moment. The sun warmed his face, soaking in past the skin for once. With Beck at his side and his fingers entwined with Nate's, he felt more complete than he had in years.

A LIGHT SNORE SOUNDED IN LINC'S EAR. HE HIKED Beck a little higher up his back as the kiddo began to slump to the side.

"Wow, he is *out*," Nate said, slipping his hands into his pockets as they walked down the main street. The sun was beginning to set, which meant Nate needed to get to his shift at the stand. Linc was determined to walk him back.

Today had been perfect in every way, more than he ever could've hoped for.

"Between the amount of sugar the kid downed and how much time he spent running back and forth trying to 'catch the boats,' there was no way he'd be lasting any longer," Linc said, offering a grin. "He's going to sleep like a rock tonight."

"After attempting to keep up with him on the first few runs, I'm going to need an exceedingly large cup of coffee to survive the night shift at the booth," Nate said. He nudged his hip against Linc's. "I've got no idea how you keep up with that energy every day."

Linc smirked. "Stamina."

The way Nate bit his lower lip sent a dose of lust rolling through him. What would it be like if this could be his life? If instead of Nate heading home to his place at the end of the night, he'd be sliding into bed with Linc?

Linc almost stopped midstride. Well, that was an escalation. He'd gone from barely daring to imagine anything beyond another day to thoughts of the future sneaking in. He waited for the thump of guilt to settle in, for the telltale grief to smack him in the face. When he looked at Nate though, all he felt was warmth and hope and light.

They stopped in front of Chesapeake Brew's booth.

"Well, this is my stop," Nate said, the air between them growing awkward. He didn't miss how Nate's eyes lingered on his lips. "Thanks for the wonderful day."

Linc leaned in, even with his arms full due to his sleeping son on his back, and he brushed his lips against Nate's. He drank in the sweetness of Nate's lips, all lemon iced tea, and the warmth of that mouth as the kiss deepened for the briefest second. When they pulled apart, Nate looked at him with a tenderness he felt deep in his chest.

"Thank you," Linc murmured, hiking Beck up again as he turned to head in the direction of the house. He was so busy watching Nate step into the booth and join Nico's bartender Mara that he almost ran smack into the couple ahead of him.

"Linc?" an all-too-familiar voice sounded.

He froze.

Marissa's parents stood in front of him. They still lived in town and took Beck once a month, unless they were down in their vacation house in South Carolina for the summer. Still, that was the amount of contact they kept in—no ill will, just too much shared grief. Natalie, Marissa's mom, glanced in the direction of the booth Nate had slipped behind. Ice slithered down his spine.

"How are you?" Linc asked on reflex, as if he could deflect any accusations, disappointment, or however the hell they might react to their former son-in-law with his new boyfriend. "Beck's passed out, or I'd offer to spend some time with you. As it is, I've got to get him home and tucked in."

"Don't disturb him for our sake," Marissa's dad, Frank, said. "We'll be taking him off your hands next Saturday anyway."

"He always loves to see his grandparents," Linc forced out, even though his insides were screaming. *Run. Run. Run.* A few drops of sweat prickled on his brow, and the rest of the chatter from the crowds ebbing and flowing around him turned to a muted buzz.

"Was that a new boyfriend?" Natalie asked, her expression unreadable.

"I…," Linc started, unable to finish the statement. "I'm seeing him, yeah." Not the proud declaration he'd hoped for, but he could barely scrape two words together right now. He braced himself for the smack of their judgement, their disappointment, their grief.

"That's good, Lincoln," Natalie murmured, her voice gentle. Even still, he didn't miss the shadowed sadness lingering in her eyes. His breaths started coming in thicker, and his surroundings fuzzed a little around the edges.

Fuck, he needed to get out of here.

"Great running into you both," Linc offered as he began to take long, loping strides down the street.

Yes, he all but ran from them. However, with the way his head buzzed and the panic surged, how his breaths seized, he needed to get Beck tucked in and safe in his bed. He needed to get home.

The walk home passed in a blur of harried breaths, the *thump, thump, thump* of footsteps or his heart, he wasn't sure which, and the cracks in the sidewalk, which seemed extra sharp and clear tonight. The racing in his chest hadn't subsided, like he'd come inches away from a car crash. He swept inside his house, and Beck blinked sleepily long enough to brush his teeth, change into his pajamas, and climb into bed. Once Beck hit the sheets, he was out.

Linc slid out of Beck's room and made it over to a chair in the dining room before his legs gave way. In the quiet of the house, his breaths sliced through the air, and when he rested his arms on the table, they trembled.

He'd thought—hoped—he was moving forward.

Yet, as he slumped forward in the firm wooden seat, chasing after his breath, the wave began to rise. The tingling buzz threatened to overwhelm him, causing his eyes to heat. Those phantom tears had been shed a long time before—now, only the memory remained.

Now, only *her* memory remained.

The gentleness in Natalie's tone, the *understanding* there—that destroyed him.

They should be furious. They should hate him. They should be so damn disappointed, because their traitorous son-in-law had buckled at last. He was moving forward, leaving their daughter behind.

Yet he should've been the one who died.

The realization didn't creep in gently. No, it plunged through him like a lath nail through the shoe. Linc hunched there in the chair, fingers clawed into his knees, everything just shaking, shaking, shaking. For the first time in years, the familiar heat behind his eyes turned wet. One tear slipped down his cheek, and then another, until they were streaming.

The sobs began next. He shoved his fist in his mouth to keep them muffled, because he wouldn't be able to live with himself if Beck came wandering out and saw him like this. Linc sat there in the dark of this lonely house, the gloom that crept here all these years coming into startling clarity.

So, so many times he'd said to himself—*Marissa could've done this better. Marissa was meant for this. Marissa would've known what to do*. Because the painful truth beat there beneath his chest all this time.

How was he supposed to exist when he'd become a ghost himself?

Linc's sobs continued, minutes, hours, he didn't know, until his chest burned from the scoured pain, until his mind was bleached clean from every thought and memory, until only the resonant echo remained.

CHAPTER 23

TAKEOUT AND A MOVIE HAD NEVER EXCITED NATE THIS much.

Not only because he was spending the time with Linc, but because after over a month of seeing each other, Linc had finally invited him over.

Nate clutched the plastic bag in hand, the aromas of sweet-and-sour chicken wafting his way as he strode up the sidewalk in the direction of Linc's place. His heart pounded harder than ever, his hopes near bursting at the seams. He hadn't missed the steps Linc was taking—from the three of them spending time together to their date in public at Chesapeake Festival yesterday. The event itself had been a total success, which had bolstered his confidence in both the store and the new roast. He should've been exhausted from the final long day of vending, but instead, his heart careened like an out-of-control car.

Maybe tonight would be the night when he could let those three little words slip free. Maybe tonight Linc would declare them official, that this wasn't just dating—they were boyfriends. Maybe tonight they'd take those concrete steps toward a future.

Nate's feet took him to Linc's home automatically, like he hadn't memorized this walk ever since he moved into town. He bit his lip, unable to stave away the daydreams of this being his walk home, of coming into a warm house filled with Linc's steadiness and Beckett's constant babbling and bright energy. When he'd first driven into Chesapeake City, he'd been searching, fumbling for something to call his own after Sam had left him.

He thought he'd been looking for a career or success, but the moment he met Linc, once he began to spend time with him and his son, the truth settled in—he'd been searching for a family of his own. A future.

Nighttime breezes swirled around him with a subtle chill, but these goose bumps had everything to do with striding up the walkway to Linc's house. He'd never felt so sure of anything in his life.

He lifted his knuckles to knock on the door.

They'd barely brushed the surface when it swung open, Linc filling the frame.

The man was the same tall, dark, and delicious as usual, but something softer lay in his eyes, a little more raw tonight. Nate's heart skipped a beat.

"Hey," he murmured, his mouth dry. He lifted the bag. "I brought the takeout."

"I've got the movie ready to roll," Linc said, the low rumble making Nate shiver every time. "Come on in." He reached out to take Nate's free hand, but when they crossed over the threshold, Nate didn't miss the way Linc's hand tightened. He didn't wonder why Linc kept people away from his place—the man guarded his past with Marissa more fiercely than a cat with prey. Based on how long Linc said he lived in this house, he must've picked it with his dead wife.

Nate wanted to know more—not about the painful stuff, but just… everything. He wanted to know about the unforgettable woman who'd captured this man's heart so hard it had shattered when she passed away. That was one subject he knew he couldn't push though.

The layout of Linc's place didn't look too different from his own, in the old two-story sense, though the interior had far more care and detail put into it. The walls had a fresh coat of cream paint, the brass fixtures were all updated and matching, and the pale hardwood floors shone. Linc clearly kept up with the place, putting his trade skills to use on his own house. Fletcher's was in disrepair, and it didn't look like the man planned on fixing it up before the sale either.

Linc guided him toward the living room, bypassing the kitchen. A flat-screen TV sat on the far end of the room with a couple of cozy brown couches set in front of it. When Nate caught the movie title on the screen, he couldn't help his grin.

"Should I be surprised you want to watch *The Dark Knight*?" Nate teased.

"I would've put on a Booster Gold movie, but he doesn't have any," Linc shot back, his brow arching in amusement. They headed over toward the couches, and Nate wove around a pile of papers— new drawings—and some plastic food and spatulas that lay scattered across the carpet. His heart warmed at the sight of this lived-in place, so different from his sterile house.

Linc glanced to the ceiling. "Beck's passed out upstairs, but the kiddo sleeps through fireworks, so you don't have to speak low."

"I believe it," Nate said, placing the bag next to the couch. "If the kid can pass out in the middle of a festival, he's got some powerful sleeping skills. Color me jealous."

Linc slid onto the couch, and Nate joined him, close enough that their legs touched. When Linc stretched out and looped an arm around his shoulders, his heart thumped wildly in his chest. While he'd lived with Sam and done the domestic thing for a while, he'd never felt this secure. There had been nights of curling up with Netflix, cuddling in bed, sure, but those had gotten fewer and fewer the longer they'd been together and the more consumed Sam got in his work.

Linc didn't seem to be like that. Not only was he a respected and well-known member of this town, but he'd made it clear from the beginning how important his son was. How important family was. Nate snuggled in against Linc's chest, the steady *thump, thump, thump* distracting. Linc's cat slunk out and settled near their feet, tail flicking a few times before he sank into deep slumber.

The movie began to play, and the time zoomed by, cocooned in Linc's heat, that inexorable earthy scent of him. They eventually tugged out the takeout and picked at the fried rice, sweet-and-sour chicken, and veggie lo mein, but everything was punctuated by the warmth that consumed him whenever they spent time together.

The big scenes exploded on the screen, but Nate barely paid attention—to be fair, he'd seen this movie a hundred times. Instead, he couldn't help but study the firm lines of Linc's face, the strong nose, those callused hands, the olive skin that deepened in the sloping shadows of his cozy living room. Their gazes kept playing tag, affection increasing in every glance. Jesus, Mary, and Joseph, he didn't know if he'd rather get his brains fucked out or keep snuggling with the man, which was a testament to how addictive Linc's presence had become.

Once the movie ended, Nate let out a yawn. Linc had offered takeout and a movie, not more than that, though Nate was dying to stay here. The idea of stretching out on the man's bed and riding to ecstasy with him, then crashing out wrapped up in each other's arms? Goddamn, it was everything he could hope for.

He cast a curious look over to Linc, not wanting to push. Even though the doubts swelled in moments like these—what if Linc was never ready—he couldn't help but hope. He was built for dreaming.

"So, is this your favorite movie?" he asked. They hadn't spoken much throughout, which came as a relief on its own. Nate had always been a nervous talker, but Linc seemed comfortable in the quiet, and the grounding presence soothed him into relaxing.

Linc's lips quirked. "*Princess Bride* is."

Nate's brows rose. "A closet romantic?"

"It was our favorite," he murmured, his voice growing a little hushed. Nate chewed on his lip, unsure if he should be pulling away to give him space or nuzzling in closer to comfort the man. He decided on the latter, glancing to Linc.

A question snagged in his throat, one he'd been longing to ask awhile now. If Linc could be brave, then he could too. Nate swallowed his nerves. "What was Marissa like?"

Linc stiffened for a moment, and Nate's insides took a nosedive. Of course, he'd pushed too fast, and now he'd fucked things up.

"You don't have to talk about it if you don't want to," Nate rushed out, trying to mitigate the damage his big mouth caused.

Linc shook his head, reaching over and settling a damp palm on Nate's thigh. With the contact on him, he didn't dare budge. Linc stared at the blank screen of the TV as if it might hold answers, but he wasn't bolting or ordering Nate out.

"I'm not used to people asking about her," he murmured. "Usually everyone either avoids all mention of her or walks on glass when they bring up past memories that involved the both of us."

Nate shrugged. "She was a part of your life. I

might not have experienced loss like that, but when I croak, I hope the people I loved still talk about me. I hope they share stories and laughs—that I bring a smile to their face, not just tragedy." He winced in the wake of those words. Of course, he sounded like a presumptuous ass.

Linc sucked in a sharp breath. When Nate dared to glance his way, those eyes were glossed over. Nate swallowed hard. If he hadn't fallen for Linc before, he'd have careened now. The sheer amount of emotion in those tender eyes struck him square in the chest. This man had stood sentinel for his deceased wife all these years. Nate couldn't imagine how much he'd suffered.

Nate placed a hand over the one Linc rested on his thigh. He didn't utter a word this time, simply waited. The man's silence was loaded, as if he summoned the nerve to speak, and Nate didn't dare disrupt that.

"We'd gone to elementary school together, though we didn't become friends until middle school. She had her circle, and I had mine. By high school, I got my first boyfriend, and so did she. I'd realized from an early age I was bi. However, we happened to go through breakups around the same time and spent a summer falling in love."

"So, she was the high school sweetheart," Nate murmured.

"Small town cliché, right?" he responded with a half smile. "We did all the normal young couple bullshit, and then I went to a local trade school while she went to the local art college."

"That must be where Beckett gets it from." Nate squeezed Linc's hand, so damn grateful for every word that poured from the man's lips.

"You asked what Marissa was like though," Linc murmured. A sharp exhale passed his lips before he continued. "She was so damn strong. In touch with her emotions in a way I'll never be, with an artistic whimsy that, yeah, Beck seems to have inherited. Like she's still guiding him. We would fight like hell too, because I've never met a woman who's more stubborn."

Linc glanced to him. "I'll admit, you and Marissa have some similarities; that drew me to you from the start. You've got the hope I never was able to tap into, and the pulse you seem to have on the people around you—that's a goddamn treasure. But you're also incredibly different. Where she'd dig her heels in, you seem to flow."

Nate's heart leapt into his throat. These from Linc, they were a gift. His eyes stung, and his chest felt full—too full—at the trust Linc bestowed on him, at the sheer pain radiating off this man, and the way he still tried, despite all his hurt.

"I might be conflict avoidant, but trust me, I've had my fair share of fights too," Nate responded, squeezing his hand again. He leaned in a little closer, his heart pounding in his ears with these feelings that rolled over him like flurries transitioning to a blizzard.

"Right," Linc shot back with a soft grin. "Like you have with Daria?"

Nate flicked him in the shoulder. "Excuse me, we're talking about your man pain here, not mine."

The tension lightened at once, and Linc let out a bark of a laugh that seemed to surprise them both.

"Fair's fair," he said, lifting his hand and turning to face Nate. "What about you and Sam? What happened there?"

"Apparently, I'm not 'long-term' material," Nate muttered, unable to hide the bitterness in his tone. Those words from their final conversation had imprinted on his mind the morning he'd discovered Sam already planned on moving out before they'd even broken up. No matter how hard he tried to talk around them, they crept in the moment he let his guard down.

Linc snorted, causing Nate's head to snap up.

"Sorry," Linc said. "The idea that you aren't long-term is laughable. You seem programmed for committed relationships."

Nate offered a half smile. "The tough part is finding someone who wants to commit to me."

Ever since he first entered the dating pool, he'd found guy after guy who pretended they wanted something real on the pretense of hooking up, or ones who tired of his awkward ramblings, his big, bleeding heart, and his neediness. "When I started dating Sam, I thought I'd broken my curse. That maybe someone would want to stick around. Yet, when he finished his law degree and started hanging out in more refined circles, what I had to offer wasn't good enough."

Truth be told, he'd been feeling for a long, long while that he'd never be good enough. To get the solid job, to keep friendships, to get the guy. Everything had been a struggle from the moment he came out this weird, awkward gay kid, and it only grew harder as he got older.

Nate stared at the floor in front of him, rubbing the same spot on the corduroy couch over and over again.

Linc's fingers slid under his chin and tilted it up until their eyes locked.

"You are more than enough," Linc whispered, his hot breath a puff against his lips. "Your ex was an idiot, because you're more than I could've ever hoped for."

Oh.

Nate's eyes burned, and a stray tear slipped down his cheek. Those words reached right in and caressed the ache in his heart that had been hurting for longer than he could remember. Linc leaned in and pressed his lips to Nate's, the kiss filled with so much tenderness he melted from the inside out. Shivers coursed through his body, something clicking into place inside him. Lincoln Lane had ruined him for any other man. He hadn't been aware, but at some point he'd handed his heart over, and he didn't want it back.

Nate gripped Linc's shirt in his fist, drinking him in deeper. He drowned in this kiss, letting it overwhelm his senses. The man's earthy scent wrapped around him like a warm blanket, and as he climbed over Linc's lap to straddle him, those hard muscles stoked his fires. The depths they'd cracked into tonight had hollowed him out, and he needed, so very badly, for Linc to fill him up again, to feel the connection of their bodies, the way they became one.

His cock grew hard, and with the way he sat on Linc's lap, he could feel the man's length stiffen beneath him, making him salivate. His emotions had run all over the place tonight, but one began to overtake the others—mind-searing desire. He wanted to be with Linc like never before.

Linc broke away for a breath, a tender glaze in his eyes that sent Nate reeling.

Love you. Love you. Love you.

Linc slid a hand to Nate's hips and squeezed. "Let's take this to the bedroom."

Nate's grin widened. "I thought you'd never ask."

CHAPTER 24

LINC'S HEART WAS HYDROPLANING ALL OVER THE PLACE as he led Nate toward his bedroom.

Any moment now, he might careen off the road and just… plummet.

When Nate first stepped inside the house, Linc braced himself for the punch to the gut he'd expected. Yet, apart from his initial discomfort, once they'd settled onto the couch and the movie began to play, Nate's hearth fire presence dominated everything. The way the man leaned into him, the warmth of his body, the bright hopefulness in his gaze—all of it soothed Linc like nothing else.

The conversation had been unexpected, and at first, panic roared so high he thought he might black out.

But then... talking about Marissa under Nate's encouraging gaze, well, that hadn't been the lash of pain he'd expected. If anything, unearthing those memories felt a whole lot like relief.

I hope they share stories and laughs—that I bring a smile to their face, not just tragedy.

Nate's words had flipped a switch inside him. He'd been dwelling in the tragedy for so damn long that he'd forgotten how to feel happy about the memories he'd shared with her. Somewhere between the moment he met Nate and now, the man had begun to help him heal, in a way he'd never expected —could've never imagined.

And tonight, he wanted to show Nate just how much he meant to him. Linc pushed open the door, the moonlight from the open window coating his bed in a soft, silvery light. The crispness from the soft breezes spread throughout the room, sending a delicious shiver down his spine. Linc closed the door behind them with a click. He swallowed the jitters traveling from his fingers down to his toes and maintained a steady pace toward the bed.

Once his knees bumped against the edge of the bed, he spun Nate around, giving him a light push. Nate thumped onto the mattress, staring at him with a hunger in his gorgeous eyes that demanded action.

The shadows accented his cleft chin, those dark lashes, and his defined, fuckable lips. The man sat on the mattress before him looking like a goddamn dream—his pale shirt highlighting his lithe figure, and those jeans doing downright nothing to hide his significant erection.

Linc hooked a finger on the hem of Nate's shirt and helped him tug it up and over to reveal more smooth skin, defined muscles, and the few dark moles along his chest that Linc wanted to trace with his tongue. He snapped open the button to Nate's jeans next, and Nate shunted those to the floor as well. Frenzy gripped him in one fierce sweep, and he tossed his tank top off, which pooled on the floor with the rest of their clothes, and he went for his belt buckle next. Within seconds, the both of them were completely bare, bathed only in the pale moonlight pouring in through his windows.

Linc licked his lips as he climbed onto the bed. He wrapped a hand around Nate's hip, tugging him down with him. His heart thundered in his ears. He'd been alone in this bed since Marissa, and the line he crossed tonight? Well, there was no going back.

Linc was moving forward.

Nate's skin felt hot underneath his palm, and Linc

soaked in his silhouette, all hard lines except for that gorgeous ass. Nate's cock hung heavy between his legs, and Linc's mouth watered. As much as he wanted to wrap his mouth around it and take a taste, he knew what they needed tonight. The conversation left them both bleeding, too raw, too vulnerable.

Nate lay back on the mattress, and Linc climbed over him. His thighs trapped Nate's on either side, and their cocks brushed together, sending a sinful thrill up his spine. Nate stared at him, those blue eyes more intense than ever, soaking in his every movement. Linc sucked in a deep inhale of the man's scent, like a fresh, running river, one that made his heart respond every time. He grabbed Nate's wrist and brought it up overhead as he began to lick and suck at his neck. He caged Nate with his body, the heat between them an inferno, their breaths coming out harsher.

Those moans ignited him as Linc continued to run his tongue along the column of Nate's neck to the spot under his ear. Nate bucked beneath him, their cocks rubbing together, all velvet-wrapped steel. Each brush sent sparks running up through him, increasing the need to bury himself inside the man. To pound his way home, to join their bodies until the connection was unbreakable.

Linc nipped at Nate's chin as he ground his cock

against Nate's just to hear the heady moan exploding from his lips. Everything about him was mesmerizing, from the way he tilted his head, neck bared in surrender, to the muscles that flexed beneath him. Linc had been stuck for far too long, unable to move, and Nate had arrived into his life, slowly, gently prying him free. Linc's lips brushed over Nate's until he slipped his tongue in, deepening the kiss. They both shifted their hips, cocks rubbing against each other as Linc devoured Nate's mouth.

"Please," Nate murmured, his voice breathy.

"What do you need, sweetheart?" Linc responded, placing a nip on his earlobe as the man continued to writhe beneath him.

Nate's gaze locked with his. "Fuck me."

Linc's mouth curled with his grin. He leaned down again and brushed his lips along Nate's neck, enjoying the shivers that exploded from him.

Nate wrapped his free hand around Linc's nape. "I need you inside me, now."

Linc brought his palm down, gliding it across Nate's waist, the firm jut of his hip, until he circled it around to squeeze that gorgeous ass. He leaned in and claimed another kiss as he glided his finger down the crack, along Nate's tight ring of muscles. The man thrust into him, another moan exploding from him, vibrating against Linc's mouth. Linc drew circles with his fingers, the desire mounting to thrust inside his tight fucking hole. His cock couldn't get stiffer, and with the way Nate's kept brushing against his, he was liable to blow just from rutting against him.

"*Please*," Nate moaned, the urgency in his voice ratcheting Linc's need.

Linc pushed up to snag lube and a condom from his bedside stand. He rolled the condom on, aware of the heat from Nate's stare, and applied a liberal amount of lube.

"Forget prepping," Nate murmured. "Just fuck me."

Linc's knees pressed into the mattress as he situated himself between Nate's thighs. He guided his legs up with a steady hand and nudged the tip of his cock against his pucker. The brief brush of contact made him gasp for breath, the pounding urge to thrust hard inside him growing with every second. With his grip tight around Nate's thigh, he eased himself inside.

The glide felt perfect, and Nate fit around him like a glove, every inch deeper increasing the intensity. When he finally slid all the way in, a groan slipped from his lips as tremors raced through him. Linc brought Nate's arms overhead, gripping them tight with his wrist to pin him to the bed. He leaned in to consume Nate's mouth in a deep, punishing kiss. From the feel of their hands pressed together, their tongues entwined, his cock buried deep inside him—every point of contact intoxicated him. He needed this. They needed this.

Linc began to move inside Nate, unable to help the escaping grunt of pleasure at how damn amazing that felt. As he drove all the way inside, Nate's eyes rolled back, his mouth open and panting. He thrust deep into him, again and again and again as he built up a rhythm. Sweat beaded on his brow, tickling as it pricked against his skin, and the inferno between them threatened to combust.

Nate looked up at him, and when their gazes met, Linc couldn't avoid the flush of affection. This was more than he'd felt in *years*. His grip around Nate's wrist tightened, as if he needed the reassurance he was still here, that he wouldn't just slip away. Linc slammed into him harder, beyond chasing after the thrill of release.

He wanted Nate to feel how deep this connection went. To feel the permanent imprint he'd left on Linc's heart. In such a short amount of time, Nate challenged all of Linc's hard and fast rules without ever even trying.

All he'd done was give him patience and understanding.

All he'd done was offer his whole heart.

Linc swallowed hard, losing himself in the pulse of sensation as he rammed into Nate again and again, the slap of their skin echoing through the room. He didn't hold back to go gentle, not with the fury of the feelings that rushed through him right now.

"Fuck, fuck, fuck," Nate moaned as Linc slammed home over and over. Nate's thighs trembled, and his thick erection was stiffer than ever, precum leaking at the tip.

"Please, touch me," Nate begged.

"We come together, sweetheart," Linc murmured, his words husky. Nate bit his lip and nodded, his Adam's apple bobbing as he swallowed down the emotion his eyes could never hide. Several of Linc's curls matted to the sweat on his brow, tickling there, but he didn't dare stop to brush them away. Instead, he leaned down to capture Nate's mouth again, tasting of coffee and sweetness. He guided his hips up a little further and drove in again, a guttural moan exploding from Nate.

Linc could feel his own release urging him forward, and he chased the coiling intensity. Each stroke inside Nate brought him closer, and he let go of his remaining tethers of restraint. He pressed Nate's wrist even harder into the mattress as he rammed home with an increasingly fast pace. His pulse thundered in his ears, and their sharp breaths created a staccato melody. Moonlight glided over every curve and angle of their bodies, mesmerizing in his darkened room.

Linc couldn't look away from Nate the entire time, the tender gaze stripping him bare. He'd been a fool to think there was ever anything casual about this. Need wrenched hard, and he reached for Nate's cock even as he continued the unrelenting pace. He slid his hand up and down the silken length, pushing him over the edge.

Linc's cock began to pulse, and Nate joined him seconds later, his hot cum splattering between their chests.

His breath hitched in his throat as he rode the waves of the orgasm, searing his mind of everything. All that remained was sheer bliss, every nerve in his body igniting at this explosion. Linc surrendered to it, keeping his grasp on Nate's wrists the entire time.

He crushed on top of him, the sticky cum pressed between their chests as he captured Nate's mouth in a softer kiss this time. The sensitized brush of their lips sent a shudder of relief through him, the sort of softness he hadn't found since… her. His heart felt lighter than it had in years, and for a little bit, he and Nate just slumped together, unmoving. His shoulders quaked, and Nate's thighs trembled.

Linc eventually pulled out, tied off the condom, and tossed it. He strode out of the room to wet a washcloth in the adjacent bathroom, and returned to clean them both off. Nate watched him, oddly quiet, a reverent wonder in his eyes.

"With how much my legs are shaking from that, I'm in for an interesting walk home," Nate murmured, a half smile at a joke he clearly didn't feel.

Linc's chest squeezed tight. He shook his head, sliding under the blanket and then tugging it over Nate as well. Nate looked over in surprise, his brows lifting.

"Who said you're going anywhere?" Linc responded.

"I… didn't want to…"

"I know," Linc said, leaning to his side. Nate settled in next to him, backing up until Linc's chest bumped against his back. Linc slung an arm around Nate's waist and pulled him close. He didn't miss the satisfied sigh that escaped Nate, one that plucked at his heart. Heaviness coated Linc's limbs as he soaked in the other man's warmth. Comfort he hadn't felt in years lulled him closer to rest, his breaths evening. Within minutes, Nate's light snore pierced the air, and Linc couldn't help his grin.

It had taken him far too long to realize it, but he'd truly fallen for Nate McAllister.

Linc's gaze traveled the length of his bedroom, the way he'd done for years. However, for the first time in a long while, the shadows didn't threaten to devour him, and the moonlight cascading through the windows didn't feel quite so lonely.

CHAPTER 25

NATE BLINKED AS BRIGHT MORNING LIGHT ATTACKED HIS senses. He stretched his arms out, and as he sat up in bed, a frown creasing his brow.

Oh. He'd stayed over at Linc's place last night.

Voices sounded from downstairs, Beckett's light, cheerful one and Linc's low gruffness. Nate's heart pounded harder than ever. Not only had he slept over at Linc's, but while his son was home.

The pure, sunlit joy that rushed through his veins woke him up better than coffee. The hope lunged forward so hard it hurt, and some small part of him desperately tried to rein it in. Linc might've never made any promises and still hadn't even placed a label on them, but this had to mean *something*. The small dissenter in the back of his mind warned this level of attachment was dangerous, that this didn't mean anything permanent, but Nate shoved it to the side, because goddamn, he wanted to bask in this progress today.

Nate hopped out of bed, tugging on his wayward clothes strewn all across the floor. Even the sex had been different—deeper—like they'd shattered whatever remaining barriers separated them.

All too easily, he could imagine waking up to this every day. Sleeping curled up in Linc's arms before walking down the road to open Chesapeake Brew. Getting to make pancakes with Linc and Nate on a weekend morning, or enjoying the chaos of everyone heading their separate ways on a workday. His heart hurt for wanting those beautiful, beautiful dreams that had always been out of reach for him.

Nate slipped out of the bedroom and took careful steps as he descended the stairs. He wove around the banister and headed in the direction of the kitchen where the voices still echoed through the room. His heart thudded in anticipation, not knowing what to expect. Would Linc pretend he'd just snuck over? Would he introduce Nate as his boyfriend? Fuck, it was probably too soon for that.

Nate flexed his fingers over and over again as he stepped into view of the kitchen. His anxiety revved on full throttle now, and the temptation to run out the door and head on home rose in a fierce way.

Beckett spotted him first. "Mr. Nate," he squealed, hopping up from his seat. "Daddy told me you'd eat breffist with us."

"Breakfast," Linc corrected automatically, though his affectionate smile made his eyes gleam.

"I'd love to have breakfast with you guys," Nate responded. "Do you guys have places to be soon?"

Beckett nodded from his seat at the circular kitchen table. "I hafta go to school."

"We've got to hustle out of here in a half hour," Linc said with an apologetic lift of his smile. "But I was hoping you'd want a few pancakes first, since I made way too many. Maybe you can eat Beck's." He cast a sidelong glance to his son, who sat with an untouched stack.

"No!" Beckett gasped, wrapping his arms around the plate.

"Don't worry," Nate said, crouching in front of Beckett. "I won't steal yours."

The kid eyed him suspiciously, which was more adorable than Nate could express.

Linc let out a laugh and gestured him over. "Grab a plate from the cabinet and help yourself."

Nate's heart thumped hard at how comfortable this felt. He could get used to this all too quickly. He couldn't resist the smile that spread across his face, one that strained his cheeks. Linc's gaze swept over him as he passed by, and the tender smirk aimed his way had him falling even harder.

Linc carried his plate of pancakes over to the kitchen table and went back to urging Beckett to eat. Nate shook his head in amusement listening to the two. He strode over to the cabinets right by a beautiful stainless steel backsplash and polished granite countertops. As he popped open the cabinets and snagged a plate, he caught sight of papers strewn over the countertop.

One looked like a job contract. Nate's focus zeroed in on the dates—next month over the course of a year… in Baltimore.

Signed and completed.

His heart beat louder, louder, louder, the sound growing deafening as his mind refused to process.

The other papers snagged his attention.

Apartment and house listings.

All Baltimore addresses.

All of the hesitant, blooming hope in his chest withered and died like flowers in the first frost.

Linc was planning on moving. To Baltimore.

He'd never said a word.

Queasiness surged in Nate's stomach, and he traced the words on the papers beneath him with numb fingertips, plate forgotten. Oh, fuck. Fuck, fuck, fuck. This was Sam all over again. Finding those listings on Sam's computer. Watching two years of effort just drain away, because his boyfriend had already signed the lease on a new apartment before breaking up with him. Before even telling him that anything was wrong between them. The bitter taste of the Earl Grey lingering in his mouth—he hadn't touched the stuff since.

And now… all of those stupid, *stupid* hopes were being dashed again.

Linc didn't plan on declaring them boyfriends, on beginning to build a future together.

No, he was leaving.

"Find the plates okay?" Linc's voice sounded. The chair screeched as he heard Linc get up, but Nate couldn't move. His throat seized as he stared in horror at the papers on the counter before him, unable to reconcile the man who hid this with the one who'd opened up to him last night, who acted like they were building a future together.

His eyes stung, and his hands began to tremble. He needed to get out, now. Before he had a breakdown in front of Beckett. Before Linc saw just how badly he'd broken him.

Stupid, stupid, stupid, he'd been so stupid. He took one step away, then another, before he bumped into something solid. He looked up and realized Linc stood right in front of him. Linc's brows furrowed, and he brought his hands to Nate's shoulders at once. The motion might've once stabilized him, but right now he wanted to vomit.

"What's wrong?" Linc asked. Nate tried to open his mouth, but no words would come. He couldn't stop shaking, like he'd stepped out in the middle of a blizzard. Linc's gaze traveled over to the counter, hardening when he landed on the papers splayed onto the counter.

"Fuck," Linc murmured low. "Look, Nate, I can explain."

Linc's face twisted in genuine concern, but goddamn, it felt like Nate stared at a stranger. How was he supposed to—no, he couldn't handle this right now. Shame fisted his throat. All those beautiful hopes and daydreams were butterflies with wet wings, unable to get off the ground.

He needed to leave.

Nate managed to thrust a hand between them. "No worries. It was nice while it lasted," he forced out. "Hope you find what you're looking for in Baltimore."

He dodged past Linc and headed for the door. Beckett's voice sounded from the kitchen, high and concerned, but Nate couldn't turn back. Not while his vision glossed over. He could barely see enough to grab the knob and twist. He stepped into the bracing air, the sunlight mocking him as he stumbled down Linc's front porch and headed to the sidewalk. His heart pounded so loud in his ears, he couldn't even hear the idle flow of the cars passing by.

He scrubbed his eyes with his palms, trying to stave off the tears. He just needed to make it home. Fuck, did he even have his keys? Nate clapped a hand to his pocket, feeling the familiar weight there. Thank god. He might've had the strength to leave, but he couldn't summon the will to return. The ground felt shaky beneath him, like a pit had opened up and he was just falling, falling, falling.

Mere moments before, he'd experienced the exact opposite.

Moving to Baltimore.

Every tender smile from Linc, every time the man opened up a little more, and last night when he'd finally told him about Marissa—Nate had been *so sure* this meant they were heading in the same direction. Had all those moments been lies?

His vision blurred again, but he turned up the walkway to his house, fumbling for the keys. After a few shaky tries, he managed to get inside, swinging the door shut behind him. The moment the door closed, he cracked.

Nate sank to his knees, his shoulders shaking, hell, his whole body trembling in the wake of this loss. He'd believed Linc knew him, that he'd seen him and accepted every part of him. The connection between them—damn, he'd never experienced something like that in his life. His fingers curled into the carpet, nails biting in deep. Had Linc never felt the same? The tears began to flow, coursing down his cheeks. Had he done something? Tried to move too fast?

Or was this just the inevitable?

Sam's words echoed over and over again, like he rocketed back to that breakup, the tang of bergamot still on his lips. For a brief glimpse, he'd thought he found what he'd been searching for. But apparently Linc didn't believe he was long-term material either. His fingernails dug into the carpet beneath him as the sobs wracked through his body, his arms and shoulders shaking.

Fucking stupid. He was always so damn stupid to keep thinking someone would want a future with him.

His throat seized as the months, the miles melted away, and he vaulted back and forth between Boston and here. Yet the way people rejected him hadn't started here—since he was a kid, he'd been too hopeful, too trusting, too damn naïve.

He ended up breaking his heart every time.

Nate's eyes burned as he tried to force down breaths, as if he stood a chance of weathering this deluge. His chest spasmed, but even as he brought up a hand to clutch it, nothing soothed that deep ache.

Why was he never enough? He grasped for answers, but none emerged in his palms.

All the pain he believed he'd left behind in Boston crashed over him again. If he were being honest though, this was worse. He'd given Sam his heart, but they'd had a chance to grow apart. This—he couldn't fathom this.

Not walking by Linc's house and peeking around to see if the man was home or seeing Beckett in the front yard. Not seeing the tender look in Linc's eyes when he watched him, as if he memorized every moment. Not feeling the man's weight crushing against him, grounding him, helping him find his footing.

From the moment he'd stepped into Chesapeake City, Linc had been attached to all his memories revolving around this place. He'd helped him find friends here. He'd helped him feel safe enough to be himself, and he'd helped him become strong enough to grow in this town. Was it even worth staying now?

He'd have to face the fresh pain every time he stepped into Cozy Corner or the Book Attic.

He'd been so damn sure. How could he trust himself now?

His phone buzzed in his pocket. Nate pushed himself up to kneel as he reached for his phone, unable to help the stupid, sickening hope that Linc had messaged him. That maybe it was all a mistake, a misunderstanding. He wiped his cheeks with the back of his palm and took a shaky breath.

Sarah had messaged. He flipped open the text to see a dumbass picture of a group of puppies in party hats. A wet laugh bubbled in his throat, and he sat back on his ass. Then another laugh ripped from him, and another, until his shoulders heaved at the sight of those dopey fucking puppies in their stupid polka-dotted hats. He dropped his phone to the ground, unable to help the reaction, even as he hit Joker-level in the sanity department.

Once the laughs ebbed away, Nate felt the pinch of hollowness in his chest, spreading out to numb his arms, his legs. He pushed himself up from the ground, rising on shaky legs to stand. His heart hurt, as if someone bashed it with a rock again and again and again, but he forced himself forward to the kitchen and began to go through the motions of getting the coffee brewing.

Losing Linc… fuck, he still couldn't even wrap his mind around it.

But he wasn't going anywhere, even if it hurt.

This place was his home, and even if no one ever wanted him for the long haul, he'd find his own way to build a future.

CHAPTER 26

LINC HAD TRIED TO TEXT NATE FOR DAYS NOW, BUT HE hadn't answered a single one.

He deserved that.

Fuck, he'd been an idiot to leave that shit out on his counter. He'd been a bigger idiot to keep it quiet, honestly. At this point, maybe it'd be better to just go through with the move. Linc sat at the kitchen table, watching Beck work on his latest masterpiece, some bug-man he'd created as a superhero. He kept glancing to the door.

Nico was coming over, but he'd be lying if he said he hadn't hoped Nate might stop by.

Linc had thought he was immune to loss after Marissa passed, but Nate crept past his defenses. After ruining things with him, his self-loathing had reached astounding new levels.

If he hadn't been such a coward, it might be Nate coming over tonight. Staying here. Linc had been so obsessed with leaving this house, with escaping this town, that he hadn't paused to see what he'd be leaving behind. He drummed his fingers on the countertop, trying to swallow the bile in his throat.

He hadn't slept since Nate walked out the door. He hadn't been able to eat, sick with the anxiety that swirled around in him. It ate away at his veins, and he only had himself to blame. Linc glanced to the clock.

"Kiddo, are you about finished? It's time to brush your teeth and get to bed," he murmured. Taking care of Beck was his autopilot, and he'd done his best to keep his emotions from the kiddo. However, he wasn't sure he did a great job. His son had been glancing to him a little more and jumping to help rather than pushing his limits like normal.

Beck bobbed his head and lifted the picture. "I drew this for Mr. Nate," he said, beaming.

Fuck.

Linc felt like he swallowed glass as he forced a smile. "Good job, Beck."

How was he supposed to explain any of this to his son? The contract for the Baltimore job sat on his counter, mocking him. After the festival, he'd changed his mind. He might've filled out some of it, but he never planned on handing it in. That was what he wanted to explain to Nate. He didn't want to leave anymore. He wanted to find a way to move forward together, even if he might need some help to get there.

Beck placed his paper in the stack, and Linc followed him into the bathroom as they settled into the motions—brushing teeth, getting into pajamas, and then climbing into bed. He floated through the routine, unable to shove away the memories of Nate's sweet smile, of the ridiculous sense of humor that always managed to make him laugh. At how the man had thrown himself all in, body and soul, even with no promises of a future.

Linc managed to get through a single book before Beck's eyes shuttered. He placed the book on the dresser and began to push himself up. A small hand grabbed his.

"Daddy?" Beck asked, those soulful brown eyes pure Marissa. Sometimes, it felt like she was speaking through their son.

"Yeah, Beck?"

"Don't be sad," Beck murmured, even as his eyes fluttered with sleepiness. "You just have to stand your ground."

Linc swallowed the lump in his throat, unable to help the way his eyes glossed over. Those words—

that was what Nate told Beck to do with the bullies. The kiddo equated the stuff that made him sad to Linc's predicament. Except he was the only one causing his pain at this point.

Linc skimmed his fingers through Beck's curls. "Love you, kiddo."

"Love you too, Daddy," Beck mumbled, drifting fast toward sleep. Linc pushed himself up and headed out of the room to wipe the water out of his eyes. His son's words echoed over and over again. Even though this was a different situation, Beck and Nate weren't wrong.

A knock sounded at his door, and his feet carried him to the foyer. The hollow thump in his chest hadn't gone away since Nate left, and he still couldn't dim the fragile hope that the man might be standing at the door. He opened wide, but as expected, Nico stood there with a six-pack in hand. When Nico paused to stare at him, concern lit his features.

"Damn, man," Nico said, ducking inside. "You look like someone ran you over with your own truck."

Unease filtered through his veins. He hadn't explained the situation to Nico yet, and he had the bad feeling his friend would be pissed when he mentioned Baltimore. He'd been so fixated on escape as the solution when it never would've been one.

Linc plucked one of the beers from the six-pack and led them toward the kitchen. He snagged the bottle opener and cracked the top, taking a deep sip of the porter Nico brought. The liquid didn't bolster his courage, but he forced himself to talk anyway.

"I fucked up," Linc muttered.

"What else is new," Nico teased while he opened his own bottle. "You're going to have to be more specific."

There was so much Linc could explain—how the bullying at Beck's school drove him out of his mind, how the loneliness had eaten away at him until he couldn't trust his own judgement anymore, or how he'd carried the memories of Marissa by himself for so long that he saw escape as the only viable solution.

Instead, he said, "Nate saw the year-long contract for a job in Baltimore and left me."

Nico leaned against the counter, blinked once, and then took a sip from his beer. "Yeah, that sounds about right."

Linc swallowed, hard. He hadn't expected gentleness from his best friend. He knew him too damn well for that. It was why he called him over in the first place.

"You introduced him to Beck—took him out on a public date with your son," Nico said, as calm as ever. They both knew what that meant. He'd *never* done that. Ever.

"I don't want to go to Baltimore," Linc admitted for the first time since the idea had taken root. The contract had been sitting there on his counter for far too long, because deep down, he didn't want to leave. He just didn't know how to move forward any other way.

Nico lifted a brow. "Of course you don't, jackass. You're just afraid of what's going to happen when you stop with the self-flagellation. Newsflash— finding happiness doesn't mean you're suddenly going to lose every damn memory of Marissa."

Linc was glad he already leaned against his counter, because otherwise the floor might've fallen from under him. He took a sip of beer before he could pull himself together enough to respond. "Thanks for holding back, asshole."

Nico bared his teeth with his grin. "That's not what you called me here for, and we both know it."

"He's not answering texts," Linc murmured, staring at the flecks in the granite countertops. When Nico laid the truth out so simply, he felt like such an idiot. As if he should've realized all of this years ago.

"The world doesn't revolve around you, princess.

He's got a business that's having a grand opening next week, and you royally fucked the trust between you. Words aren't going to cut it here."

Linc tilted his head to look at the ceiling. "What would?"

Nico shrugged. "He was your boyfriend, man. It's up to you to figure out how to win him back."

"Remind me why I put myself through this?" Linc responded, sarcasm flowing freely.

"Because you love me." Nico smirked. "If you wanted bullshit, you could've called… well, no one. Ever notice you surround yourself with mouthy assholes?"

Linc snorted. Nico's words had his sluggish mind beginning to tick again. Nate deserved better—Linc had admitted that from the start, and yet, through Nate's patience, through the way he took care of Beck, and through the gentle way he opened Linc's heart, he'd proved he wanted him regardless. It was time for Linc to do the same.

"Do you think it's too late?" Linc asked, even though the answer didn't matter. He needed to try either way.

"Your stubborn ass is going to do whatever you see fit, anyway," Nico responded. "You'd be a lucky man to reel in a guy like that. I've never met anyone as genuine as him."

"I know," Linc murmured, his heart twisting at the onslaught of memories. Of teasing conversations while he worked at Chesapeake Brew, of the love shining in those beautiful blue eyes, of the hikes, the lunches filled with laughter, of a thousand stolen kisses.

And Nate thought he was willing to toss all of that aside like garbage. Like their relationship hadn't meant the world to him.

He needed to prove him wrong. That he wasn't going anywhere. An idea filtered in, and his lips began to lift. This would either work, or it could go catastrophically. But he'd never know if he didn't try.

CHAPTER 27

CHESAPEAKE BREW WAS OPENING IN THREE DAYS.

That should've filled Nate with so much excitement, but little held thrill as of late. His day had already started off with a devastating blow. Linc's house went up for sale. He'd stopped midstride and almost buckled then and there at the sight of the red-and-white sign. Even though he hadn't responded to Linc's texts, he hadn't realized how much it would tear him apart to see the stupid thing on Linc's lawn. This was real. He was leaving.

And when he arrived at the shop, his day continued on that trajectory. With the mess that stretched before him, he was about to spiral into a full-blown panic attack.

Open boxes stretched before him—five-pound bags of coffee ordered in preparation for their first week. All from the wrong vendor. Daria had been in charge of putting through the order, and after the constant complaints she'd made about switching vendors, he knew she hadn't ordered from Uncle Harold's old vendor by mistake.

The click of the lock sounded in the door as Daria entered.

When her gaze landed on the boxes, no surprise registered. The woman kept her features schooled.

"You ordered from the old vendor," he said, fighting every ounce of anger to keep his voice level.

"Guess we're just going to have to go with that coffee," she responded, with the audacity to sport a smug smile.

This was going to fuck up a large part of his push for the new business. She knew that, yet she didn't *care*.

He'd been patient. He'd tried to reason with her. He'd tried to compromise and make her feel like she still had a say.

Yet she'd badmouthed him around town. She'd fought him on every change. And now she was sabotaging his opening day.

If he wanted to stay here for the long haul, he needed to make one more change.

"Daria, you're fired."

Daria opened her mouth, shock spreading across her features. "But we're opening in a few days."

Nate shook his head. "I'm opening in a few days."

"You can't do this," she tried to argue, placing her hands on her hips. "Your Uncle Howard hired me, and he would've wanted me to be running this place."

Nate jutted his chin forward. He'd reached the end of compromising with her, begging her to try and understand, and smoothing over her temper. "If he wanted you to run the place, you would've been in the will. You've made my job difficult from the moment I moved to town, and I can't have you continuing to sabotage the future of this shop. Despite what you think, we've got a damn good chance of success here."

He sucked in a deep breath, even as her hands balled into fists. "If you've got anything back there, grab it before you go. I'd rather do this on my own than fight with you every step of the way."

Daria let out a guttural noise and called him something under her breath before she stomped to the back.

Nate's heart raced. What had he just done? Sure, Linc had been hinting at firing her for a long while, and Nico had given him warnings as well, but… his timing couldn't be worse. How the hell was he supposed to manage this store opening by himself?

Daria stomped past him with a hoodie she'd left here in hand, shooting him a filthy glare as she headed for the door. "I hope this place is shut down within the month." She tossed her key to the ground and slammed the door behind her.

Nate swallowed, hard. Ugliness washed over him, but his limbs already trembled from the monster of a task that spread before him. He took a seat on the cool hardwood floor. First things first—he went on the website for the new coffee vendor and put in a rush order. When he finished with that, he opened up his texts, skimming to the one Nico sent a few days ago, asking if he needed any help.

Yeah, he did.

Nate typed out a quick text to Nico and then shot out one to Eliza, sitting on the floor of his coffee shop, surrounded by boxes of coffee he shouldn't be using. Fuck, what if the new order didn't come in time? Would he even be able to return this stuff? Chances were, the old vendor had a shit return policy.

He'd just fired his only employee.

A hysterical laugh bubbled in his throat. He should be feeling far worse about that, but after all the strife Daria put him through? Honestly, he felt lighter. Freer. He should've done that from the start rather than trying to push through with her out of obligation.

Nate shook his head. He glanced around the room, to all the care put into the details of this place, from the metal fixtures to the stainless steel back-splash. All reminders of Linc. Tears welled in his eyes, his mind whirling at the whiplash of the emotional storm battering him. He missed him. So damn much. No matter how things ended, Nate couldn't help the sharp twist in his chest every time he thought about the man.

He only wished they still had a chance. He'd been planning on responding to Linc at last—he'd just needed a few days. But after seeing the For Sale sign in front of Linc's house, he couldn't bring himself to do it. Explanations wouldn't matter in face of a reality where Linc left him behind.

He let out a heavy sigh and pushed himself up from the floor.

Time to get to work.

OPENING DAY HAD ARRIVED.

Was he ready in the slightest?

Fuck no.

Was he going to do his damn best anyway?

Absolutely.

Nate brought out the other five-pound bag to the front, sitting it next to one of the misordered ones. After a quick brainstorming session with Nico, Nate had realized he could still do something with the coffee order. Until the old supply ran out, he would offer two different types of brew. The Throwback coffee for the old customers who might take some time to adjust, and then the new and improved Chesapeake Brew. Once he phased out the old stuff, everyone would have time to try the new blend and get used to his version of his uncle's old coffee shop.

"Ready for this, boss?" Rachel asked, setting a steaming cup of coffee out from the first batch of the day. Eliza's niece who'd returned home from college had been a godsend. Since Cozy Corner had a full staff and Rachel was looking for a job, the timing couldn't have been more perfect. She possessed a sarcastic sense of humor, enough piercings to belong in a tattoo shop, and coffee shop experience. Adjusting to Nate's espresso machine and the new menu had taken a single day.

"We'll find out when we open the doors," Nate responded. "If you find me cowering in the back and crying, clearly, I was underprepared."

Rachel snorted and made her way over to the door.

Nate soaked in the sight of Chesapeake Brew—his store, his new beginning. Sadness saturated into the pride welling in his chest as he soaked in his surroundings. A part of this place would always, always remind him of Linc. He'd fallen hopelessly in love, but he couldn't help if those feelings weren't returned. Still, it hurt.

"Go ahead, Rach," he said. "Open the door."

She flashed a bright grin and clicked the lock before flipping the neon sign to open.

A few of the early risers in town had trickled in before Rach even stepped behind the bar again. He recognized a few of them already—Mr. Peabody who took his black lab on walks every morning at sunrise, Mrs. Rhodes who lived down the block from him, and Kerry who opened the bank Sarah worked at. Nate plastered on his best customer service smile and stepped behind the register.

"Welcome to Chesapeake Brew," he said, feeling those words stir something deep inside him. "What can I get you?"

The rest of the morning whirred by in a blur.

It felt like he'd seen most of the town in a short span of time, whether they were swinging by for a muffin and black coffee or to sit and enjoy the new seating with a cappuccino. So many familiar faces strode in through the door. While a few grumbled at the new prices, the new coffee, the new... everything, most of the customers were thrilled. His ears rang from the sheer number of folks who'd gushed about how he'd transformed this place. Rachel was a refreshing change of pace to work with, cracking jokes the entire time, easygoing and creative. He'd never been more relieved over firing Daria.

The scent of coffee clung to him at this point from the dozens of espressos, cappuccinos, and cups of brew he'd made over the course of the day, and his cheeks hurt from smiling so often. But an exuberant joy filtered through his veins, one he couldn't suppress.

Though, every once in a while, he'd glance to the swinging door and hope for one man to walk on through. Somehow, Linc not being here on his opening day felt wrong, even after everything had crumbled between them.

The dinner rush had just started to come through when he happened to catch the flash of blond hair pulled back into a familiar utilitarian ponytail. His gaze landed on someone he hadn't seen in *months*.

"Laura?" he called, his tone incredulous. The sight of his best friend in the middle of his coffee shop felt surreal. "Get on over here." He slipped out from behind the bar and had Rachel take over as he crossed the distance to Laura.

He threw his arms around her, pulling her into a crushing embrace. She hugged back just as fiercely, smelling like her favorite Chanel perfume and looking like she could take the world on with her pinky as the weapon. Fuck, he'd missed her.

"What are you doing here?" he asked, nearly breathless.

Laura flashed him a huge smile. "I drove down. You think I'm missing your opening day?"

Nate buried his face in Laura's shoulder, trying to hold back the tears of relief threatening to escape. "You have no idea how good it is to see you."

"Do I get to meet your man?" she asked.

He winced at the splash of vinegar on those open wounds. "It's a long story." Truth be told, he still wished he was Linc's anything. Their connection—he wasn't sure he'd ever find something like that again.

"Well, I'm hanging here for a while before I go and nab some sleep at the hotel," Laura said. "So, if now isn't a good time, then we're catching up over breakfast."

"I'm all yours," he said, squeezing her into one more hug. With that, he raced behind the bar to help Rachel with the line. The rest of the night zipped along as fast as the day had, and Laura got to meet

Nico, Sarah, and Jer. Like he'd suspected, Laura and Sarah hit it off from the start, and he kept ducking into the conversation when he could. Everyone had showed up.

Everyone except Linc.

Eventually, the last few stragglers exited, and closing time had arrived.

"You're welcome to head out, Rach," he called as he finished cleaning the counters. A static buzz still filled the air from all the chaos from earlier, the residual presence of all the people who had come to Chesapeake Brew lingering. All he needed to do was count up and he'd head home for the night. The exhaustion that cloaked his body threatened to knock him out the second he got home, but it competed with a hum of satisfaction from what a glorious day the opening had been.

"Thanks, boss," she called out. Rachel paused at the door and swung around. "There's one last customer here to see you."

Nate bit back a sigh. He just wanted to curl up in bed at this point. "Hey," he started, looking to the open door.

Linc stood in the doorway.

He looked handsome enough to knock the air from Nate's chest, but even he noticed his sunken cheeks and the weary look in his eyes. A small part of him twisted at the sight—that maybe Linc had been heartbroken too.

Rachel glanced between the two of them and offered a wave before ducking out the door and heading home. Linc stepped inside, and as he approached, each footstep echoed through the empty café.

Nate's throat dried. Now that Linc was here, he didn't know what to do. What to say.

Those feelings came rushing back, strong enough to stagger him. He chewed on his lip in an attempt to try and stave off the way his eyes threatened to water. He wasn't going to cry in front of Linc. He'd cried enough over the past week.

"Hey," Linc said, the soft, husky voice causing him to shudder. "Congratulations. I saw lines out of here all day."

"Yeah." Nate nodded. Don't cry, don't cry, don't cry. "We did well."

Linc skimmed fingers through his hair. "Can I walk you home?"

Nate's brows drew together. "Is this some final goodbye before you move or something?" His chest ached stronger than ever when he caught the familiar earthy scent he'd buried himself into so often.

Linc shook his head. "Just… come with me."

"Give me a sec," he said, leaning in front of the

safe to begin the count. Linc strode around the café, his steady pace sending his nerves sky high. Nate fumbled the count three times and had to start over with the way his nerves jangled. He should be rejoicing at the numbers of what they pulled in today, but nothing pierced past—this. He didn't know if Linc had showed up to break his heart further or…

He couldn't afford to hope again.

When Nate finished, he pushed up from his crouch and headed toward the door. "All right," he murmured. "Time to go." Linc followed him out the door as he turned off the lights and locked up.

In silence, they began to walk down the sidewalk, side by side.

"There's a lot I've wanted to say to you," Linc murmured. "Starting with sorry. I am so sorry I hurt you."

Nate's throat tightened. He didn't know how to respond, because he wasn't getting any damn signals from the man. What was he sorry for? Breaking his heart? Signing on to move away without telling him?

"I had myself convinced that if I didn't escape my house, this town, I'd never be able to move past Marissa," Linc continued, his dark gaze focused on the ground in front of them. "I'd become so obsessed with it, that I never realized I already had." His gaze flickered to Nate, and they stopped walking. "You were the first person who made me hope again. The first one I felt bone-deep comfort with, who got me. The one who had me breaking all the rules I'd set in place to guard my heart."

Nate sucked in a sharp breath. "Why are you telling me this, Linc? I saw the For Sale sign."

The inches between them tensed, but neither one of them moved.

"Because I fucking miss you," Linc said, the deep voice resonating through him. "Because every day I've woken up without you, I realize how much goddamn joy you brought into my life. Because I'm not going anywhere."

"What do you mean?" Nate asked. His heart raced a thousand miles a minute, but he couldn't pull himself away from the intense look in Linc's eyes. He'd never been able to.

Linc reached up, his fingers hesitant as they skimmed Nate's jaw. Nate nearly collapsed at the touch, from how damn badly he'd missed this man.

"I put the house up for sale because I'm moving. I bought Fletcher's house," Linc murmured. "I spent enough time not telling you how I felt, not touching you in public, not calling you my boyfriend, even though you were. I should've told you how I love spending family time with you and my son—who's been asking for you all week."

Nate's chest expanded and contracted hard as his heart stopped and restarted again. "You bought Fletcher's house?"

Linc brushed his fingertips under Nate's chin. "If you need to walk away, I'll understand. We'll be your neighbors, but nothing more. But if you still want this… want me… I've spent enough time punishing myself. I'd love nothing more than to wake up next to you every damn day."

Nate's eyes watered, and a few traitorous tears slipped down. His lip trembled as he stared into Linc's tender gaze.

He hadn't been wrong. The connection between them had never been one-sided. There was no way something this powerful could be.

Linc had bought the house. He wasn't moving away. He was moving *in*.

Pure, unfettered joy sang through Nate's veins as he closed the distance between them. He consumed Linc in a fierce kiss. His heart ached, and his soul sang. Riding on this thrill, he could easily reach for those distant stars above. He drank in Linc's familiar taste as the man swept his tongue in his mouth, deepening the kiss. Their chests collided as their hands moved all over each other, the touch a reassurance that this was real.

This was happening.

He lost himself in this kiss, all-consuming, scouring away the persistent ache that had filled his chest ever since he'd walked away. Warmth raced through him, like stepping out to watch the river sparkle under the sunlight on a spring day. Nate had never had a chance against this man. Linc might be stubborn to a fault, but he didn't make a decision on a whim. This was real. This beautiful man who built houses and raised one of the kindest kids he knew wanted a future with him.

Nate pulled apart for a breath, alight with a fierce thrill that refused to subside. He hoped it never did.

"So, is that a yes?" Linc asked. His tone might sound confident, but Nate didn't miss the vulnerable look in those deep brown eyes.

"You're everything I've ever wanted, Lincoln Lane," Nate murmured against his mouth. "Yes, I'll be your boyfriend. Yes, I'll live with you and Beck." He sucked in a sharp breath. Was he going to do this? Before he could second guess himself, the words escaped him. "I love you."

Linc's jaw dropped, and for a moment Nate wanted to grab those words out of the air. Before he could descend into a panic, a breathtaking smile slid onto Linc's face.

"I love you too."

Nate blinked, barely able to believe he'd heard

those words back. "Fuck, you're going to make me cry again."

Linc snorted. "Before you do that, why don't we get to my place so I can relieve Nico. He offered to watch Beck while I went to try and win you back."

Nate shook his head. "Should've figured he was involved." A stupid, goofy smile rose to his face unbidden. God, was this even real?

Linc reached out and slipped his hand into Nate's. "Come on," he said. "We're just a block away."

Nate floated the entire way there, basking in just being near Linc again after their time apart. He'd learned he could survive on his own, that he'd built his own foundation to thrive here, but Linc and Beck made his life better, richer, like grayscale to technicolor, and he wanted to bask in all that glorious, beautiful color.

Linc unlocked his door and stepped inside, drawing Nate in behind him. Nico and Beck approached at the sound, because they'd both clearly been waiting.

Nico glanced between them, and a smile grew on his face. He offered a wink to Nate and clapped a hand on Linc's shoulder. "I'll leave you to it." With that, he exited out the door.

"Daddy, did you bring Mr. Nate so I can give him his picture?" Beck asked.

Nate swallowed hard. He'd missed that kid so damn much.

Linc nodded. "Yeah, kiddo. I've got something to tell you though. Mr. Nate's my boyfriend."

Beck wrinkled his nose. "What, like kissing?"

Linc let out a laugh. "Yeah, but if you want, it also means we can move in with Mr. Nate and get to see him every day."

Beckett glanced between both of them, and Nate chewed on his lip, hoping beyond hope that he didn't hate the idea. "Can I bring all my toys?"

Nate grinned, trying not to cry for the thousandth time today. "Yeah, you can. And we can have pancakes together and draw whenever you want."

Linc placed a hand on his shoulder. "Don't go making any promises before you see how often that kid draws."

Beck nodded and hopped up to throw his arms around Nate's legs. "Let's move in now," he exclaimed. Jesus, Mary, and Joseph, this kid slayed him every damn time. Nate didn't know how he was still standing after the emotional ride today had been. He reached down and mussed Beck's curls.

He caught Linc's stare on them, unrestrained tenderness that made his heart thump hard. Linc slipped his arm around Nate's shoulders and squeezed tight. Nate basked in this warmth, stronger than he ever could've believed.

Every time he thought about what he longed for, this was what he'd imagined. Building a life, a family, a home with the two of them.

When he'd first driven across the bridge into Chesapeake City, he'd seen a horizon full of promise stretched before him, and this—this aching, beautiful future was everything he'd hoped for.

EPILOGUE
THREE MONTHS LATER

LINC STOOD AT THE GRILL, WATCHING THE BURGERS sizzle. Shrieks sounded behind him, but unlike the way it'd been for years, he was able to relax. Ever since he and Beck moved into Nate's house, life had been brighter than before. The warmth that flooded through him at the thought felt a lot like Marissa's smile. If she could've picked anyone for him and Beck, it would've been Nate McAllister.

While Nate made Chesapeake Brew a popular place, Linc continued his local business with swarms of home projects on his agenda this summer. Beck had been taking art lessons with other kids his age, something Nate suggested. Every day they weathered life's curveballs together, day-to-day things growing far easier with a partner at his side. And at night, they were fire between the sheets.

A pair of hands snaked around his waist as Nate rested his chin on Linc's shoulder. "Hey, handsome. Those going to be done anytime soon? The tyrants are restless."

Linc cast a glance to where Beck raced around with Everly's daughter Raven and Jessica, a girl from his art class. The sight of his son exploding in laughter sent such a fierce sweep of joy through him. With those two girls going to school with Beck next year, Linc had faith his son would be able to not just survive but thrive. And any time the doubts or worries grew too strong, Nate was there to smooth his brow and promise it would all be okay.

"You sure you're not the one who's hungry?" Linc asked. Nate's sweaty chest plastered to his back, and his shoulders heaved from exertion. Linc couldn't help the amusement that welled in his chest.

"Starving. How the hell do they have that much energy?" Nate leaned in and kissed him on the cheek. Fuck, he was so in love with this man it hurt. He soaked in the sight of Nate's long, long lashes, the strands of dark hair plastered to his forehead, and the bright, happy grin that he'd sacrifice anything to keep on his face.

"You are allowed to hang with the adults, you know," Linc reminded him, casting a glance over to where Nico stood with Sarah, Taran, Everly, and

Jessica's mom, Ruby. A few others were coming over later, and his folks had already stopped by. He'd been so excited for this barbecue—the first one he and Nate threw together in their new place.

Nate pecked at his cheek again before he pulled away to stand by the grill, keeping an eye out at the backyard to where the kids raced around. "I could, but I want to spend time with Beck. I've been so busy at the coffee shop recently that we've been missing out on quality drawing sessions."

Linc reached out and placed a hand on Nate's hips. "Did I mention I love you?"

"You didn't, but you can always show me later," he said, wiggling his brows.

A laugh escaped Linc as he tilted his head up to an achingly blue sky. The clouds were bright, bright white, and the scent of the cooking meat mingled with the fresh-cut grass of their lawn. He sometimes still felt a twinge when he passed his old house or stopped by one of the places he and Marissa used to visit all the time. But then Nate would ask him about it, and instead of stuffing the memory down, he shared those experiences with him, keeping Marissa's memory alive in a far better way.

He'd spent so many years on autopilot, not believing he could find happiness again after getting so lucky with Marissa. And as the years progressed, that loneliness had cemented inside him until his wife hadn't been the one who'd become a ghost —he had.

Until this accident-prone, anxious, absolutely amazing man almost ran him over and changed everything.

Nate had brought him back to life.

GET READY TO CHECK OUT BOOK TWO, **STRONGER THAN PASSION**! Plus check out Katherine's delicious M/M romantic suspense **MIDNIGHT HEIST**.

ALSO BY KATHERINE MCINTYRE

ACKNOWLEDGMENTS

Stronger Than Hope wouldn't have been possible without first and foremost, my husband, Rob. He's a rock in our family, and after I'd started this story was when we all got put through the wringer during the turbulent delivery of our daughter. He's a constant inspiration and a team player, which helped us get through all the insanity.

I also need to shout out to my crit partners, Landra and Jaqueline, who offered their ever valuable insight on this book as well as my author tribe who just keeps me sane on a regular basis.

And last but not least, a huge thank you to my editors and the team at Hot Tree Publishing for believing in me and taking a chance on my stories.

ABOUT THE AUTHOR

Katherine McIntyre is a feisty chick with a big attitude despite her short stature. She writes stories featuring snarky women, ragtag crews, and men with bad attitudes—and there's an equally high chance for a passionate speech thrown into the mix. As an eternal geek and tomboy who's always stepped to her own beat, she's made it her mission to write stories that represent the broad spectrum of people out there, from different cultures and races to all varieties of men and women.

Website: http://www.katherine-mcintyre.com

Newsletter sign-up: http://eepurl.com/duIScb

facebook.com/kmcintyreauthor

twitter.com/pixierants

instagram.com/authorkmcintyre

bookbub.com/profile/katherine-mcintyre

ABOUT THE PUBLISHER

Hot Tree Publishing opened its doors in 2015 with an aspiration to bring quality fiction to the world of readers. With the initial focus on romance and a wide spread of romance subgenres, Hot Tree Publishing has since opened their first imprint, Tangled Tree Publishing, specializing in crime, mystery, suspense, and thriller.

Firmly seated in the industry as a leading editing provider to independent authors and small publishing houses, Hot Tree Publishing is the sister company to Hot Tree Editing, founded in 2012. Having established in-house editing and promotions, plus having a well-respected market presence, Hot Tree Publishing endeavors to be a leader in bringing quality stories to the world of readers.

Interested in discovering more amazing reads brought to you by Hot Tree Publishing? Head over to the website for information:

www.hottreepublishing.com

facebook.com/hottreepublishing

twitter.com/hottreepubs

Lightning Source UK Ltd.
Milton Keynes UK
UKHW040946160223
417122UK00002B/442